THE RETURN OF SOMETHING LOST

MARK SKIEN CHAPLIN

CHICAGO SPECTRUM PRESS
LOUISVILLE, KENTUCKY 40207

This is a work of fiction. The characters, incidents, dialogues, and some settings are products of the author's imagination and are not to be construed as real. Any resemblance to actual events or persons, living or dead, is entirely coincidental.

The author's profits from the sale of this book will be given to medical research.

For Kirsti

CHAPTER ONE

No garment covered her, no sheet. The umbilicus stood up as a summons; something sought to escape. A stripe of pigment halved her swollen belly, and stretch marks wrapped her flanks, row on row. Her skin soon paled. Her hands turned blue. Fingers plucked at the pad on which she lay.

Her eyes roved and twitched beneath closed lids. Lips parted, and then came a moan. She struggled to rise. From around her neck, a gold cross, hung on a chain, bobbed against breasts laden with milk. The eyelids opened. She propped herself on an elbow and wobbled for just a moment, before falling back.

The clock was started. Blood began flowing. The skin recoiled at the blade's slash, and the flesh beneath sprang apart. Her torso flexed, and the cross, which now lay on her chest, glinted twice in the light.

"Oh!" she said. She covered her mouth with a closed fist.

A spray of droplets from cut arterioles landed in a red mist on the surgeon's gown. Crimson and cyan swirls of blood mixed and pooled before they could be sucked up. A hemostat crushed a large vein. The cautery seared it. The vessel popped and hissed, blood boiled, and tendrils of smoke wafted up until they faded away, leaving an odd scent of roasted flesh.

The nurses were transfixed. Not a word passed among them.

The door banged against the wall when Dr. Tyler Ashton rushed in. He snapped on gloves, and latex dust mixed in the air with alcohol. The aerosol thus formed gave off an odor peculiar to that place. He approached the table, picking at the gloves' rubber digits until they formed a second skin. He clasped his hands. No alarm showed on his face. In his eyes was no fear, yet his voice was thin, less than certain.

"Tyler Ashton, ER," he said.

"Thanks for coming, Tyler. Stuart Conrad. We've got a cord prolapse. Fetal heart tones dropped out."

"How much?"

"Sixty."

"Suction. Three-point-five ET tube, stylette," Ashton said to the nearest nurse. "Call the ICU."

Heather Laird winced, but made no sound. There was madness in her eyes. A tear glistened on her cheek. Her head reared up from the table and turned fiercely, side to side. "Am I going to die?" she said finally. The surgeon answered, "No, you're not!"

"Don't be afraid," Ashton said. "You'll be all right."

"Oxygen, five liters," Conrad said to the nurses who scurried about the room and tore at instrument packs.

"Suction. Turn up the damned suction!" The V-shaped lines bulged on Conrad's forehead. His neck veins stood in relief.

"Run the IV wide open. Start a second. Give one unit O-negative, packed cells. Order two more units."

Conrad cleft the mutinous tissue with three strokes. Globules of fat sparkled under the light. Bleeders popped up. Her cut flesh oozed. Blood ran in runnels down her belly and spilled to the table before splashing on the floor. The doctors' clean, white shoes changed, by degree, to spattered, sticky red.

"I can't see. Move the damned light!" Dr. Conrad said.

A nurse grabbed a glove without putting it on, reached to the handle, and levered the beams, focusing them on the cavity. She turned to the patient.

The woman's strength was a wonder, given her small size. Her power seemed scaled for another dimension. Legs kicked. One slipped off the table. The nurse wrapped a nylon strap around her thighs, cinching them together. Heather twisted and arched against the restraint like a snared beast. A second strap restrained the chest and arm, while the other arm, uncaught, flailed about the pad.

Trembling gave way to hard, shaking chills. She managed to pull off her oxygen mask and cried out, "Move the damned light! I can't see. There. There it is. Thank you, thank you. No! It's a wolf! Run! I'm trapped! Get away! No! Get out! The curtain. Move the curtain! Change the light!"

The nurse clamped the mask over Heather's nose and mouth. She held it there as her patient twisted and shook. With her free hand, Heather clawed at something invisible on her cheek. Muffled curses, interspersed with shrieks, rose from the steaming mask. Her head flopped back and forth.

"More oxygen, wide open. Get the respirator. Where is anesthesia?" Ashton said. "If they don't come soon, I'll have to tube her."

"What about the kid?" asked Conrad.

Ashton looked up with a puzzled stare.

Conrad split the fascia and divided the muscles until he brought the uterus into view. Snarls of dark veins covered its convex surface. It shone like a huge tumor. Ashton held the bladder blade as a shield while Conrad's knife opened a half-inch wound in the uterine wall. Bandage scissors extended the gash laterally to six inches. Conrad thrust his gloved hand deep inside, seized, and then rotated the fetus until a hairy shape filled the gap.

The baby's head erupted with a sucking noise. Its bruised scalp, covered with blond hair, had absorbed fluid like a sponge. At its pierced center was a cut wire electrode. Cone-shaped and lumpy, the skull rose alien as the surgeon grappled with it, pulling at the jaw, stretching the neck. Though hideous, the infant's form suggested no pain, and indeed, was strangely serene.

The rest then flopped into the world. It was a girl. Olive green sludge coated the torso and smelled like something rotten. They waited to see if she would breathe, and for a moment, everything was quiet, eerily calm.

Two feet of off-white cord, an inch in diameter and gelatinous at its center, hung serpentine from her belly. Ashton squeezed the cord for a six-inch section and stripped blood from its spiral arteries and vein. Kelly clamps crushed the cord at each end before Conrad's scissors sliced through the middle. The clamp dangled on the stump.

He passed the baby to Ashton who, trained in adult medicine, stiffly held her. She was warm and wet, as mute and limp as a pale blue rag doll.

"Get the gas-passers up here *now*," Conrad said. "Where the hell are they? Mop up the blood. Get us some shoe covers before we shock ourselves with the cautery!"

Still she made no sound. Olive liquid drooled from her mouth. Her disconnected eyes seemed to regard nothing. She was an émigré from a strange and forbidding place, having fallen into the world by dreadful mistake.

Ashton carried her, wrapped in a towel, a distance of three steps to the warming table. He sucked the slime, first from the mouth, and then from the nostrils. A neonatal nurse, Keely, one of three present, towel-dried the baby's fissured skin, and some on the soles of the feet came off in strips. Heat radiated from the warmer, and after a few seconds, sweat dripped from the heads of doctor and nurse to the tiny bed below.

"ET tube." The other nurse handed him a tube the size of a straw with a curved wire inside. "Three-point-five with stylette."

"Heart rate, forty. Want to start CPR?" Keely slapped the baby's peeling feet. Shock waves ran up the legs. Then stillness.

"Let's tube him first. Suction."

"It's a she."

Ashton nodded. "A she. Okay. Tracheal traction. No, not that way."

"Like this?"

The floppy babe was on her back, head toward Ashton. Her shoulders overlay a warm, rolled-up towel. A laryngoscope in his left hand swept her tongue aside. The right hand slipped the tube through the vocal cords into the trachea. He withdrew the guide wire. Suction brought forth more of the green goo. He fit the anesthesia bag to the tube, and with every squeeze of the bellows, pumped oxygen into both lungs. Keely's two fingers on the infant's sternum compressed the tiny chest one inch as they coordinated the CPR. She mashed the sternum three times in succession for every breath of pure oxygen.

"She's pinking up," said Ashton.

The bellows bag sent a splendid wind, a breeze to a dying ember. They stared in awe when she changed from mottled blue, to faint pink, then to perfect crimson—glowing, as if she were invested with a divine spark. Even her toes became brilliant red, except the toenails, which were stained with olive grout. The nurse's face burned under the heat and light of the lamp, and Ashton grinned like a man redeemed.

"Heart rate, one-twenty," she said. They stopped the compressions.

"Watch the chest."

The baby's breath, weak at first, strengthened in force and frequency. As life took hold, legs quaked and arms trembled. The baby twisted and arched her back. Her limbs thrashed. Ashton had hold of her head and mouth and held the little conduit that gave oxygen in a firm grip. He pinned her to the table.

She seemed so fragile—butterfly fragile—a marvel that stirred his imagination. Some wet chrysalis, collapsed random from a quantum void, encoded to grow, to fly, to beget, and to fade. The torso turned clockwise about her flaxen head and then swiveled back.

"You have the right to remain silent," he said. "Anything you say can and will be held against you in a court of law."

"Miranda. She looks like a Miranda to me!" The nurse tried to suppress a smile.

"You've had your warning," Ashton said, still speaking to the infant.

After a few minutes, he removed the tracheal tube. He held the free-flow oxygen under the nose of the changeling, whose ravenous nostrils flared wide, sucking up the gas. The baby gasped. She grunted with each breath. Her ribs retracted, and her tiny abdomen pulsed.

Vernix clung to the skin until a warm cloth smudged it away. Her skin color shifted. The torso was a patchwork of red and white marble. Limbs were splotched like faint mauve lace. Legs bowed, and the forefeet, wrinkled on the soles, bent inward, molded by an irresistible force. She blinked with bewilderment, staring at the overhead light. With his ring finger, Ashton touched her palm. Her five digits surrounded and grasped it. Connected by their fingers, he raised his hand and hoisted her chest from the table. She refused to let go.

"Forgive the imposition," he said. "Welcome to the abattoir."

She frowned and uttered a plaintive cry. He lowered her gently, but she clung to his finger, as though wishing to recover something lost.

"Easier to talk without that thing stuck down your throat," said Keely. She stroked the baby's face with a warm towel.

"Can a good end come from such a beginning?"

"What do you mean? You saved her. A perfect rescue."

"I'm not sure we deserve any praise."

"That's an odd thing to say, coming from a doctor."

"If there's a first sin, is it being born, or is it, after all—" He hesitated.

"What?"

"Giving birth."

"You need a vacation."

"Can I skip my stress test this year?" He chuckled as he disengaged the baby's hand, and when he released it, her arms shook for a second or two.

"Take some time off."

"Mind-reader."

The baby's chest sang with crackles and wheezes, heard throughout both lung fields. Frothy spittle, blood flecked, spewed from nose and mouth. It was syringed with a rubber bulb. Ashton unscrewed the scalp electrode. He turned down the oxygen to sixty percent. In a few minutes, like adjusting the burner on a stove, her skin changed to dull red, except the tattered hands and feet, which returned to cyanic blue.

"She needs a line and some gases," Ashton said.

"Here's the cath tray. Do you want a three and a half or a five?" She turned and drew the drape from a wheeled cart.

"Call for the transport isolette. The Unit can place the line."

The operating room rapidly filled. Doctors, masked men named by tags clipped to their clothes, swarmed into the room. One, an anesthesiologist, Dr. Selsnick, observed the spectacle. His mouth was agape.

"What the hell? What's going on, Conrad?"

"Cord prolapse. No time. Fetus in jeopardy."

"No anesthesia? You cut her open with nothing?"

"Nothing is all I had. Still have."

"Outrageous!"

"The kid was about to croak. Mom's lost a lot of blood. One unit up. She needs another."

"Good luck with peer review."

"Hey, man, I had no choice. Maybe if you'd been here, she would be asleep."

"I can't be two places at once."

"Betray the mother, or abandon the child. We made our choice," Ashton said.

"Don't blame me, damn it!" said Selsnick.

"Maybe the lawyers, given enough time, will figure out what we should have done," Ashton added.

"You're scaring my patient."

"Give her something, then. What are you waiting for?" said Conrad.

Heather's blood pressure was ninety over sixty, and her heart rate and rhythm were normal. The anesthesiologist checked the two IVs, now open wide, and injected fentanyl into one line. Her crazed orbs twitched in a brief disconjugate stare and turned up, looking dense and white as stone. Her breath stopped. The jaw sagged, the tongue lolled, the face stared blank.

He removed her oxygen mask and suctioned her mouth. He clasped the mask over her nose and squeezed the bellows time and again, forcing the gas into her lungs. Her chest heaved as the clock's hand ticked away the seconds. He placed the tracheal tube and inflated its cuff, then set the ventilator, turning its blue and green dials. The machine's sibilant breathing and the suction wand's slurp spread through the room as the men tracked blood on the floor.

The crisis passed. The one who had cleared her airway, given her oxygen, and induced her sleep, now muttered darkly. He seemed to debate an issue. A drug ampoule flew to the wall and pinged off the tiles. It crunched like ice under his shoe. Even after fitting his mask, his jaw moved, mouthing silent words. The fluids and cells he gave Heather raised her pressure to 120/70. Her ashen face colored, and her jugular veins filled.

Clothed head to toe, cap to gown, Conrad's partner entered the room and approached the table. He sewed while Conrad scrubbed again and dressed. Housekeepers mopped the floor of dying blood, and afterward, there remained no sign of ill-starred deeds.

The surgeons dragged the placenta from Heather Laird's womb. Ashton examined it. The disk of liverish flesh, its laces of leaking vessels, its noisome smell, all seemed inhuman, vaguely malign—a grotesque but cunning organ that had fed the fetus unflagging those many months, but now its days were done, having been cast into a large, steel bowl.

Ashton held up the bowl. "To the lab?"

"Can't you see she's asleep?"

"I see. I suppose it can't be recycled."

"She's lost her appetite." Conrad chuckled.

"The hunger always returns." No one could see if Ashton smiled.

Conrad sewed shut the torn uterus and closed the peritoneum. He found bleeders and tied them, burned others, and suctioned what blood remained. He repaired her abdominal muscles, fascia, and skin. With the fetus removed, the abdomen decompressed, and the stretched tissues, now lax and wrinkled, prefigured old age, as though the tumult, once begun, forced some inevitable end.

A neonatal nurse, happy as a schoolgirl, arrived with the transport isolette. Ashton picked up the infant, held the green tube under her nose, and placed her on the heated pad. He threaded the tubing through a side panel hole and closed the Plexiglas window. The nurse turned the oxygen to eighty percent. They hurried to the intensive care unit, trundling the isolette and its cargo of muffled cries.

As they entered the ICU, Ashton gazed on the newly born, some housed in crystal wombs. Others, squirrel-small, were attached to machines, and were stuck in a tangle of wires. A few, having fled their cages, clutched at their mothers. Ashton stared at the baby in the next bed—spare, lank, and bilious orange—who lounged mute under banks of light, her eyes patched, wearing a bikini fashioned from a mask.

The nurse took her charge from the incubator. She placed her under the heat and fit the oxygen hood over her head. The infant gulped the air. Her arms were out flung. Nostrils flared, the rib bones sank. She grunted, blowing mucoid bubbles from nose and mouth, bursting like primeval ooze from a boil. Her greedy lips pursed. She whimpered. Someone from behind yelled, "Three thousand, six hundred ten grams; fifty centimeters."

A neonatal fellow arrived, a black woman in her early thirties—Dr. Beatrice Young. She wore a scrub shirt and pants and moved with a dancer's grace. Ashton found himself admiring her face and figure when he shook her cinnamon hand.

He related the history and afterward said, "See the art; know the artist." He extended his hands, palms down.

"What?"

"Never mind."

"Did you just make that up?"

"Mrs. Courtney, seventh grade."

"You've got blood on your shoes. What would your teacher say about that?"

"My hands are clean." He held up his hands again, palms forward.

"You'd better change before OSHA finds out."

"Aye, aye, ma'am." He saluted and did an about face and walked over to the labor hall. He put on shoe covers and grabbed his coat.

Ashton left the obstetric wing and skirted the intensive care unit. Outside the nursery window, a throng had gathered, resembling penitents. As he passed, hoping to get away, the mob came close and pelted him with questions. An old woman, the great grandmother, ordered him to save the baby. A lady with a kind face moved lips in silent prayer. Unsettled eyes devoured him for signs of a sanguine prophecy. A slight smile was all they needed, some omen. Ashton demurred, asking them to speak to the pediatricians, but they persisted in their entreaties, and finally he relented.

"The umbilical cord fell into the birth canal. The baby's head came down on top of it." He formed his hands in demonstration. "The baby's blood supply was cut off. Her heart rate dropped."

"It's a girl?" The question came from a woman who listened to his recital with large eyes.

"Yes, it is a girl. Dr. Conrad was forced to operate immediately to save the baby's life. She wasn't breathing. I had to breathe for her. She was covered in goo, and some of it entered her lungs. I think she'll be all right, though. Time will tell. She does have pneumonia. But she pinked up right away and is better. You can see her in the intensive care nursery."

"How much does she weigh?"

"Eight pounds or so. Big girl. Strong, robust. They'll weigh her in the ICU. Her skull bones are molded." He formed his hands again. "She has an elongated head, but that will resolve. Mom is stable. She's been through quite an ordeal. Dr. Conrad will tell you more."

"Eight pounds!"

From the back came a man's voice.

Ashton studied the concerned face—lined not young. "And you are? The father?"

"Maternal grandfather. One wife is enough for me."

"The odds are with her."

"What about the mother?"

"She's still in the OR. I think she'll be all right. Dr. Conrad will talk to you in about an hour."

Ashton had been awake for nearly twenty-four hours. He was unshaven and unwashed. From the assemblage, he heard someone say, "Thank you." He excused himself, absorbed in the insane thoughts of recent events. The sounds of the hospital dissolved to white noise and then became silent.

When he walked, his long, white coat, covering blue scrubs, flapped like vestments. Red script lettering over a breast pocket read, "Tyler Brooks

Ashton, M.D." Underneath read, "Emergency Medicine." A stethoscope protruded from a side pocket. A small book occupied the one opposite. A clip-on pager clung crookedly and bounced on the front of his pants.

He walked quickly down the hallway, and as he approached a staircase, hugging the corner, eyes down, he bumped into someone wearing a red beret. Her face collided with his chest, knocking her beret awry. They recoiled, more from surprise than impact. He recognized the young woman, Whitney Laird. He had treated her in the emergency department many times over several years. She was a senior at the university. She suffered from a chronic lung disease, but despite her illness, possessed beauty of wondrous delicacy.

He tried to comb his gray-fringed hair with his fingers. He put his palm to his cheek, feeling the thick stubble that might have been put to better use on his head's crown.

She smiled and adjusted her beret. "Hello." Her voice was gritty. "I'm glad we weren't moving any faster."

"Might have been serious," he said, returning her smile.

Her gaze moved over his tall frame and on to his identification photo. He looked like a renegade, a man who had perhaps breached some law or forsworn some oath. Horn-rimmed glasses peeped above his pocket's edge. At the front of the coat, a fountain pen leaked a blue stain. On his lapel dangled a radiation badge. Her scrutiny went to his face. His eyes were bleary. He looked spent.

"Do you know anything about Heather Laird? Did she have the baby?" Her breathing was short, her speech halting.

"Yes."

"Is something wrong?" She coughed long and hard.

"You might say that."

"What is it?"

"We had to perform an emergency C-section. Fetal distress. The baby refused to breathe. She's in the intensive care nursery now. Mom lost a lot of blood."

"So it's a girl? She's my half-sister. Is she going to be okay?"

"I think so, but we'll have to see."

"What about Heather?"

"I didn't realize you were related."

"My father remarried."

He nodded. "Heather's stable, still in the OR. But it was a close call. She'll be moved to the ICU on the second floor."

Whitney Laird continued to study his face.

"You look really beat, Dr. Ashton."

"Thank you." He forced a smile. "I've had better days."

"I thought you worked downstairs," she said with iambic breath.

He leaned against the wall and put his hands in his lab coat. She picked at the top button of her dress.

"Usually, unless I'm lucky. Like today. There was no one else."

"I know about luck."

Her lips, painted red, formed a slight smile. Foundation make-up coated her face.

"How are you doing?" he said.

"I'm doing okay. I see my lung specialist, Dr. Bourke, again next Wednesday."

"Wednesday? That's a long way off. I can examine you now in the ER, if you want, to get you through 'til your appointment."

"I don't want to be a bother."

"No, no. No bother. I'll meet you in the ER. Tell the clerk I'll be down. I do need to take a shower and shave and change clothes." He looked at his watch. "I'll be there in twenty minutes."

"Okay. I just want to look at the baby, the cause of all this fuss. I'll see you downstairs."

He left Whitney Laird standing in front of the elevator, opened the staircase door and descended the stairs fast—three floors to ground level, where he turned left, past the CT scanner. He entered the emergency department, behind trauma bay one. At the back were six small doctors' offices in a row, flanked by two bathrooms.

He showered and shaved, slipped into street clothes, and put his blood-stained clogs in a locker, exchanging them for another pair. He went to the front nursing station and inquired about Whitney Laird. After reading her chart, he entered treatment room three and found her sitting in a chair. Her legs were crossed, her hands clasped in her lap. The beret had disappeared, along with the red choker. Two pencil-like rods pinned her long hair up, now braided and gathered in the back. She had wiped away the make-up, lipstick, and rouge. Covering her thin figure was an azure dress. It reflected the light and added to the cyan pallor of her face. She pointed to her lips with a blue finger.

"See?"

Ashton studied the isosceles lips, the short philtrum. He held her right hand and examined her nail beds. He sat facing her in a swivel chair.

"Tell me about your cough."

"It's getting worse. It keeps me up at night." Her lips kissed when she breathed.

"How long has this been going on?"

"All my life."

Ashton raised his eyebrows. She looked away and then back.

"Three or four days."

"Why didn't you come in earlier?"

"I'm not a whiner, okay?"

"Any fever?"

"101. It started yesterday."

"How is your peak flow?"

"I didn't do any."

He nodded. "Taking your inhalers?"

"Yes."

"Which ones?"

"Albuterol and the new one."

"I'll need to examine you. We'll get you a gown. You can hop up on the table. I'll be back in a second." He rose and turned to leave.

"Don't bother. You've seen me before. Anyway, blue breasts don't turn anyone on."

She abruptly stood, unbuttoned, and removed her dress. She threw it onto the chair, stepped out of her shoes, and except for underpants, sat on the table naked.

Unease crept over him like a fog; it fought with fatigue as he mulled whether to call for assistance. He stood with arms crossed and placed a forefinger to closed lips. Seconds of silence passed, his thoughts having found no voice, and he began his examination, pretending he was accustomed to such behavior.

She was five-feet-seven, 105 pounds. Turned sideways, she was paper-thin. Her forehead was round, nose straight, eyes large, translucent blue.

The skin, almost diaphanous—that of a sandy blonde—had become faint cyan. Her face, he thought, seemed formed by a god, so refined it was. Her ribs protruded. Muscles attached to them pulled and sucked on her gaunt ribcage. The scapulae jutted as tiny, flawed wings. Heard with a stethoscope, fine rales in all lung fields crinkled like cellophane. With great effort, her breath rose and fell. She hungered for air.

His eyes fixed on her and followed her movement. He looked perplexed, as though pondering some mystery. He recalled that as a youth, he had seen in a woman's form nothing but desire. Then in medical school—disease. But now there was some third thing, inscrutable, beyond desire and disease. He mused whether he should have such thoughts, but there they were, compulsive—and she, magnetic.

When he finished his exam, he turned and sat, rolling his chair from the table to the desk, where he studied her chart. She folded her arms and watched him closely, like a ghost.

He looked up and stared vacantly, and then he turned to her. "Pneumonia again."

"Big surprise."

"Both lungs."

"Are they still on warranty?"

"No return policy, I'm afraid."

"Is it bad?"

"I need a chest x-ray and culture before we start."

"How bad is it?"

"I don't know yet."

"Don't. No. No, don't! No hospital!"

"We have to, Whitney, for a short time, anyway. You'll feel better after some oxygen, nebs, and antibiotics. We'd better get blood gases, too."

"No more x-rays! I've been x-rayed enough. No blood gases! I won't be admitted! I must defend my show. I'm graduating." She dabbed her wet eyes and stared listlessly at the floor. Her lower lip quivered. "Can't you give me something? I'll get better."

His baritone voice dropped to a whisper. "Whitney, you won't get better at home. You'll get worse, maybe a lot worse. I'll write the school. You'll be all right. You'll go home soon. Don't be afraid."

"I'm not afraid." She wiped her cheek with two fingers. The muscles around her jaw clenched. For some seconds, there was no sound apart from her breathing and the tick of a clock. Outside in the hall, nurses laughed, an IV pole rattled against a gurney, and then someone groaned.

Whitney stepped from the table and stood motionless, eyes downcast. She put on her dress and fumbled with the buttons, leaving two of them undone. She stood in her shoes and took a deep breath. She combed her hair and adjusted the wooden pins. With one hand touching her throat, she struggled to remain calm. She forced a slight smile.

"I'll find out who is covering for your doctor. Bourke, right?"

She nodded.

He reached for his pen with his left hand and lifted the cap. "I'll write your orders, and we'll get you started. Wait here just a moment. You'll be fine up on 3 North. I'll stop by to see how you're doing before my sabbatical."

"Sabbatical?"

"I'll make sure you're taken care of." His hand held her chart as he groped for the doorknob and backed out of the room. He extended his other hand, clutching the pen, in an awkward gesture of farewell.

"Nothing lasts," she said.

CHAPTER TWO

On the room's north side, visible through a huge window, the leaves of a tree stirred in a breeze. On a limb, a cardinal sat, puffed up in her feathers, and swayed in the morning mist. The gray, liquid sky roiled with gloom. Sleet hit the panes like thrown rice. The framing in the window was perfect, and Ashton began to dwell on the image. He followed the bird to and fro and became lost in its movements. The bird peered in his direction. There was the faint noise of the wind. The bird's feathers bent. She ruffled them.

"I wonder if she sees me framed in the window," he said. The bird flew away and vanished into the field, leaving the tree limbs shifting in the wind.

"She?" said his personal lawyer, Michael Amberley. "Get a grip, Ashton. It's just a bird."

It was Monday, half-past nine, two days after the C-section. Ashton and his defense attorneys waited in a third floor conference room of the law offices of Clement and Warren. Among others, the firm retained six subalterns whose job involved pressing injury lawsuits. Hundreds of bound volumes filled walnut caseworks lining three of four sides, designed by spiders, Ashton said, to trap the unlucky in their web.

The walnut conference table stood among a dozen matching chairs. In addition to the defendant, present and seated were seven attorneys: three for the plaintiff, three for the defense, and one for the hospital. With them sat a stenographer and a videographer.

The plaintiff's lead attorney was Joel Clement. His dialect suggested New England, perhaps Boston. He had a habit of clicking his ballpoint pen. He jabbed with it when speaking to his associates, whose responses were almost military in their brevity and respect of his command. They might have worn uniforms and had their ranks sewn like flags to their noses.

"Where are the accountants, insurance men, and tax collectors?" asked Ashton.

"Clement is the big dog," whispered Randolf Black, the main defense lawyer, who had been selected by the underwriters of Ashton's liability coverage. It had taken eighteen months to meet Black. Until now, he had dealt with the newest member of the firm, Ms. Thompson, a twenty-nine-year-old with only a handful of cases tried. She had struck him as sincere, but green. No one had bothered to tell him that a team waited behind her, that she was, in effect, an intern. Recently, he had learned that Black was the most well regarded medical defense attorney in town.

"Watch my body language," Black said, close to his ear. "If I move my left hand in front, don't answer right away." He demonstrated. "I might raise an objection. During the deposition, I can't give you advice."

Ashton nodded.

"Remember, don't teach. Don't volunteer. Think before you speak. Never exaggerate. If they ask your name, don't give your address and phone number. If they ask what you would do in a hypothetical case, say you can't decide without more data. Stick to the facts."

Again, Ashton nodded.

The defense attorneys sat on either side of Ashton, Black and Thompson to the right, Michael Amberley to the left. The plaintiff's men sat opposite. Ashton had retained separate counsel to ensure that his interests were not subsumed to those of the insurance company. "The man who pays the piper calls the tune," Amberley had said.

The cameraman fit Ashton with lapel microphones and readied twin cameras, joined on a rolling stand. When the three legal teams agreed, the deposition began. With wires dangling about him, Ashton mused about being fixed for electric shock if he were to give wrong answers.

"Doctor, please state your full name and address."

Ashton did so. Clement used his mellifluous voice, soothing, yet authoritative. He seemed to have a binary personality, harsh at times, paternal at others; now mean, now nice.

"Your CV states that you graduated from medical school in 1975, and that you completed your residency in 1979. Is that right?"

"Yes."

"How many years have you practiced?"

"Twenty-one."

"On the night of June 7, 1996, you were employed by Merced University Hospital and treated the plaintiff, Walter Slade, for chest pain. Is that correct?"

"It is."

"Why did you send the patient home with chest pain? The next day, he died of a heart attack, Doctor." The avuncular manner of the lead attorney had turned cold and accusatory.

"I did not think then, nor do I now, that heart disease caused the pain."

"He died the next day of a heart attack, did he not?"

"Yes."

"Do you concede that the patient had heart disease the night you treated him? Otherwise he couldn't possibly have died the next day from a heart attack."

"I do acknowledge longstanding, and silent, atherosclerosis. You might have it this very minute. His history, exam, and various tests did not point to impending infarction, but to other causes."

"He did die from a heart attack the next day, Doctor."

Ashton looked at his attorney, then looked back and smiled a small smile as his eyes shifted to the video camera.

"Asked and answered, sir."

The lawyer sitting next to Mr. Clement, his hand over his mouth, whispered something inaudible into Clement's ear. "What do you think caused the pain, doctor?"

"Reflux esophagitis."

"A person doesn't die from that, does he, Doctor? You don't think the patient had unstable angina?"

"No."

"Why do you think Mr. Slade died?"

"The pathology report, which I believe you have before you, indicates infarction. That happened later, not when I treated him."

"Why do you say that, Doctor?"

"The EKG and muscle enzymes were normal. The physical exam was normal. He had a history of esophageal problems. Having excluded cardiac causes, I diagnosed esophagitis as its probable cause."

"Our experts think otherwise, Doctor."

Seconds of silence followed. The lawyers looked at the defendant, who looked back.

"Was there a question?" Ashton said.

"Do you think it's possible Mr. Slade had angina and that this condition worsened?"

"The word 'possible' troubles me. It's possible an elephant might run out of these woods, but how likely is it? No, his history of esophagitis, as well as a normal physical exam, EKG, and enzymes led me to another conclusion."

The lawyers grilled him for three hours, examining the chart line by line. They attacked, they feinted, they doubled back, they waited, they were congenial, they were rude; they groped for any inconsistency, any opening.

The attorneys broke for lunch, returned, and chewed on him for another three hours. When they finished, they invited others to take a turn. None took up the task, but they reserved the right to reconvene. When the meeting broke up, Black told Ashton that he had done well, and the four men took the elevator to the first floor. When they exited the building, Amberley and Ashton went one way, Black and Thompson the other.

Amberley turned to Ashton. "Care for a drink?"

"Sure, I could use one."

"Across the street there's a good place. Nadja's."

They jaywalked in the rain across Limestone Street, entered the bistro, and ordered drinks—a beer for Amberley, a gin and tonic for Ashton.

"What do you make of it?" asked Ashton. As he put the temple of his glasses between his lips, he studied Amberley's crooked bow tie.

"They're just trying to 'put the sceer' in you." He held up and bent two fingers of each hand. "You need an expert witness to bring suit, but you don't declare him until after deposition. They probably don't have one. They're fishing."

Ashton nodded. "I have three, from different sources."

"Black told me. I believe you are a hundred percent defensible. At trial you should win."

"They want to settle, though, right? No 'litigation stress.'"

"The plaintiff does. The insurance company might."

"Never. I have right of refusal."

"Well, there's no reason you should settle."

"What about filing a countersuit? Let's sue *their* butts. See how they like it."

"If you win, you could file for 'malicious prosecution' or 'abuse of process,' but that might not sit well with the judge. Piling on, you know."

"Who judges the judges?"

Amberley shrugged.

"People want perfection," Ashton went on, "and they don't find it. They feel wronged, then they sue. They look around for the money. A jury of your peers, with a tenth-grade education, decides the case after five years of legal bullshit, and by the way, here's a hundred fifty thousand in fees. They find in your favor, maybe, after five or six years of crap, and then everything is just fine?"

"Right, then you're vindicated." Amberley held up fingers like quotation marks again and smiled. He sipped his beer.

"I heard somewhere juries are apt to judge you, not on facts, but on severity. Last time I checked, this is pretty severe." He raised his eyebrows and smiled, gesturing with an open left hand.

"Dead is severe, that's for sure. Sympathy for the deceased."

"Tell me—what's wrong with my reasoning? If I can't trust the jury, impaneled from my own community, I really can't trust the people, and if I can't trust the people, why the hell would I want to be the people's doctor?"

"Have another drink, Tyler."

"Can you tell me that?" His voice was raised. The bartender and waitress looked up.

"The system works, but like medicine, it isn't perfect." Amberley regarded his client and close friend. "You're really jacked up, aren't you?"

"I guess you could say that."

"We learn the first day in law school, 'No facts alone, just opinions about facts.'"

"I see. Everything is a debate. Everyone is up for grabs. Truth is a five/four decision."

"We have to live with it."

"I used to talk about the doctor-patient relationship. Now it's the doctor-plaintiff relationship."

"If this goes to trial, the jury will probably find for you, but you can never be sure. Jurors aren't independent. Usually one or two dominant people carry weight, and the others are persuaded. Groupthink."

"They aren't on trial. They don't care."

"It's not that so much, Tyler. They usually do a good job."

"How many votes do you need for a finding? Is it unanimous?"

"Only in criminal cases is conviction 'beyond a reasonable doubt.' In civil cases, it's the 'preponderance of evidence.' Judgment is given by majority."

"Swell."

Ashton ordered a second gin and tonic. Some seconds lapsed, and neither spoke. Both seemed deep in thought. Ashton's eyes focused on an infinite distance.

"It seems nothing moves without force. The force of problems or the problem of no problems." He suppressed laughter. "Everyone wants the absolute."

"Or absolution. We'll find that only in paradise," Amberley said.

"What would a person do there?"

"What?"

"Without any needs. What would you *do*, Michael?"

Amberley looked quizzical. He shifted in his chair and smiled nervously. Ashton broke off the discussion and tossed down his drink.

"Shall we go?"

"Do you need a ride?"

"No. Thanks."

Ashton drove to the hospital and walked to his office. Having cleaned his desk out days before, he considered how to deal with what remained—three cases of books and papers. He had saved *The New England Journal of Medicine*, twenty-five years worth, and every two or three years had bound them, even when they were available in the library. There was a solemnity about the volumes, giving his office a solid sense of place. He had loved to read them; he had signed every one. For some minutes he sat, elbow on desk, palm to chin. He rose and selected a dozen volumes. He placed them in a cardboard box and carried the box outside, via the back door.

In a corner of the parking lot, a dumpster squatted under a heavy lid. He opened it with a clang, dumped the books, saved the box, and went inside for a second load. After several trips, he noticed three people, one with green scrubs, two with coats and ties, who stood behind a window. They watched with the intensity of eagles. They talked, motioned, and seemed to consult each other. He ignored them.

He disposed of about two hundred items: texts, journals, PDR's, and formularies—the last of the bunch. He sat at his desk for a minute, swiveled in the chair, then walked out and closed the door. He turned and looked at the sign on the wall, Tyler B. Ashton, M.D., before sliding it from its holder. He put it in his pocket.

He went to his locker in the men's dressing room and dialed the combination. The shoes, spackled with dried blood, perched on a shelf. Two white coats hung on pegs. He wrapped the shoes in the coats and tucked the wad under his arm. Now manumitted, he strolled through the department halls, passing a nurse who said hello. He moved his lips in a perfunctory smile.

In a wastebasket at the hall's end, he tossed away the lock. It thumped in the bottom. He left the ER and walked down the stairs into the hall and through a doorway, into the daylight. He squinted as he put on his sunglasses. The power of the sun warmed half his face. He walked on to his car. The three people watching him earlier had lifted the lid of the dumpster and were picking through its contents, as if they had discovered something long lost. He avoided their stares and got into his car. In the rear view mirror, he looked for a moment. He removed his sunglasses and saw a hard face, nothing like his own.

CHAPTER THREE

It was past midnight. The airport served Cantwell, population 8,000, the county seat of 65,000 souls. A penumbra of city light, two miles away, shone in humid diffusion. Though an airport in name, it was more like a lone asphalt strip adjacent to two hangars. Inside the first hangar were three Cessna and an old Beech. The second was empty. Heard from a great distance, a mournful whistle sounded as a locomotive passed. For a minute or more, remote clacking pierced the silence, diminished, and faded out.

Light spilled onto the tarmac from two hangar bulbs and a sodium vapor light bolted to a rusted stanchion. Sulphur butterflies circled the lamp. A bat lunged at them from time to time, and the butterflies scattered then returned, drawn endlessly to the light.

Four men with hand-held strobes stood in shadow on both sides of the runway. One talked on a cell phone. A van was parked on the driveway, and the driver listened on a static-filled radio to a female voice dispatching curt orders.

After a few minutes, the man with the radio turned on a flashlight, signaling the others, who did likewise. They pointed their strobes skyward. Distant engine noise increased until a twin engine Cessna 421 Conquest, white with red markings, hit the runway and taxied closer to them. It had no running lights, and the only illumination came from the cockpit's instrument panel.

A silver Mercedes sedan, rocker panels caked with mud, sped onto the tarmac, and stopped before hangar number one. A man with wild, red hair and an ungroomed beard climbed out of the driver's seat. His name was Juan Moreno. He moved slowly under the light, hands in pockets, head forward, determined, as if trudging through mud in the rain. The bats fluttered and checked. Butterflies scattered. He looked up. His beard partially hid fleshy cheeks that were covered by a wolf-like red stain. He bore the same affliction on his twisted nose, and yet somehow, he was handsome.

The pilot, Jimmy Blaine, a man in his late twenties, strode under the lamp and stopped next to Moreno. He rotated upward his night vision goggles. There was no handshake, no physical contact. Bolstered by a bulletproof vest, Blaine swaggered with confidence, but his eyes gave the lie.

They went to the plane. In the pilot's untied shoulder holster was a Beretta 9mm. A CZ Skorpion machine pistol lay on the passenger seat next to a military parachute.

They strolled between plane and car. "Did you bring my duffel?" the pilot asked.

Moreno popped the trunk of the Mercedes, while Jimmy Blaine retrieved the bag. Balancing it on the trunk lid, he rummaged through food and drinks, at last finding a green nylon flight jacket, which he put on. He walked around to the plane's passenger side, grabbed the parachute, and lifted it onto his shoulders. He fastened, checked, and double-checked the harness.

A blue SUV pulled alongside the Mercedes. It carried only the driver, Brendan Coulter, a muscular giant who wore jogging shorts and running shoes. He opened the truck's gate, and struggled with a brown box with a volume of three to four cubic feet. Blaine helped him carry it to the Cessna, from which the rear seats had been removed, creating a cargo bay. There were four other boxes, not quite as large or heavy.

"What denominations?" Jimmy said.

"Twenties in the big one, hundreds in the small ones." Coulter went back to the SUV.

A bent, oblong object, wrapped in a tarp and shaped like a three-dimensional boomerang, lay in the truck. Five feet in length, and weighing more than two hundred pounds, it required two men to remove and carry it to the plane.

"What's going on here?" asked Jimmy.

"Unscheduled express delivery," said Coulter in a nasal tenor. He made turtle-like movements with his head and poked Jimmy's shirt with an index finger.

Coulter and Jimmy carried the bundle to the aircraft. They eased it around the door and shoved it, sliding, onto the floor. Moreno watched them with some detachment, then from Coulter's truck, he gathered up a boating anchor and chain, walked to the plane, threw it inside, and fastened the anchor to grommets in the tarp.

"See, stout as the bull, just as smart," he said with a Spanish lilt. He gesticulated with his hand, now holding a cigar. He flicked the ash with the nail of a ringed, fifth finger.

"Almost as big," said Coulter.

"But better looking!"

"What's in the tarp?" Blaine asked.

"Bad memories," Coulter said. He looked at a jogging watch on his wrist, half-covered by a stand of coarse hair.

Blaine shook his head. "Damn! I don't like this."

"Get way off the coast and dump it," Moreno told him. "With the extra tanks, you shouldn't have trouble. If you do, take the strip in Rodrigo. Ditch it. Don't get caught."

Coulter nodded his agreement.

"I know what I'm doing. After the night scopes and radar you ripped-off from Madison Field, how can we lose?"

"Don't be over-confident. That's when you screw up," Moreno said.

"Who's in the tarp?" Blaine said.

"Clyde's fingers were in the pie," said Coulter. "He skimmed over a million. Thought he was clever."

The corners of Jimmy's mouth turned down. His brow wrinkled.

"How does that involve me?"

"As you can see, we have a disposal problem here."

"Hey, I didn't sign on for this."

Moreno said, "Sometimes, Jimmy, you must cope with the unexpected. Make the adjustment. Loyalty has its virtue. Money is also good, yes? An extra fifty thousand. I have it here." He gestured with his open hand. "I know this will help persuade you." He put his arm around Jimmy's shoulder for a moment, moved his hand to the cigar in his mouth, and then inhaled.

The pilot said nothing. He paced back and forth under the light. Moreno stuck one hand in his pocket and fingered the cigar with the other. Coulter leaned against the stanchion and watched as the plane was refueled. Jimmy said finally, "All right. I'll do it."

"Dump it deep," Moreno said.

"Damn! With all this weight, I just hope I don't crash."

"Once you've made the drop, get to Morelos. The crew will be there at five. Don't leave anything. Like last time with Richard. Especially since we're selling the plane."

"I can't believe he left his damn suitcase down there." Jimmy said.

"We were lucky we found it in time. Mistakes like that might get us nailed," added Coulter.

"Unbelievable."

Moreno puffed on the cigar and then flicked the tip. "Call about the return flight. Coulter will see you at the airport."

Coulter nodded. "I told him. Three days."

"When will you need me again?"

"Not for one month. At least. But we do need another plane. You can work on that."

"They've got one over in Jaeger. The guy needs money, real bad. DC-4 in pretty good shape. We can retrofit in Savanna, starting next Friday. Should be on line in two to three weeks."

"How much?" said Coulter.

"Two-seventy-five, maybe two-fifty."

"All right," said Moreno, and he handed Jimmy a briefcase and a cashier's check for fifty thousand dollars. "Here is your bonus." He opened his palm, and Jimmy took the briefcase key.

Blaine swiped off the goggles and stuck them under his armpit. He opened the case on the car's hood. His eyes moved over the stacks of hundred-dollar bills. He closed it. He removed a pack of cigarettes from his jacket, used his lips to draw one out, and lit it with a lighter. His eyes darted to Moreno.

"What am I supposed to do with a check for this amount of money?"

Moreno chuckled. "You won it from me in a poker game, if anyone asks."

"I'd rather have cash."

Moreno's blue eyes glowered. "Jimmy, take the check. It is cash. You know where you can cash it."

Blaine sighed and accepted it.

The two men finished refueling. Moreno gestured with a twist of his neck, and the three men moved away about twenty yards.

"If you have any problems, call Coulter. I'm not going to be available for a couple of days. All right?"

"Got it."

The headlights of a car appeared at the entrance to the airstrip. A Jeep with a woman driver pulled up, and she parked a few yards from the three men.

"Who the hell is that?" said Coulter. He started to move toward his truck, but thought better of it. After a pause, he added, "Isn't that your car?"

Jimmy threw the check inside the case and locked it. He jogged to the car. He held the girl's hand briefly, kissed her, and then handed her the briefcase. He walked back, smiling, toward the two men, while she quickly drove away.

"Jeez. You don't bring your girlfriend here. What the fuck's the matter with you?" said Coulter. His feet did not move, but he rotated his trunk toward the pilot.

"Come on, man. She doesn't know squat! She thinks I'm doing earthquake relief."

Jimmy went to the plane, his eyes downcast, his thin lips pressed together. He entered the cockpit and closed the door. Muttering to himself, he went through a pre-flight checklist and waited for the ground crew to finish. He adjusted the goggles, gave the thumbs-up sign to the crew, and then turned off the running lights.

Moreno and Coulter moved backward, approaching the Mercedes. The engine cranked, sputtered, and started, and the plane turned and taxied onto the strip. The throttle opened up as the plane gathered speed, going into the wind, south-southeast, still with no lights on board, and they listened as the engine noise faded, and the plane lifted, unseen, into the dark, until all traces of it had vanished.

"Except for that unfortunate breach of loyalty, this is going well," said Moreno. "A man could grow fond of it." Moreno's laugh was a kind of squeal. "Having to buy a larger plane is a nice problem to have!"

Coulter said nothing.

"About Clyde—I told you to convince him, not kill him." Moreno ran his lips around the cigar.

"He fought back. He tried to run."

"Tried to run, eh? Clyde was wrong, but so were you. There were other options. Don't let it happen again. Understand?" said Moreno.

Coulter pinched the bridge of his nose. "Understood. About Jimmy—should we train a second pilot? The way he's been acting, I wonder if he wants to split."

Moreno ignored the question. "He's good. But anyone can be replaced. Except me and thee, right?"

"A hundred thousand per run is like a million to him."

"A hundred today, a hundred tomorrow. Yeah, it is millions. I don't think we need to worry about him staying. But let's keep an eye on that girl of his."

Coulter nodded. "I'm sorry about Clyde. I thought he could be trusted."

"Sharks have no liege, Mister. Still, we don't need to kill. Blood draws other sharks." After an interval, he said, "Send Enriche and Hector back to Cartagena."

"Do we have enough men?"

"If you can't trust the leader, you can't trust the led. We have to replace the whole section."

"Who's going to come in their place? And when?"

"I've made inquiries," Moreno said. "I'll let you know."

"All right." He paused. "Well, I must be off."

"Off with you, then." Moreno chuckled.

They drove away. It was quarter-past one.

Moreno drove the thirty miles downtown to the Grayson Hotel. He occupied a penthouse suite on the seventh floor, where most weekends, an adjacent room was used for high-stakes poker. He went to his suite, got into a blazer, and from his open safe, picked up a mahogany box. He walked down the hall to another room, entered, and found several men sitting around a green felt table, studying their cards. At a bar behind the table, he fixed himself a straight bourbon whiskey, and then sat.

"I hope you have room for one so poor," he said to the four players.

"Now Juan, just because last time you lost a few pesos—"

A bespectacled man, his eyes looking over his cards, grinned and said, "Yes, just a few pesos."

"I think it was a hundred and eighty-three thousand dollars," said Moreno. "I'm not as smart as you are, but I do remember the amount." His laughter did not reach his eyes. He finished his cigar and threw the wet butt into a wastebasket. Producing a curved pipe and tobacco, he filled the bowl. He tamped it with an enormous finger. He torched the contents with a butane lighter while sucking mightily on the pipe's stem. The pipe jutted from the corner of his mouth and bobbed when he talked.

The door opened, and a black man with white hair, wearing a black suit, entered.

"Gentlemen, something from the grill?"

"Hot Brown," said Moreno. "In this company, you must keep up your strength."

"Anyone else?"

"Turn on the fan, please. Clear this smoke out." The man with glasses passed his hand back and forth in front of his face.

"It is on, sir." The man shook his head.

No one else ordered. The five men played stud poker for the next three hours. Moreno wagered boldly, losing much, winning much. In either case, his mood was high. He was ensconced in a comfortable chair, smoking by turns cigar, pipe, and cigarette. At intervals, he hummed and sang fragments from lyrical, if obscure, Argentinean folksongs.

At four in the morning, they concluded the evening and said their farewells. The wits among them bantered with the less fortunate, and some feigned graciousness, while others smiled without meaning it, and after all columns were tallied, the winner, a Mr. Marr, tried to suppress his glee at winning $113,000—payable in cash. Moreno won $128,000 and change, and notwithstanding the tremendous losses of a prior meeting, said, "The evening is young. Perhaps I might entice you to a game of blackjack—winner takes all?" There were no takers, but as was their custom, they agreed to resume play the following week.

Moreno went back to his suite, made a phone call, and drew water for a bath. He opened a drawer, took out a thermometer, and checked the temperature before closing the faucets. One hundred degrees. He slid the thermometer into the soap dish. He turned on a shelf CD stereo, punched a button, and music filled the room, Vivaldi's *The Four Seasons*.

He undressed, got in the tub, and soaked in the water, which covered everything except his navel, face, and beard. Now floating oddly on the surface, the head seemed disembodied. An empty wine bottle sat in a bucket half-full of water on a stand next to the tub. After a time, he reached for a towel, dried his hands, and grabbed a rolled-up magazine entitled, *Brainteasers*. There was a pen clipped inside. A torn page of the *New York Times* crossword puzzle, filled out in ink, dropped into the water. He cursed, fished it out, wadded it up, and tossed it into the sink.

He scribbled in the magazine, stuck it in the bucket, and refilled the tub. He closed his reddened eyes twice, as though trying to rest, but they would not stay closed. He finished his bath, dried, and dressed. In his closet, he opened the door of a heavy safe, and threw in the box, filled with soldier courses of hundred-dollar bills. He counted ten bills, folded them, and stuffed them into a pocket.

An hour later, the doorbell rang. A young, voluptuous woman, wearing a black dress, stood pigeon-toed on platform shoes and smiled sweetly at him. It was half-past five.

"Hi. I'm Adelaide." She fiddled with keys in a delicate hand. "Did you call?"

"What a beautiful name. Yes, yes. Come right in." Moreno ogled her as she stood there. She was a woman of quality—a joy to look upon, and not as costly as a wife. He wondered what she might look like in ten years, and then decided not to think about that.

"You poor, poor dear. I'm here to help. Even at this hour." She giggled and held up a bottle of champagne, saying, "Food for the mind." She swept by and entered the room, and as Moreno closed the door, she slowly removed her wrap.

CHAPTER FOUR

In the morning, Tyler Ashton went to University Hospital to check on Whitney Laird. He paused at her door, noted the "Respiratory Isolation" sign, and stopped at the nursing station. He smiled at a student nurse, who was dressed in white and wearing a charming starched nursing cap. He fumbled around the chart rack until she asked if he needed Laird's chart, and after he nodded, she said, "Sorry," and handed it to him.

"Quite all right. Thank you."

He knocked on the door and entered. Whitney sat in bed. A clear fluid ran through the IV to her arm. Green tubing hung from her nose. Her skin was pink. Her breath came easily; she was calm. An aluminum notebook computer was perched, open, on her lap; when she saw him, she smiled and closed the lid. She placed it on the table next to a small printer and a stack of typescript pages.

Ashton returned her smile. "You're better!"

"I am better." She unconsciously preened her hair, still damp from washing. It fell to her shoulders. She wore make-up, carmine lipstick, and sported rings on two fingers of the left hand and the thumb of the other. Having severed the sleeves from a red sweater, she used them as arm coverings.

"I forgot to thank you. You didn't have to help me. I know I'm a pain."

"No, you're not."

"Out of the blue zone, back in the red."

"Yes, yes, I see."

"Give me day, or give me night. Not this shadowy stuff in between, okay?" She was laughing. "I'm not complaining."

Ashton bent down and opened the hospital gown. He placed the stethoscope's diaphragm on her skin, asking her to breathe deeply as he listened to her upper back. He adjusted his earpieces and listened again with the bell placed on the anterior chest wall. Friction rubs crackled and scraped, but less so. Air moved well, the ribcage relaxed. Her respiratory rate had reverted to normal. The fever had gone. He held her warm hand and pushed on the pad of her index finger, noting the capillary refill.

Her deep breathing triggered a paroxysm of coughing. The room swayed in front of her eyes. She reached for a tissue and coughed in staccato barks for twenty seconds. Ashton sat on the bed's edge as she wheezed and sucked air. She was blue about the mouth, and he rose and opened the oxygen valve, increasing the liter flow. He walked around to the other side of the bed and sat in a chair, scooting it close.

"It's okay," she said. "It's breaking up."

"Your lungs sound much better."

"Can I go home?"

"I checked the cultures. The usual suspects—Staph and Pseudomonas. No need to change antibiotics."

"I guess that means 'no.'"

"It will be up to Dr. Bourke. He's your attending physician."

There was a pause. She looked down at her computer. He put his hands on the chair arms and started to rise.

"Are you going to teach any? Here, at the university?" she asked.

She looked at him, and he did not get up.

"I don't think the dean would approve of my comments."

"Like what?"

"Too much hierarchy. It's a medieval institution. You're on both ends of a leash."

"What then?"

"Not exactly a sabbatical. More like a leave."

"Leave of absence?"

"Permanent. I have satisfied my needs. A weight has been taken away." His eyes seemed unfocused.

"Seen it all, eh?"

"See one. Do one. Teach one. There must be something else."

She studied his face. "You don't seem too pleased."

"Passions come and go. I'm fine."

"Changing venues is nice—except for one thing."

"And that is?"

"You have to take yourself with you," she said.

"A grave observation for one so young." He ran a thumb and finger over his upper lip.

"Oh. I didn't mean you, personally, and I'm not so young."

"Everything is personal." He blinked, and his eyes closed a full second.

"Maybe I can see you out there, somewhere." She smiled. "Wherever you are."

He did not respond. His eyes cast about for something to look at on the floor.

"What does your wife think about all this?"

"No wife."

She was picking at the sheet. She looked up.

"I'm divorced," he added, after a pause.

"Oh."

"Back in the nineteenth century. So long ago, I barely remember."

"What will you do?"

"Do? Ponder meanings and essences, I guess." He forced a smile.

She raised her eyebrows, continuing to study him. "I know of a Trappist monastery, not far from here."

"That might work."

"You don't have any plans at all?"

"I bought a farm in Stuart County. It needs a lot of work. Still, it's a labor of love. I'm also a fine art photographer."

Her fingers were ever combing her hair. "Really? What kind of subjects?"

"Landscape. Black and white, some color. I'll photograph around the state a few days, then somewhere else."

"Do you need an assistant? I'm available."

He sucked on a tooth. He couldn't tell whether she was joking.

"Can you fix it with the board?" he said.

"What?"

"Medical examiners. They have a clerical zeal against doctors traveling with their patients."

"I'm Dr. Bourke's patient. You're retired, remember?"

"You're splitting hairs now."

"Do you know Dr. Bates?"

Ashton shook his head side to side.

"Dr. Bourke's new partner. He thinks I'll be off oxygen tomorrow, and then I can be treated at home. I finished my paper. I'm going to defend my show. I get my BFA next week. You could come!"

"Well, I don't know—"

"Please." She reached out and almost touched his forearm before pulling back.

"Maybe."

"The show is in the Hart Auditorium at Armistead. Opening is six on Friday."

There was a knock at the door. It slowly opened, and a man's face protruded through the crack. He asked if he might be disturbing their conversation. Whitney said no and invited him to enter. She introduced her father to Ashton without actually greeting or looking at him.

Geoffrey Laird was youngish-looking, and he smelled of expensive cologne. He wore a pinstripe suit with a spread collar, a regimental tie, enameled cufflinks, and cap-toe oxfords. Ashton thought he was someone defined by possessions, probably numerous. Laird strode to Ashton, grasped his hand in a firm handshake, and smiled.

"Dr. Ashton saved your baby girl," said Whitney.

"Well, Dr. Ashton, thank you. It was touch and go there. What an ordeal. Dr. Conrad says Heather and the baby will be all right. Did he really have to operate without an anesthetic? That seems impossible. I can't imagine. Isn't an anesthesiologist supposed to be on call at all times?"

"Maybe you could give him a nanosecond to answer, Dad."

"There were emergencies, trauma cases," Ashton explained slowly. "Three people in a car wreck were trying to die. They got shipped to the OR right before your wife's sudden downturn. We had to call in second and third teams. Had we waited, even for a few minutes, I'm afraid the baby wouldn't have made it."

"How often does this happen?"

Ashton's eyebrows gathered; his brow wrinkled.

"During a pregnancy, I mean."

"Not often, but if it happens to you, it happens all the time. We did use a drug that induces a partial amnesia. Your wife won't recall too much."

Laird nodded. "That's why she can't remember the pain or much of anything else."

"Nature also suppresses the fear. Makes the unbearable bearable."

"Maybe we all should take some. Can you send it to the bank?" Laird's mirth produced visible tears. Whitney and Ashton began laughing. Laird tried to control himself, but he seemed giddy, out of control.

"Dad!"

"Isn't there a saying, 'First, do no harm'? How often do you make the wrong choice?" Laird pulled out a handkerchief, mopped his brow, and began wiping his glasses.

"I'm perfect," Ashton said. "Aren't you?"

"Now that you mention it." Laird looked at his daughter as he folded his handkerchief.

"Medical decisions can be difficult," Ashton said. "Nothing looks good. Everything is chancy. I don't like it, but that's the way it is. Things turned out well, but we might have lost the mother, the child, or both."

"We have to hope for the best," Laird said finally.

Whitney looked at her arm and abruptly raised her hand. "My IV!"

The tubing had come loose from the stopcock, and the blood had backed up and had leaked onto the sheet, blooming into a red spot, saucer sized. As Ashton re-assembled the line, Laird began swaying, groping behind him for balance. He suddenly slumped to the floor, and his head bounced against the wall. His glasses flew off.

"Dad! Dad!"

Ashton laid him on his back and propped his feet on the chair. There were no scalp wounds. His face was pale and damp. Ashton listened to Laird's heart and checked the blood pressure.

"He fainted."

"Are you sure?"

"He'll be all right. It's a common occurrence."

Laird began to talk a few seconds later and excused himself for having caused trouble.

"How do you stand all this?" he said, his voice weak.

Ashton shrugged. "It's part of the job. There are sights you shouldn't see. Some you can't forget."

"I want to see everything," Whitney said.

Laird sat on the chair's edge, where he looked more embarrassed than injured. The color had returned to his face.

"If you feel dizzy, get your head below your heart, and quickly," Ashton told him. "Put your head between your knees."

"I'm okay now." Laird sat in the chair.

Ashton stood beside Whitney's bed. "I must be going," he said, smiling down at her. "Best wishes on your graduation. It's been a privilege to know you. You're so brave."

"You talk like I won't see you again."

"I'm sure our paths will cross."

"Don't forget my show."

He reached for his wallet. He removed a business card, wrote something on it, and handed it to her. He stayed for a few seconds more, and then excused himself.

When the door closed, her demeanor changed. The muscles around her eyes tightened. Her lips pursed. She clenched a fist around the sheet.

"Did you get what you wanted now? A wife upgrade. A new baby. Are you happy at last?"

"I know how you feel, but you have no idea how I feel. I'll look after you. I'll still be your father. You don't know what you would do until you get there."

"I'm not getting there, am I?"

"I only meant—"

She shook her head. "You only care about yourself. You're completely cold—totally indifferent to the pain you cause others. Totally careless. Other people exist only so you can use them."

He moved his arms in a gesture of dismay. "Haven't I always taken care of you?"

"Material needs. Money. But never the real thing. Now you're just throwing me away."

"No. That's not true. Let's not argue. It never helps."

"You should know. You and mom did enough of it."

"I have to go to work." He sighed. He got up, wiped his brow again, clutching the wadded cloth in his fist.

"I need to talk to you about that, too."

He shot her a quick glance. "What about?"

"Ever since last spring, maybe longer, I've sensed something was wrong in the bank. I've been a teller over three years, so I know the ropes, Dad. I can't put my finger on it, but there's something fishy going on."

"What do you mean?" He folded his arms around his chest.

"Guys are coming up to my window, giving me huge amounts of cash. This goes on almost every week. Sometimes every day. They seem to prefer coming to me, more often than not. The funds are transferred to a master account. That account is on the Exempt Businesses list."

"How much money are we talking about here?"

"Eight or nine thousand per deposit. Always under the limit. Jewelry stores, antiques, and rug stores. There's a movie theater, too. They can't make that much money selling stuff in this town. No one else does."

"Do you know their names?"

"Oh, sure. I can give them to you."

"Did you mention it to anyone else?"

"I mentioned it to Ms. Fritz, but she didn't think we needed to file a report. Didn't she tell you? She's not the most organized person around. She said she would."

"I'll talk to her. It's probably not what you think. You have the names and account numbers?"

"Yeah, I've got them. Somewhere." She reached for her purse, rummaged through it, but found nothing. "It's at the bank. Fritz must have it."

"I'll check with her. I'll look into it today. Thanks for telling me." He paused, then added, "I'd appreciate it if you'd keep this to yourself."

"You can have your computer back." She handed it to him. "Thanks. And say hi to your new wife."

He wheeled without a word and rushed out of the room.

CHAPTER FIVE

Whitney talked Dr. Bates into continuing her treatment as an outpatient. She was to receive oxygen as needed and daily IV injections of antibiotics, given by a nurse twice a day. Melanie Laird invited Whitney to stay with her until she recuperated. Divorced six months, Mrs. Laird lived downtown, alone. After two days, Whitney no longer needed the oxygen. She returned to school and resumed her job as teller.

After work each day, she drove to her mother's townhouse in a red VW Cabrio adorned with bumper stickers that read, "Mean People Suck," and "Capital Punishment is a Hate Crime." Written on a chrome plaque was the command, "Bare feet, not arms."

Behind the townhouse, surrounded by ivy-clad brick walls, was a small garden Mrs. Laird had planted. She nurtured it with continuing passion. Constructed as a parterre, its paths formed a central diamond, and in the interior, successions of daffodils, azalea, flox, and daisies bloomed. Clipped boxwoods were massed at the periphery, interspersed with hollies and Japanese maples. When the weather permitted, mother and daughter took meals on the patio, especially when Melanie Laird felt the need to smoke.

Whitney resembled her mother, who at forty-seven years was still a beautiful woman. She had Whitney's sandy-colored hair, untouched by gray, and brilliant blue eyes. Having little need of makeup, she wore it sparingly.

"I had a surprise the other day," Whitney said. "Dad showed up at the hospital."

"You didn't tell me."

"I'm telling you now, okay?"

Melanie ignored her daughter's sharp tone. "I guess he had three people to see, all in one place." She hesitated. "I shouldn't say that."

"Yeah, it's like seeing a friend on your way to your real destination."

"Did you see the baby?"

"Through the window, right after birth. She was hooked up to machines."

"Maybe she won't live."

"She will. Dr. Ashton thinks so. You know she can't have an illness like mine."

"Dr. Ashton? What does he have to do with it?"

"He was called to the operating room at Heather's delivery. Right before I saw him in the emergency department. He was there again when Dad came."

Melanie put her finger to her chin, and then nodded.

"What in the world attracted you to Dad, anyway?"

Melanie started to answer, but said nothing. She put her thumb and index finger over her lips. A heavy silence settled over them. Whitney's eyes remained fixed on her mother. Her mother looked up.

"We met in college," she said finally. "I was a freshman. He was a junior. French class. We were seated alphabetically. He sat in front of me. Laird and Logan. We had to recite dialogue. I was his partner." There was another pause, as if she were remembering something. She looked away.

"Well, what happened? Did sparks fly? Was that it?"

"In the first week, he asked me for a date. Very confident. Very charming. Sincere. He kept saying my name. And of course I was flattered. We began to date. He bought me presents. He was smart. His mind was quick. A fast talker. He told me I was beautiful. He said, *'Je t'aime,'* in class one day."

"Oh, brother." Whitney rolled her eyes. "He seduced you."

"He took up all of my time. He opened doors for me—put his hand on my waist. Now that I think about it, he touched me a lot. But he was moody, especially when he drank. He hated my friends. He called me constantly. And was very jealous. He had a way of interrupting me and ridiculing what I said. It hurt. With him, wit was a sport. He made a game of poking fun at everything. And everyone. Good people were dupes."

"A real smart-ass, Mom. That must have been hard."

"He started his MBA, and I went to work. I didn't finish my degree."

"Why not?"

"I don't know. I wanted to get married. A career didn't even occur to me."

"Didn't you date anyone else?" Whitney took off her sweater and threw it on the table.

"He took up all my time. 'His woman,' you know."

Mrs. Laird adjusted her sunglasses, frowning at them. "The woman should choose. Let them chase; you choose. The first one to the door, the aggressive one—watch out for him. He may be not the best. But of course, I was young—not that wise."

"The devil come for your soul?"

"He wasn't the devil, but he wasn't a gentle heart, either."

"We can agree on that."

"He always craved success. Beating other people. It got in the way of everything."

"Other people are just props."

"What?"

"He's a total narcissist, Mom."

Melanie sighed and reached for a cigarette.

"You should quit smoking. It kills your lungs."

Melanie smiled sadly at her daughter. "I'll quit tomorrow."

Whitney put her hand on her mother's arm. "Do it now. Why wait?"

"I don't know if I can."

"You can. Just do it."

Melanie put the cigarette back.

"When did you know I was sick?"

"You were the healthy one, not at all like Mary. They said she had an intestinal blockage. She lived three days. "You got pneumonia every winter, and when you were five, they finally did tests. I was devastated. I'm sorry." Her eyes welled up. She dabbed them with the napkin.

"Sooner or later, you discover things aren't as important as you thought. Sooner, in my case." Whitney reached for her mother's hand. "Tell me more about Dad."

"He had lots of affairs. The last one with Heather—when he got her pregnant, that did it. I had no choice, except to get a divorce."

"Dad wanted to change the gene pool. Then he could win!"

"I considered leaving earlier, but I didn't because of you. That's what I told myself. It didn't hurt that your father made lots of money. The truth is I was afraid of being on my own."

"Well, it's over now. You're back in school."

"I want my degree. Life has more meaning."

They sat in silence for a few seconds, listening to the birds chitter.

"Guys," Whitney said. "Some are so shy; others are so brash."

"Women need to flirt. You make the first move."

"Be the aggressor. Attack."

"Be positive. Be agreeable. Listen. Is that so hard?"

"Yes," Whitney said. They laughed.

"When people are attracted, they may hesitate, not wanting to be rejected. They look for an entrance. That's where flirting comes in."

"If the guy doesn't hold back, he's looking for another kind of entrance."

"Really, dear. Are you trying to shock me?"

"I think it's hard to slake a man's thirst."

"Why do you think that?"

"Most men want children."

"Not everyone is like your father."

"You don't think so?"

"Some women, especially those with careers, don't have children. And then marriage isn't everything."

"That's true. Every fourth person seems to be a lesbian."

"Oh my word! Don't mention that."

"Look on the bright side. It might prevent a population explosion."

There was a long silence. Melanie lit a cigarette in spite of Whitney's frown. Soon, a gray pall of smoke wafted overhead. Whitney's cat, Cheshire, wandered in, lay on the warm bricks, and then licked his foreleg.

"You look deep in thought," said Melanie.

"It's nothing."

"Tell me."

Whitney leaned forward. "Did Dad do anything illegal at work in the years you were married to him?"

"Why do you ask?"

"I have my reasons."

"He was sued once by stockholders." She looked away.

"Go on."

"Another, larger bank wanted to buy his bank. He wrote several of the stockholders, mostly widows, and offered to buy all their shares. He didn't mention that if they held onto them, they would make a whole lot more money. Some did sell. Six months later, he liquidated and almost doubled his money. There were complaints. That led to a civil suit. He settled and had to return half the profit."

"Anything worse than that?"

"There was another time. The SEC investigated him for insider trading. He was on the board of directors of another company. The general counsel, his friend, told him the company was going to go down the tubes soon. Geoffrey sold everything—thousands of stock options and shares—and made a small fortune. Three months later, the stock sank, and the bankruptcy led to an SEC inquiry. Of course, there was no hard evidence. Actually, they just asked him for an explanation. No interview, no investigation. No charges. He knew the guy at the SEC, too."

"Guess what, Mom? He's up to his tricks again. I read his e-mails. I know. I shouldn't have. He's getting a ten percent cut on overseas, multi-million dollar wire transfers."

"You read his e-mails? When?"

"I borrowed his laptop to polish my senior paper. While mine was being fixed."

"I'm not surprised he's doing something dirty. He thinks he's untouchable. I guess he is. Nothing bad ever happens to him. He always seems to come out on top." Melanie squashed out her cigarette in the ashtray. "He's not an honest man."

Whitney's eyes flashed. She raised her voice. "I have to do something, Mom. I'm not going to stand for this. The way he's treated us. Getting that girl pregnant and everything. I won't take it."

"But what can you do?" Her mother reached for another cigarette, and holding it with three fingertips, placed it between her lips.

"I can blow the whistle on him. That's what."

"No, no, dear, don't do that."

"He ran off with what's left of my life." She paused and squeezed her eyes shut. "I'm just a castaway, a discard. And you are, too. It's not right." She opened her eyes and wiped her face.

"You matter to me, Whitney."

"He won't get away with this, Mom. I can tell you that right now."

CHAPTER SIX

Ashton napped much of the day and slept through the night. He rose at half-past five, before the sun. He stored in his backpack his cherished view camera, a 1944 Deardorff, made of walnut and brass, and three lenses, housed in their respective boards, a dark cloth, a light meter, filters, cable release, and loupe. In a changing bag, he loaded twenty sheets of five by seven-inch black and white negatives into holders.

He took the pack and a battered wood tripod to the trunk of his five-year-old convertible, a steel-blue BMW 328i. He left the city going west on Barret Parkway, shifting through the five gears, reaching speeds of over ninety miles per hour. Dead black enveloped the headlight beams.

With little warning, he came upon two lanes of stalled traffic, forcing him to brake hard. He slowed to a crawl, and the line crept forward until it approached a wreck in the median. Two cars had been in a head-to-head collision. EMTs hurried to aid the victims. Firemen cut into the wreck with great hydraulic pincers. A woman, attended by a man in uniform, lay crumpled on the grass; her blouse was open. Four cones of light, cast up from the trucks, limned the scene in an eerie glow, and changed the kneeling men into beggared apparitions.

Curiosity seekers had gathered—benumbed witnesses to the spectacle. State police kept them at a distance. While passing the crowd, Ashton peered into their shocked, yet intrigued faces. For a reproachful moment, he debated whether to stop. His car traveled on as if self-determining. As the wreck receded and vanished, time converged to memory, and he passed through a curtain into the unbroken night.

After an hour, Ashton passed Sawyer and then Maryville, turned north on highway 617, and parked his car. As dawn broke, the land became a palate of grays. He took his backpack and walked with a flashlight along the trail to Hampton Arch, but exposed no film. He went back to the car and drove to a stone bridge. He wandered into the Smith Creek area, and as the sun cleared the horizon, he explored Rudd River tributaries, bleeding arteries winding through a body of trackless wilderness. In a clearing, next to the stream, he disturbed a silent killdeer running back and forth, feigning a shattered wing.

At the bottoms of ravines, lying far beneath sandstone ridges, narrow rills ran cold to creeks lined with smooth rock. Tulip poplar, white oak, and shagbark hickory grew on steep slopes. Under a canopy of trees near the red stream, mountain laurel and rhododendron grew wild amid ferns and moss. A steady rain had fallen in the night. Water beaded on the surfaces of leaves. Needles of young pines bent under strings of droplets, glinting in the dawn like so many pearls.

Shafts of diagonal light pierced the tree canopy. Gold pooled on the ground. He trod on carpets of moldering leaves and dodged saplings without number. A moist cloud enveloped the forest; mist rose from waters that eddied and purled. Chittering birds alighted on the branches; blue-winged and yellow warblers crooned lovelorn in the new day.

When the sun cleared the cliff, Ashton placed the tripod spikes in muddy water. Smoke hung over the brook, diffusing all color; he could scarcely discern the forest's bent trees. He fastened the Deardorff to the tripod's head and mounted a green-filtered lens. He opened the lens wide, and under the dark cloth, focused on the ground glass, using an eight-power loupe. He placed the rear standard at vertical, and kept the film plane parallel to the trees. He determined the exposure, taking three readings with a spot meter, and then set the f-stop to 32, the shutter speed to two seconds. After loading a sheet of black and white five by seven-inch film, he fired the shutter. He exposed a second negative at four seconds. Detail loomed in shadow, in an otherwise lambent cathedral.

He sat astride an uprooted tree near speaking shoals. He watched the red salamanders as plants toiled, animals devoured, and each in the wet air breathed in the others' breaths. The world seemed cast in beautiful order, a born and grown machine of tellurian calm. The thought sprang unbidden from some neural circuit, while its dark twin, the notion all things were chaotic, all were fighting all, came next, and both took up residence in his mind like unwelcome quests.

After eight hours, drifting through dappled woods, drinking from his canteen, eating nothing, he had exposed the twenty sheets of film. He put the camera in the backpack, hoisted it onto his shoulders, and folded the legs of the tripod. Tired and hungry, he began his return.

As he descended the hillside along a slick and muddy path, a noise came from behind, like a stick breaking. He turned, looked, and then continued. Again, there was a rustling, closer now, and he veered off the path and stood motionless behind a beech. After some moments, a large, female dog appeared—a herding breed of some sort—shaggy, bone white, bedraggled, and without a collar.

The dog spied him, stopped, and whimpered like a foundling. She neither growled, nor bared her teeth. She crouched, forelimbs on the ground, nose pointed upward, rump up, tail down, and ears pendant. Ashton talked nonsense to the dog. She lowered her head. Her tail wagged. He went onto the path and petted her, and she abruptly lay on her back. When he continued walking, the dog followed, six feet behind.

At length, he came to his car, opened a cooler, and unwrapped a chicken sandwich. Ashton gave the chicken to the dog while he ate the bread, lettuce, and tomato—an easy compromise, since he held vegetarian leanings, sometimes practiced, sometimes not. The dog snapped at the meat and devoured it in an instant. She sat on her haunches. Her tail thumped the asphalt. "Go home," he said. "Go on, now."

Ashton climbed in the car and drove away. In the mirror, he saw the dog sitting at the roadside, becoming smaller and smaller. Two miles down the road, Ashton came to a country store. He studied the shelves for something to eat, found nothing, and bought a Pepsi instead. He got back in the car.

"Damn it," he said aloud, pounding the steering wheel, as if he had arrived at some onerous decision. He drove back, and when he arrived, she was still there, still glued to the roadside. He placed one of his white coats on the front seat and opened the passenger door. The dog looked to the left and the right, and then whined.

"Last chance, pal." The dog jumped into the car, and the two headed to town. It was hot in the car, and after a while, the dog began to pant. "You're drooling on my lab coat," he said. The dog cocked one eyebrow, her mouth ajar, her tongue dangling.

Rather than turn on the air-conditioning, which he disliked, Ashton pulled over to the roadside and stopped. He lowered the convertible top. He then drove south eight miles to Courtland, a town of 4012 people. She stuck her head outside the windshield; the wind whipped her ears as they drove onto the main street. Ashton took a room at the Potts Creek Motel, a ramshackle enterprise of thirty units. The clerk, also the owner, said, "We don't take no dogs. They kindly make a mess." Ashton changed the man's mind with an offer to pay double. He left a deposit for any damages.

"Compared to some people, she's a treasure. Looks like most of the damage here is done." He smiled.

"You pay double for a damned dog?" the man asked.

"Maybe I'm a fool," Ashton said. "Lack of a proper upbringing."

The clerk recommended Quinn's Place, a bar and grill, as the best bet for dinner.

After taking a shower, Ashton left the dog in the room and walked less than a block to a tiny store, where he bought dog food. He returned, fed her, and put an ice bucket full of water on the floor. The dog seemed not to have eaten in days. She had muddied the carpet in brown splotches where she had lain on the floor. She rested her head on her paws. One eyebrow rose.

He thought for a moment before starting the shower. He removed his clothes and urged the dog to stand. He dragged and cajoled her into the bathroom and lifted her into the tub. Her aversion to water was as sheep to wolves. Like lifting a big lamb, he picked her up, placing her in the tub. She growled and tried to jump out. When he washed her beard, she tried to nip his hand, but he clamped shut her muzzle. She gave up. She hung her head, stood still, and continued to whine. When he was finished, he began drying her with a towel, but she broke loose, jumped out of the tub, went into the hallway, and shook sequentially, nose to tail. He used three towels to dry her, and afterwards, she looked like an unshorn ewe with a strange jaw and funny hooves.

Ashton put up the top and drove about a mile from the hotel to Quinn's Place. It would garner no awards, unless Quinn or his friends were to bestow them, in the fashion usual to American society. Quinn saw himself more as critic than architect. A pink neon sign flashed, "Bar." When you walked inside, floorboards, worn in places, caved in others, and painted a uniform soil-brown, squeaked under drunken boots. From the stained drop ceiling, wires in chains led to naked, red bulbs housed in black, inverted cones. Behind the bar was Quinn himself, splashing beer into frosted steins.

Revelers with cracked necks and tobacco-stained nails sucked on wet cigarette stubs. Ashton listened to one man tell an obscene tale with a drunken voice. Four-letter words floated about like flatulence as men swapped insults.

Transected heads of glass-eyed deer stared enigmatic from two walls. Electric fans blew stale smoke through the dead air. Ashton strolled to an empty booth, wherein someone had scratched "Lord" on the table. He put his jacket over the back of the chair and went to the bar for a beer. He took it back to the booth and watched the people over his cold glass.

A teenaged girl sat among the regulars, chewing gum and twisting her bleach-blond hair with a finger. Nail polish flaked on her ragged nails. She wore a braless dress, exposing on her back a tattoo of a dragon breathing fire.

Claudia, an aging waitress with a youthful bounce to her gait, came to his table. Her face was sallow, her lips thin, and smoke clung to her clothes. She stifled a yawn as she groped in her apron for a pad and pencil.

"Hidy," she said with a grin. Ashton nodded.

"I found a stray dog," he said. "Know where there's an animal shelter?"

"There ain't one here, son. A lot of animals, though, if you take my meaning."

"Know anyone who wants a cute dog? Very friendly."

"We already took one. Yonder." She waved with her raised hand toward an odd looking dog, a shapeless, forlorn beast recombined in a bizarre gene drift, slumped on the floor, snoring.

"You think he might like a friend?"

She shook her head. "One's enough." She studied Ashton.

"You don't seem from around here."

"I'm not."

"Where are you from?"

"East of here, sixty miles."

"What kind of work do you do?"

"Doctor."

"So what brings you to these parts, Doc?"

"Solitude."

She scowled. "Say what?"

"I need some time for myself."

Ashton reached into the bucket of unshelled peanuts sitting at his table, crushed one, and popped the nuts into his mouth. He chewed quietly, as the waitress went on.

"We could have used you back a spell. There was a fight. One guy got hisself cut up pretty good."

"Hmmm, that's a shame."

"Yeah, a doctor would've come in right handy."

"I'm not on anyone's payroll just now."

"You taking it easy for a while, huh?"

"Looking out for my own needs. Like everyone else."

She puckered her lips and sighed. Her eyelids narrowed reprovingly. She pointed a bony finger, began to speak, then thought better of it.

"Take your order?" Having found nothing in her apron, she took the pencil from behind her ear, opened a ragged pad, and stood, one leg bent, on thick-soled shoes.

He ordered a salad. As the waitress turned, he swept a pile of peanut shells off the table. When the salad came, he removed the bacon bits and black olives and left them on the plate's edge. An infirm horsefly spiraled down. It buzzed and spun on the table. It righted itself, wobbled for an instant, then flew to the top of a crouton.

Ashton pulled out his eight-power loupe, and like a god, studied the fly's iridescent eyes as its proboscis mopped up its spew. Approaching the fly from the rear, he used his loupe's rubber band, and shot it away with a loud snap. The crouton launched off the plate and dropped toward the floor as the doomed fly bolted across the room in a looping arc. They hit the floor in synchrony. From across the room, Claudia looked at him and shook her head. He smiled.

Ashton gulped his beer, ordered a second one, and listened to the music. His thirst was unquenchable. The jukebox lyrics began to make sense. No one knew where he was. No one noticed him. No one cared. The waitress seemed determined to shun him.

A man and a woman in their early twenties entered the bar and began playing nine-ball. They seemed like happy lovers. Her eyes held the young man's in a radar gaze. He placed his hand on her belly, below a red tube top, above her nude navel, which was pierced with a gold ring. She wore headphones. Ashton studied her as she danced alone in a pirouette, arms upraised, chin down, eyes closed. Another man, head thrust back, wearing leather pants and Harley boots, held a black helmet, and he stood over the jukebox mouthing the words of some country song. When the tune ended, Ashton sidled up to the young couple and watched them play pool.

She laughed drunkenly. They exchanged introductions. She lisped, having also had her tongue pierced with a gold stud. Ashton kept staring at it. After two games of straight pool, the couple invited him to join. They were, all three, good, drunken pool players. Typical Americans, each relayed his or her life story in five minutes or less. Adrian and Nell Ferguson, high school sweethearts, had been married three months.

It was well after midnight when Ashton left the bar and returned to the motel. The dog had eaten all the food and lay asleep at the foot the bed. She looked up, and her tail bounced on the floor. She had not destroyed anything. There were no unusual odors. He took the dog outside and returned, patted her, climbed into bed, and fell asleep in seconds.

Before dawn, he rose, used the changing bag to place new film into their holders, and at first light, returned to the gorge. He and the dog, now named Piper, parked in the same place and disappeared into the forest, empty of man and dog—save for themselves. Piper sniffed at the edge of the forest and squatted. Then she followed him, sometimes running ahead on the path in a zigzag pattern. He photographed the rock outcroppings, cliffs, and arches for much of the morning. In the distance, a murder of crows called. After some hours, he stopped, sat, and rested a moment, leaning against a tree; after a few minutes, he dropped off to sleep and into a dream.

When he awoke to the calls of the raucous crows, the sun was overhead in a cloudless sky, casting harsh shadows on an indifferent landscape. One bird, perhaps attracted to the glint of his wristwatch, swooped down, landing in a branch overhead. It bounced up and down. Ashton waited, not moving, coaxing it to come closer, but it never did. Piper got up and licked Ashton's face. The bird flew away.

Light, shifting randomly through the canopy of rustling leaves, mottled the forest floor. The light's brightness exceeded his film's dynamic range, so he could make no exposures. Instead, he sat for a long while, like a cat in the bush, indolent, breathing under the sun, looking at nothing in particular. He resolved to return to town.

On the way back, he passed a veterinarian's office, and without giving the matter much thought, pulled into the parking lot, which was vacant of cars, except for an old pick-up. He and Piper went inside, where no one waited, not even a receptionist. He sat in one of a dozen or so chairs and looked around. She lay on the floor at his feet.

On the table were cut-up magazines for knife aficionados and motor-cycle devotees. On a cracked wall, a stuffed trout swam crazily. A rude aquarium's murky water bubbled without a sign of a fish. Two bison skulls were copper-nailed to plaques. On its side, lay a rigid vixen. Ashton stood, preparing to slip out the door, when the veterinarian shambled into the reception room. He wore an odd cap, no socks, and looked as if he were Trotsky's brother.

"I'm afraid I don't have an appointment," Ashton said.

"Never mind. Come on back. Receptionist is out." He stuck out his hand. "Dr. Stuart."

"Tyler Ashton."

The vet opened the door and ushered them into an exam room, where Ashton lifted Piper onto a waist-high table. The dog whined.

"I found a stray. I'd like to get her stuffed."

"What?"

"Just kidding. She needs an exam. Shots."

Stuart grabbed Piper's jaws, pried them open, and peered at her inci-sors. "I'd say she's four, maybe five." The dog growled. Her lips curled; her jaw flexed and twisted. The vet's arms swung wildly as Piper struggled to her feet, snarling. Stuart squinted and grunted, making unseemly animal noises in equal measure.

"You're not going to stick your head in there, are you?"

The vet looked up, but continued grappling. His nose wrinkled, mouth opened. Ashton looked at the vet's inflamed gums. The dog voided on the table, and Stuart released the dog, and then wiped the urine away with his hand.

"Interesting. Not unlike some of my practice," said Ashton, smiling. "They growl or pee on your tie."

"You a doctor?"

"Yeah."

"What do you do?"

"Emergency medicine."

"We're in a bad way here. Old Doc Hayes quit the clinic, retired after fifty-two years of practice. Then he up and died."

"Poor bastard. Died, eh? Damn. Well, *C'est la guerre.*"

Dr. Stuart finished his exam, recommended three vaccines, gave them, and they were out the door in twenty minutes, with Ashton holding preventive medicine for heartworms.

Ashton was back at Quinn's by five o'clock. He ate the same meal as the previous night, while listening to the first set of a bluegrass band. He debated whether to return in the evening to photograph, but was seized by a strange lassitude. The moment was lost. At about six o'clock, Adrian and Nell Ferguson entered and went right to the pool table. After a couple of beers, Ashton returned to the motel and slept the night through.

CHAPTER SEVEN

He began his return to the city at dawn, a Friday, the day of Whitney's BFA show. He took an alternate route and drove with the top up along Paris Pike. Black roads twisted through an unbroken greensward, undulant, like rolling seas. Copses of trees arrayed themselves in pastures, forming park-like savannahs.

He could not imagine sights more beautiful. White shelves of clouds floated languidly. On both sides of the road, dry-laid limestone fences guarded soft, verdant fields. Miles of ashlar fence, made by Scots, the English, and then Irish masons, wound along the roadside, forming dual gray ribbons.

He made it to his small townhouse and parked in the driveway. He grabbed Piper's neck, guided her across the yard, unlocked his door, and passed under the lintel. When he released her, she bounded through the rooms, upstairs and down, and at last satisfied, followed him into the living room, where he stood sorting the mail. An announcement about the University BFA and MFA shows caught his attention. Whitney Laird. Opening, half-past six.

An hour later, thinking about the importance of making a good impression, his mind turned to the sartorial. He dressed in a hounds-tooth sport coat, faded blue jeans (but not too faded), and a white dress shirt. No tie. He looked into the mirror and then decided the outfit was absurd. He considered wearing something else, then thought about not going at all, and concluded by keeping the same jeans and jacket. "Damn it," he said to Piper, who sat cocking her head. "Aren't appearances trivial?"

He drove to the university, located in the city's center, and found a parking place in a lot across the street from the Sarah Building, an old tobacco warehouse converted into art studios. He entered a side door. Two students in advanced, Bohemian decay guarded the entrance and took five dollars in "extortion" money.

He climbed the stairs leading to a wide, long hallway, creaking under tons of weight, where a crowd milled in calculated dishabille. They picked over buffets filled with a miscellany of snacks and soups decocted from nameless ingredients. He found the red wine, poured it into a plastic glass, pretended to inspect the food, gulped the wine quickly, and refilled his glass twice. He knew no one, but smiled at the few faces that smiled at him.

Two-thirds of the way down the hall, a lone woman sat on a bar stool— a waif—and sang with great passion while picking on a guitar. Her soprano penetrated to the rafters, and when she sang "Lily of the West" and "Wayfaring Stranger," Ashton leaned against the wall, deeply moved, not knowing why.

Two hundred or more drawings and paintings were displayed. Jutting at right angles to the walls stood eight-foot caseworks, some adorned with ceramics and clay pots, painted in a manner like the ancient Greeks. Other cabinets held sculptures, both metal and stone. The floors were speckled like a clown's suit, splashed with generations of random paints.

Rooms with sixteen-foot ceilings, supported by twelve-inch-thick oak posts and beams, opened on either side of the hall. He surveyed the rooms one by one, discovering people in the printmaking studio, with its Bavarian limestones and etching presses. In galleries, artist proof monotypes, lithographs, and woodcuts hung on three walls. Many were for sale; some few had red dots, indicating a deal had been struck.

He wandered to the Hart Gallery, where the BFA students opened their shows. He stopped at the entrance and spotted Whitney Laird among the three presenters. He wrote a congratulatory note on a deckled-edge card and tossed it in a glass bowl. He went left, studying the paintings and prints of Gretchen Hill, to whom he nodded and made awkward and indulgent conversation.

Whitney Laird's work occupied the entire rear wall. He looked first at the prints and then the paintings. He stopped before one, a monotype showing a pregnant woman with a transparent abdomen and uterus. The fetus, which encroached on the woman's heart, pushed it to the side, squeezing it. Two enigmatic figures, apparently men with mantis-like faces, stared at the viewer. A big cat sat on the floor, completing a pyramidal form, thrust before a background matrix of swirls, like Munch. The artist needed anatomy lessons, but the more he looked at it, the more he liked it.

He moved to the next, a painting. A clothed figure, alone and small, stood before a murky tree line under a brooding sky, black with clouds. The next, an acrylic, showed three figures huddled apart from a child, whose huge, forlorn eyes stared straight ahead. The sun was oppressive. At the exhibition's middle, a series of monotypes of fractured nudes hung in a collage, self-portraits, Ashton decided.

She spied him and broke off her conversation with a middle- aged man. She rushed up to him, and smiling, held out her hand.

"You came!"

"Surprised?"

"I got my show hung, after all."

"Well hung."

"Are you being suggestive?" She picked at the top button of her blouse and giggled.

"No, no. I think I'd like to buy one of your works."

"Which one?"

"The pregnant one." He went to the one with the transparent uterus and pointed to it.

"It's called 'Feral People.' Turned a few heads."

"Wrap it up for me."

"Really? I haven't sold anything yet. I overheard one woman wonder how people could put this stuff in their living rooms." She had a huge smile, and she could not decide what to do with her hands. She held her fingers, interlaced, at her waist and then slipped her thumbs in her pant's belt loops.

"I know just the place to hang it."

"Where?"

"The dining room. You see this green? A hint of viridian? Matches my curtains perfectly."

She looked quizzical.

"Just kidding. I don't have any curtains."

"You have a strange sense of humor, Dr. Ashton."

"I guess it's true."

"I'm cleared to graduate! My professors liked the show."

"When?"

"Next Saturday. Will you come?"

"No promises."

"Please!"

"Send me the details."

"Okay."

"How do I pay for this thing?"

"You can pay me. I'll get you a receipt."

He took out his checkbook, filled in the amount for four hundred dollars, and handed it to her. She gave him the receipt.

"I'll make sure you get it. The show lasts one week."

"Fine. Fine. Splendid."

She studied his face. "And how do I get in touch with you?"

"Do you still have my card?"

She nodded.

"You can call that number, and my address is on the check. I'm not always available, though. I wore a beeper for so long, so people could always find me, that now, sometimes, I don't want to be found. I don't have a cell phone."

"That's okay."

A couple whispered and laughed, moving close, and it was apparent that Whitney wanted speak to them. Ashton excused himself and looked at the remainder of the show: the sculptures, photographs, ceramics, paintings, and prints. He ended up at the bar. He left an hour later, saying goodbye to the "extortionists."

Showing prudence not given to ordinary boozers, he abandoned the car and ambled home in an alcoholic mist. He arrived safely, twenty minutes later. Piper sniffed at him oddly. There were few furnishings, nothing on the walls, no carpets. He had divided his furniture between the townhouse and his new country place, about thirty-five miles away. Neither place was elegant; they were spare but clean. His housekeeper and sometime cook, Ms. Wilson, had worked for him for eighteen years, and she kept both places spotless.

A week later, he received an invitation from Whitney through the mail slot. It had no stamp. Graduation would take place at two PM, outdoors on the Commons, at Armistead University. A handwritten note folded around the envelope directed him to the garage, where she had left his painting. She suggested they meet for dinner afterward to celebrate "A mutual end, a beginning."

Ashton had skipped his own graduation. His diploma had been sent in the mail. He had still less interest in someone else's graduation, but the dinner invitation intrigued him. It was not entirely innocent, not strictly ethical, but neither was it an assignation. He did not know what it was, exactly, but to find out, he resolved to go.

At the ceremony, he met Whitney's parents, Geoffrey Laird and Melanie Laird. He found the graduation ritual predictably boring. At the valedictory, a naive first among equals spoke solemn words about character and duty. No mention of money or power, command and control, arrogant, petty, or corrupt bosses. Nothing about betrayal. He stayed long enough to confirm dinner's time and place. No one else was invited.

They were to meet at seven o'clock at The White Orchid, perhaps the best restaurant in the city. There was a white tablecloth, a wealth of forks, knives, and spoons, a gaggle of black-tied waiters, the works. He was seated when she arrived and had already drunk a glass of Bordeaux. A waiter appeared instantly and poured for them both. Ashton held the glass by the stem, swirled the bowl, and inhaled the vapor. She sipped her wine, leaving a red smudge on the rim of the glass.

"Sorry, I'm late."

"You're not late. I got here early."

"Did you like the ceremony?"

"Nice."

"Nice? That's a pretty weak word."

"I'm not much for ceremonies."

"Well, I'm happy you went, anyway."

"You look well, Whitney. Much better in the red zone."

She rolled up her jacket sleeve, hiding an IV catheter.

"A red sweater helps, too. I lose the IV in two days."

"This is a rare pleasure, being invited to dinner by a lovely, young woman. To what do I owe such a privilege?" Ashton adjusted his tie as he spoke.

"Sorry for being forward. Everybody says I'm pushy, even my parents. 'She's strong willed.'" She laughed and unconsciously groomed her hair.

"Forward yes. Froward no."

"Well, here's to new lives!" Whitney lifted her glass, studying the smudge on the rim, and quaffed the remaining wine. "This is super!" she said.

"Quite a thirst you have, my child." He raised his eyelids, looking amused.

"I'm not a child."

"Yes, yes, I know." He opened the fingers of his left hand. The sommelier appeared at their table, and Ashton ordered a second bottle, same vintage.

"I'm glad you're so much better," he said.

"I snap back once the drugs kick in. I'm tough."

Ashton smiled and said nothing.

"You're still leaving practice?"

"I've left."

"But why?"

"I'm not really sure." He played with his fork. He looked at her eyes, glanced away, then looked back.

"Come on, tell me."

"Let's say I've formed an opinion."

"Which is?"

He thought a moment. "My eleemosynary feelings have turned to their opposite."

"What was that fifty-dollar word?"

"Charitable."

"Why don't you just say 'charitable'?"

"I'm a pompous ass?" He grinned.

"What does 'pompous' mean?" she said with a half-smile.

"Tell me which words to avoid, and I'll make substitutions."

"Smarty pants."

"I'm not as conceited as you think."

"That's what they all say."

The waiter came, opened a second bottle, and filled both glasses. He gave them cards written in French and English and then recited a litany of culinary specials.

"So what didn't you like about practicing medicine?"

He thought for a few seconds. "Vast unpleasantness, too horrible to relate."

"Don't you feel guilty about quitting? How many years of school?"

"Twelve."

"You are trained to save lives."

"How many lives do I need to save?"

"Until you can't save any more. Everyone needs something to work for."

"Everyone needs something to work on."

"What do you mean?"

"Work depends on opposites. You need a substrate."

"No criminal, no sheriff. Is that it?"

"Yeah, good or bad depends upon which side of the teeth you're on."

"Are you a cynic?"

"Maybe." He smiled.

She had a charming giggle. "You're a funny man. I think you may be one. Devout, I'd say."

They sipped wine. The waiter took their orders. Ashton seemed distant, like a man who struggled to read the unreadable.

"You don't say much, do you? A quiet guy."

"Medicine is the most respected form of indentured servitude. Patients are like the sun, always out there, burning. Somewhere. They never give up."

"You act like they're not worthy of your concern. A bother."

He said nothing.

"You don't like people, do you?" Her face took on a perturbed look.

"I'm present when people are changing, usually in some hateful way."

"That's natural. You're a doctor."

"People resist change."

"Okay."

"Frustration, physical pain. It causes anger, then aggression."

"You didn't answer my question."

"People are fickle."

"Fickle?"

"Selfish. They see things with an eye to advantage. Especially the sick. Everyone is pissed. It's a pissed-off world."

"I'll take that as a 'no'."

"I afraid I don't have a definite answer for you."

She paused, and then said quietly, "I think you want to avoid attachments."

He placed his hand to his chin and leaned forward, as if to convey a confidence. He whispered, "No colon, no colitis."

"Just what is that supposed to mean?"

"A surgeon told me that. We were discussing a patient's treatment."

"But what does it mean?"

"No people, no problems."

"You're becoming an old coot! There's still time for excitement, something new!"

"Things attract, get close, then repel. It's the way of the world."

"Don't torture yourself, okay? You'll make things worse."

"I shouldn't be talking this way. I'm drunk."

"You get drunk after two glasses?"

He made a face. "I've been here a while. I'm way ahead of you."

The appetizers arrived. They busied themselves eating for a minute, saying nothing.

"You certainly are different."

"I'm a heretic. I've known it for a long time. Make the most of it."

"A heretic and a mutant. We're a pair."

The waiter seated two couples at an adjacent table. Whitney glanced in their direction. The couples talked loudly and laughed, but fell silent on receiving the menus.

"My mother told me I was negative," Ashton said.

"Your mother?"

"Then I challenged her to read the dictionary, rating words as negative or positive, discarding the neutral. We did, finding equal parts 'good and bad'. For every thing or idea there is its opposite, its shadow."

"You sure spend a lot of time looking for things that can't be found."

"I haven't found some things. I did find other things I didn't want to find."

"What do you mean?"

"Nothing."

She pulled at a lock of hair, seeming to consider whether to press the issue.

"Okay, you've had your ten minutes."

"Ten minutes?" His tongue was numb, the air flammable.

"Of griping."

A different waiter removed their plates, and a third arrived with the main course.

"I should keep these thoughts to myself, shouldn't I? I forgot you hate whiners," said Ashton.

"You're digging a pretty deep hole."

"It usually takes more than a bottle of wine and a ready ear. Shall we change the subject? I'll be pleasant. I promise. Let's talk about you."

"Remember, you can't choose your fate, but you can accept it. I know."

"I'm sorry. I wasn't thinking."

He looked away and began to wonder just who it was using his voice these last minutes, someone ignoble and mean. He turned his head toward her. Their eyes met. He returned her smile.

They finished their meal. Neither of them said much. When they got up to leave, Whitney suggested they see a movie, a Bunuel film, *Belle de Jour*, playing at the Milroy Theatre, the only art theater in town. He said, "What the hell? Might as well be hanged for a sheep as a goat," and she replied, "A sheep as a lamb."

In the movie, a French surgeon's beautiful and priggish wife, Severine, dissatisfied with mundane duties and seized with masochistic fantasies, worked secretly in a brothel, where, like an incubus, she used men to sate her salacious desires. That she was impelled by irresistible urges mattered little. "I can't help myself. I am lost," she said.

They left the theater and walked along the sidewalk. "That was uplifting," Whitney said.

"Why don't I ever meet women like that?"

She elbowed him in the ribs. She suggested they go to a café, which they did. They walked across the street to Nadja's and ordered espressos and dessert.

"I didn't invite you to dinner to give advice," Whitney said. "I guess I'm going to do it, though. My mother's just a mom. You're someone I think I can trust. I don't know why, but I do."

"I'm listening."

"My dad and I are having some bumpy times. Since the divorce. He married a twenty-four-year-old. She's my age! That was their baby you helped deliver. How could you forget, right? Here's the thing. For him to have a normal child, he had to change wives." She paused. "Now I'm an orphan."

"He still cares for you. The other day in the hospital—"

"It's all about him. His ego. He wants someone perfect to carry on the Laird legacy."

"Hmmm."

"We had a little argument. That's what I want to talk about. I work at the bank, part-time. He's the president."

"He's the president."

She nodded. "I used his laptop to finish my senior paper. It never occurred to him that I might read his e-mail. No. He thinks he's immune. Or that he can weasel his way out of anything. Anyway, I shouldn't have read his e-mails, but I did, and I found out something really bad. At least I think so. I don't know whether to call the cops or bank regulators or just what to do."

"What is it that you think your Dad's involved with?"

"Men are making huge deposits into various accounts in a single day. Four guys that I know of, maybe more. Small businesses. Never any deposits over ten thousand dollars. That triggers a federal form. The whole staff is required to attend courses about this. There is this one guy in particular. Young. Spanish accent. He keeps coming to my window. He flirts with me."

"Go on."

"Anyway, I thought this was suspicious and told my Dad. We're supposed to 'know' our customers. He said not to worry; it was nothing. He would look into it."

"Did he look into it?

"He had one of the vice-presidents investigate."

"There you have it."

"The money is transferred to other accounts inside the investment division. And get this, all the money eventually goes to an off-shore bank. Some sort of holding company. Don't you think that's strange? What do little antique stores and jewelry stores have in common with foreign banks?"

"I couldn't say. But it does sound shady."

"The name of the holding company is Newcastle. That's where my father's father is from. One e-mail, titled 'Newcastle,' said 'transfer to you on Friday afternoon, 500K, usual protocol.' What do you think that means?"

"I'm afraid this is way out of my territory," he said.

"I looked up the account number."

Ashton muttered something unintelligible.

She breathed deeply and added, "It's the same account as the one the Spanish guy is transferring money to.

"Right." Ashton stared at the table, toying with his drink.

"Are you listening? Don't you care?" She moved her hand and knocked over her espresso, which conveyed a wet stain onto the tablecloth. Her mouth curled in annoyance as she threw her napkin over the spot. A waiter came and offered to replace the cloth; she refused, asking instead for another napkin. He returned with it and another espresso.

"I've never been good at riddles, Whitney. I don't know what to tell you."

"My Dad's no good."

Ashton's eyebrows rose above his glasses, but he said nothing.

"Isn't it obvious? He's involved, somehow, in this scheme. Whatever it is."

"I thought you said money was being transferred out."

"In or out, it's all the same."

"What do you want me to say?"

"What would you do? Report it to somebody?"

"Ask your Dad again. See what he says."

"Just tell him I've been spying?"

"Then pretend you never saw it."

"But I did! I'm involved."

"Don't take sides. Time will sort it out. Concentrate on your work."

"I have to tell somebody."

Ashton shifted in his seat and coughed. "It's probably not what you think. How is this your problem? Look at it as a confidence, like that between priest and parishioner, or doctor and patient. Or father and daughter."

"But he hasn't confided in me. He's concealing something that might be serious."

"Avoid pain. That's my advice. Haven't you had enough?"

She looked down at the table and drummed with her spoon.

"Believe me, there are things a person shouldn't know," he said. "Don't look for trouble. Don't open closed doors."

"You don't think I'd be guilty, too? I want the truth!"

"Guilty? I don't know about that. The truth is, we didn't make ourselves. Just like Severine, we're not nearly as free to choose as we would like to think."

"You talk like you're some kind of robot." She sniffed and tilted her head. "I guess you can't help yourself."

"We don't create our desires. That's all I meant. And it's almost impossible to understand other peoples' complex motives."

"We judge ourselves. We have values."

"It's best not to probe so much."

"I disagree."

"You're not the police, Whitney. You're not on their payroll."

"You think morality is relative?" Her face reddened and her lips compressed with anger.

"Nature has preferences. But no ethics. We try to rise above it, but we can't. We're part of it. You can't figure it out. Try to relax. When you think about it, it's really a consolation. I'm speaking here as my own therapist."

"I didn't think you, of all people, would say something so wrong-headed."

"You think so?" He smiled.

"Don't make fun of me."

"Rewards and punishments. That is a thorny issue. It's unknowable." He took off his glasses and placed the temple to his mouth.

"How can you say that?" Her brow gathered.

"You're shocked, still capable of indignation. As you grow older, you learn to become more unregenerate."

"You mean degenerate, don't you?"

"Maybe. But what I'm trying to tell you is that you don't need to blow the whistle."

"So do nothing—is that it?"

"You could quit your job."

"I'm not a quitter, okay?"

"Remember: if it's raining, you're going to get wet. You really want to get wet? I'm not so sure."

They lapsed into silence, picking at their desserts. After a time, her mood lightened. "Well, at least I got the question off my chest," she said. "No answers, though; it's unknowable." She started laughing, and when she stopped, she retained a grin.

He returned her smile. "What are you planning after your graduation? A career in art?"

"Take a vacation. Travel for a month or so. I'm not ready to settle down just yet. Maybe get an MFA."

"Traveling. I know someone who's planning to do the same. Quite a coincidence."

"Maybe you could put me in touch with this person. We could do it together."

"Do what? Travel?"

"Whatever."

"He's an older guy. What do you think the neighbors would say about a young woman traveling with a geezer?"

"I know what you're thinking."

"Here we go."

"You're not a father figure. I hope you realize that."

"You're thirty years younger than I am."

"I'm a mature twenty-three. I don't care what the neighbors think. I don't have a lot of time to burn."

"You have time."

"You don't believe that, do you?"

"Who can see into the future?"

"I have to live now. I'm worth something, aren't I?"

"Of course you are."

She sighed. "I feel like a discard."

"You're not. Don't say that."

"Other people are happy."

"And so will you be. You will."

"Look. I have to spend some time with my mother, and I need two more days of IV antibiotics. I could leave Tuesday. Is that too late? Where are we going?"

"However much I might want to travel somewhere with you, it wouldn't be right."

"Look right, you mean."

"That too," he said.

Ashton called for the check, and they left. They walked to the parking lot behind the White Orchid. She made him promise to call her after he returned from his trip south.

It was nearly midnight when he started the engine. He stared hard at the white stripe in the center lane and drove slowly home. He parked at the curb in front of his house. He went through an unlit hallway, past bookcases holding nine hundred volumes, walked slowly up the stairs, and into his bedroom. He lay on the bed fully dressed. Finally, he switched on the lamp over his bed and reached for the uppermost of five books stacked with open spines. By the third page, he was asleep.

He awoke at seven the next morning, undressed, took a shower, and swallowed two aspirin with a gulp of chalky antacid. He shaved and dressed in fresh clothes. It occurred to him that it was Sunday. Not bothering to get a glass, he drank orange juice from the container. He paced back and forth through the dining room, then sat on the sofa, his legs crossed and kicking, for more than thirty minutes. Piper came in and lay on the floor. He watched her for a long time. She closed her eyes and swallowed several times.

Rousing himself with effort, he went to an oak desk near the sunroom, unlocked the top, and removed a box of engraved stationery. He picked up a fountain pen and removed the cartridge, opened another drawer, and grabbed a bottle of blue ink. He procured a syringe, pulled off the cap with his teeth, filled the syringe with ink and then squirted it into the cartridge. When he had put the pen together, blue ink smudges stained two fingers. He sat and wrote:

> Dear Whitney,
>
> The dawn brings a harsh light to my remembrance of yester-day. I was terribly unkind, worse than a boor, telling you many unwelcome things. I hope you will forgive me. I am sorry. No excuses. A bad confidante is a worse doctor. I sensed much that is awry with the world. Truly, it is I who am unwell.
>
> Don't believe all I said. In fact, you'd better forget most of it. Perhaps one day, you will allow me to make amends. You deserve a pleasant evening. I do sense we are fellow travelers. I still recommend not adding to your injury, replaying it, bringing it to the fore where surely it will demand a reckoning. Yes, I believe some doors should not open to terrible secrets. Don't look for ogres;

you might find one. Prevention is cure. Use the eraser if you can.
Best wishes, your churlish friend,

TBA

P.S. I love your work.

He put the letter in an envelope, addressed it, affixed a stamp, and placed it on an end table near the front door. Then, fearing that he would change his mind if it were to sit there until Monday morning, he walked with Piper to the mailbox one block away and dropped the letter in the slot.

CHAPTER EIGHT

A man of middle height and dark complexion, insouciant, wearing a linen sport coat but no tie, strode across the carpet. He waved and grinned at a secretary dressed in a retro 50's skirt and blouse seated at her desk. He surveyed the lines at the teller windows. Clutching a green, zippered, cloth bag, he approached the window with the shortest line, where Whitney Laird was sitting behind the window on a high swivel chair.

He stood patiently, waiting his turn.

"Good afternoon."

"Hi!" he said, approaching the window. He had pearl-white teeth. He unzipped the bag, produced a number of checks, but mostly cash, along with a deposit slip.

She entered the account number, showing a balance of $271,658.59. Over the last month, twenty-three deposits had been made, valued in excess of $200,000. Whitney took the deposit money, counted it twice, and, eyes to monitor, punched buttons on her calculator. She added up the checks, and then the cash. The total was $9823.16.

"Your fingers are like machines. How do you do that?" The man rotated a diamond ring on his fifth finger. He was pleased with himself.

She looked up at him. "Business must be good."

"Spring sale. Yes."

"You have several stores?"

"Several. Import, export."

She handed him a paper receipt, and they exchanged automatic smiles. The man turned to leave. "Thanks," he said. "See you next time."

He pivoted, brushed against an old woman, excused himself, walked across the floor, gestured to the secretary, and went out the door. As he did so, Whitney turned to the adjacent teller.

"Can you cover?"

"I'm always covering for someone," she said.

"I'll be back after lunch, okay?"

"Sure. You owe me one."

Whitney closed her window, walked across the room, went up one flight of stairs, and entered the investment banking division. It was a small department, having been in existence just a few years, established after the repeal of Glass-Spiegal. She waited there for Claire Hawthorne. Executive assistant to Brendan Coulter, Claire helped supervise investments both domestic and foreign. When she left Coulter's office, she was frowning. Her eyes rolled as she closed the door, and then she put on sunglasses.

She went to her desk, saw Whitney, and greeted her. She opened a drawer, pulled out her running shoes, and said, "Let's go."

They walked out a side door and headed for The Neutron Cafe. Although bank employees conformed to a dress code, Claire's taste was *sui generis*. Wearing a short skirt silk suit, high heels, and painted and perfumed, she looked seductive, if not provocative. They stopped outside, where Claire stepped out of her spike heels, stuck them in a huge purse, and laced up the running shoes' red shoestrings.

"What was that about?" asked Whitney.

"That jerk thinks he owns me."

"Maybe it's your dress." She raised her eyebrows.

"He's under the fat illusion I'm still his woman."

"Oh?"

"Believe me—that's so over."

They walked through a parking lot and crossed Baker Street, when Claire lit a cigarette and somehow managed to smoke half of it before they arrived at their favorite eatery. She threw it on the pavement, stepped on it, and swept it under a bush with her shoe. They entered and sat next to a window.

Whitney looked at Claire's face. The sunglasses hid her eyes. Seen at an angle, a green bruise oozed outward from the corner of the frame.

"He hit you, didn't he?"

She removed the glasses. "Nice, isn't it? Green clashes with my dress."

"He did hit you! That son of a bitch."

"Staying here is bad for my health. I'm going to split. Soon."

"You mean leave town?"

"I've said too much already."

"What are you saying?"

"Your dad's the president of the bank, right?"

"What about it?"

"You don't know, do you?"

"What don't I know?"

"Coulter isn't what he seems. He's a bad ass. Believe it. And there are others. You ever wonder why foreigners sit on the board? It's a total fraud, you know. The whole thing. Your father's the frickin' president."

"The whole thing's a fraud?"

"Coulter told me to keep my mouth shut. Or maybe he would shut it for me. He wasn't kidding around. No joke."

"But what about my father?"

"I didn't mean your father."

"You just said so."

"What's gone down is big. Big. If he doesn't know, someone should tell him. But it won't be me. That's for sure. I'm out of here. And I'd like to leave in one piece, thank you."

"What's going on at the bank, Claire?" Whitney's mouth twisted in a perturbed look.

"Maybe it's better not to know. For both of us. But you might want to find another job. I can tell you that."

"You're exaggerating."

"Look. You handle the deposit boxes, right?"

"No."

"I thought I saw you in there last week."

"Jeannie lets me do it sometimes."

"Could you get me a box without anyone knowing?"

"Without anyone knowing?"

"Use a false name."

"You know I can't. Why don't you use another bank?"

"I want you to keep my key so if anything happens to me you can get to it."

"In case you're abducted, held for ransom?" She smiled sarcastically.

"I'm dead serious, Whitney. This is no laughing matter."

"Maybe you should go to the police."

Claire shook her head. "The police look into things after they pay you a courtesy call in the morgue."

"What's with the box?"

"An insurance policy. Or a way to get even."

"Maybe you're right. I don't need to know anything more."

They sat in an uneasy silence for a moment.

"What do you want me to do, Claire?" Whitney said, breaking the tension.

"Just get me the box."

"I can get a one for myself. You can put your stuff inside mine. Locked. We'll each have a key."

Claire's face brightened. "All right. That's good. That'll work."

"Jeannie has to approve all deposit boxes."

"Fine."

They finished their lunch and returned to the bank. The next morning, Whitney opened a medium-sized box and paid the rental for one year. Claire gave her a check for the locker fee and a gray metal box with a tiny padlock, which Whitney, the next day, placed inside her box. She taped the key inside a light fixture in the kitchen. Claire kept the other key.

CHAPTER NINE

In darkness, he removed the sheet, rolled it, and put it inside a polymer cylinder. He filled six tubes with developer and affixed the tops. With the light on, he threw them into a water-filled tray, rolling them like logs for eight minutes. He switched off the light, opened and drained the tubes, then added an acid stop bath, rinsed them, and poured in the fixer. After five minutes, the negatives were put under a washer for one hour. Developing twenty sheets took most of the morning.

The next day, he selected negatives, the best two images. The first negative sat in its carrier, which he put above the lens in the enlarger's slot. The image lit the paper-filled easel. An eight-power loupe confirmed focus. Viewed closely, welters of halide grains made no sense. They were just dots. He lapsed into a reflective mood, listening to Townes Van Zandt, wondering whether the span of his life defined any order, as the fleeting days, which droned on, like dots, did not.

The light of successive blue and green wavelengths illuminated the sixteen by twenty-inch silver gelatin paper. He immersed it in the developer. The image emerged. Like magic, the chaos of the grains, made whole, produced a picture so permanent that it would resist for centuries the mockeries of time. He placed it in an acid bath, followed by two baths of fixer. After five or six exposure refinements, the final print was washed in running water for over one hour. A day's work produced only two prints of exhibition quality.

The following morning, he took Piper to Michael Amberley's home. He then left for Wycliffe, at the southeast edge of the Spoon National Recreation Area. At three in the afternoon, he arrived and checked into Harmony House, a bed and breakfast with four guest rooms, each with a fireplace. He flopped on the bed and dozed for two hours before changing to hiking clothes.

He grabbed the Deardorff and drove west to Middle Creek. He parked at the Limestone trailhead and walked the trail to the arches. Dogwoods quaked in the wind above a floor of wet leaves, interrupted by throngs of stargrass and wood-lilies. He exposed one negative of the arch before returning to the car.

He wandered about gravel roads, reaching a tributary of Constance Creek. Rills ran in rapids, and in places formed sheets of water over falls. Two leaves were caught in a whirlpool. A spectral mist rose above the stream; arched over it was the faintest of rainbows. A skein of Canada geese honked in the distance. Their calls grew louder. He looked skyward through a gap in the tree canopy as their wings pumped overhead, and he listened for a time, as all their words faded after them, swallowed up in a cold breeze.

He trudged on, coming upon small, listing gravestones gathered in gray rows amidst an uneven thicket, enclosed by a tumbledown fence. There stood a colony of mayapples. He recalled Professor Davis, who so many years ago had admonished the class, "Young doctors make lumpy churchyards." He attempted to straighten one of the stones, smaller than the others, but it would not budge. He cleared the brush until he could see the lettering, worn much with the years—a girl of three, Ruth. Next to her, John, age five. About half the stones announced the surname, McWilliams. He sat before the graves a long moment in deep absorption, wondering what devilry could be the cause of such abomination.

He rose and looked to a branch where a mourning dove sat silently over its clutch, watching him. She had been there all the time. He set up the tripod and camera and inched closer. The bird was steadfast. In a short while, wings whistled overhead, and in the same tree, behind the stones, the dove's mate landed on a limb, where a tangent of theatrical light struck it like an intelligent bolt. With great solicitude, he made two negatives before slowly backing away.

He had sealed himself against reversals. He resolved to withdraw. He would care for no one. At least for now, before his real nature might emerge again, like seeds bred true. He envied the young, the risk takers, and the generous, who embraced dangerous journeys with no regard for the cost.

At Harmony House, he showered and dressed. He spent no time before the mirror. Though two days unshaven, he went downstairs and sat alone in an alcove. He ran his eyes over the financial section of the *Wycliffe Gazette*, and after a short time, he walked to his car, got a sack out of the trunk, and went back to his room. Soon thereafter, downstairs, he consulted the innkeeper about a place to eat. There was only one restaurant, and it was across the street. He went there and ordered dinner and a glass of red wine.

Having nearly finished the wine, giving thought to a second glass, he looked up as Whitney Laird, wearing a red beret, marched to his table and stood over him. Skin-tight blue jeans stretched over slim legs, and she wore a white sweatshirt with the word "Armistead" printed on it in an arch on the front. Her fingers poked through cut-off woolen gloves.

"Don't be mad."

"Madness, that's next."

"I got your letter. It was sweet."

"How did you find me?"

"I asked somebody."

"No one knew my plans."

"No one but your housekeeper."

He raised his eyebrows. "How did you get those on?" He nodded toward her jeans.

She made a funny face. "With great difficulty."

"I should imagine." He waved to a chair. "Sit if you can."

"Don't get all worked up over a pair of tight jeans, okay?"

"I promise I'll try not to."

There was a pause. She sat.

"What are you thinking, Tyler? I hope you don't mind if I call you by your first name."

"I don't mind. You've been plotting. There must be a conspiracy."

"I thought if I don't interfere with your work, I could join you."

"Does anyone know you're here?"

"No. Why?"

"I suppose you can. There's no harm in it."

"I see your resistance is fading." She smiled coyly.

"Is it?" When he glanced up, she was watching. He looked away and back again. Her eyes seemed to see beyond the surface. Her face was familiar, though much was hidden.

"Watch out," she said. "Something might happen, something you didn't plan." Her triangulate mouth stayed open.

"I wouldn't want that to happen."

"I could paint while you photograph."

"Where are you staying?"

"At Harmony House."

"That's my place."

"Tyler, there aren't many hotels around here."

He ordered another glass of Merlot. She ordered a first, then a second with dinner. She had spent a lot of time preening, making herself sleek as a bird. Her eyes locked on. At times, she fidgeted and unconsciously groomed her hair. Leaning forward, she smiled with red painted lips, teeth aglitter.

"Why are you doing that?" he said.

"Doing what?"

"Puckering up your mouth."

"Like this?" She paused. "Can I tell you a secret?"

"Just when I was beginning to think there weren't any."

"My mother told me to."

"To flirt?"

"Yes."

"Now why would she do that?"

"You know what else?"

He said nothing, but shook his head.

"You want me to flirt." Her chin was down, eyes up, and her sclerae peeped under pale irises. "You really do, you know."

"What makes you think so?"

"I know men."

"Do you? Like mother, like daughter. Experts."

"You're a boy who wants to pet the dog, but thinks she might bite him."

"You are cunning. Don't you think this boy might be too old to pet dogs?"

"No."

"I'm not an old man, but I can see him from here."

"No, we're the same, really."

"How do you figure that? Still a girl. I mean no disrespect."

"I'm twenty-three! Men my age aren't serious. They're superficial—frivolous. They have time to burn."

He picked up his glass, drank, and watched her over the rim of the glass. "There are lots of good, young men out there."

"When they find out about me—well, you know."

"As beautiful as you are, I should think you might need an unlisted number to get any peace. At the least."

"Do you think so?" She looked down, covering her mouth with two fingers.

"I'm not trying to flatter you. I don't want anything."

"Everybody wants something."

"I seek no advantage."

"You think you're really smart."

"I'm not trying to annoy you."

She gazed at the table. "It's all surface, right. The truth comes out."

"Your life is intense, Whitney. Maybe more meaningful than mine."

"I told you before, I try not to complain. But more meaningful? You must be insane!"

"Well, it's not boring, is it?" They stared at each other for a time. A waitress inquired about their orders.

"I feel like doing something wild," she said. She looked into his eyes.

He laughed nervously. He twisted his mouth, trying to suppress a grin, but he failed. She reached for his hand, but he moved it away.

"What are you thinking, Tyler?"

"Nothing."

"Please, tell me."

"When I was in medical school—this was back in the eighteenth century, I shared a biochem project with a PhD student. She was beautiful, prim. Tidewater." He imitated her Virginia accent.

"She taught in histology lab. A very smart girl, a couple of years older. We were mad scientists in training. She was beautiful. I was intrigued, but I couldn't read her. She gave no signals. She was impassive, proper, reserved, mysterious. She was older."

"You said that."

"No flirting, no body language, no subtle invitations, no touching. She was beautiful and accustomed to lots of attention."

"Was she beautiful?" She held up her hands in mock surprise.

"On the last day of class, before finals week, and our last day together, she announced she wanted 'to do something wild.' She looked at me, and then she stared at the floor and said nothing. I waited what seemed like minutes. She acted as if she had said something wrong. I was amazed. I was attracted, but it was also the weekend before exams. I had to study."

"Did you kiss her?"

"Are you serious? I was speechless. We stood frozen in the middle of the laboratory. I can still see her eyelids. After a time, we pretended that nothing had happened. I debated. The afternoon passed without either of us saying anything."

"That's it? You still see her eyelids!"

"Over the weekend, I thought about it. I thought it was a signal; what the hell, she could only say 'no.' I decided to go to the registrar, tell him some cock and bull story about needing her phone number."

"You didn't have her number? You must be joking."

"On Monday, as I left the exam, heading for the Registrar's Office, students milled outside in the hallway, and I heard one of my classmates say she had been accepted to another medical school. She would start in the fall, a second-year student. I didn't even know she had applied to medical school! That was why she wanted to 'do something wild.' She had just received her acceptance letter. It wasn't me at all. I didn't go to the registrar. We never met. It's just a memory now."

Neither said anything for some moments. They ate and sipped wine.

"If a woman is beautiful and mysterious," she said, "you may project your own image—like onto a doll. You don't see her anymore. You see the object of your fantasy."

He watched her closely, cupping hand to mouth. He seemed surprised. He ran his finger over the upper lip.

"I see. You mean, patriarchy and oppression, housework and motherhood?" He had a half-smile.

"Just the first three." She laughed. And after a moment she said, "Do you have children?"

"No."

"You don't like kids?"

"It's the most important question, isn't it?"

"Your wife didn't want any."

"I wanted certainty, but ended up undecided. It's not enough."

"Was it her career?"

"No. Not that." He paused, trying to make his thoughts behave.

"Are you going to tell me or what?"

"Complicity."

"Complicity about what?"

He raised his eyebrows. "I hesitate to say. I don't want to write any more letters." He began laughing.

"I'm interested. Go ahead."

"I know I should accept the world the way it is. But I can't. I can't give my consent."

"Okay."

"On a pilgrimage, you should call for volunteers. We don't ask children, do we? We make them go."

She looked puzzled. She shifted in her seat. Legs crossed. Her brow wrinkled, and she rolled her thumb and forefinger. "You seem like you haven't convinced yourself. Like you're not sure."

"But you should be sure, something definite, not something studied. Like driving on the highway. Twenty miles to Dayton, ten, five; do I want to get off at Dayton? The next thing you know, you're in Toledo."

She leaned back in her chair, ran her hand through her hair, drank from her glass. He sat in naked silence.

"Doctors intercede. To intercede is complicity. You obviously don't think that is wrong. You must think what you do is good."

"I suppose so. I never looked at it that way." His eyes focused on his fingers, now playing with the saltshaker. "I think it's the difference between preserving and creating."

"If something's worth preserving," she said, "it must be worth creating."

"Hmmm." He spread his arms and shrugged.

"You mean I thought of something you haven't?" She uncrossed her legs, then crossed them.

"I guess you did. Although I should point out, that's no great feat."

"Do you feel responsible for those you helped?"

"No, I don't think so. At best, I'm a link in the chain."

"I think I've given you a bone to pick, Doctor." She tossed her head and raised her eyebrows.

He leaned on an elbow, hand under his chin.

"I think you're plagued with doubt."

Ashton appeared deep in thought. He looked to the side and pulled at the tablecloth.

"Hello?" she said.

"Doubt is the one thing I'm sure of." He paused. "And kindness, which does imply moral choice. I'll give you that."

"What about sex?"

"What about it?"

"It leads to children."

"My brethren seem to have solved that problem. For the most part."

He sensed he was talking too much again. Control, he thought, maintain control. After a time, he said, "Let's talk about you."

"If I weren't sick, I'd never have known you."

"How fortunate." His features softened. "That's quite a trade-off. I'm happy we met, definitely not happy about your illness."

She rolled her eyes. "I'm going to the powder room."

She stood, turned, and walked away, knowing his eyes were following her. She turned left, looked over her shoulder, and smiled at him.

When she returned, she walked up behind him, put her arms around his neck, and slipped something into his inside coat pocket.

"Don't look now. Do it later." She went around the table and sat.

He pulled the object out. She had written her phone number on her panties. His face reddened, he gave her a lopsided grin, and then stuffed them into his sport coat side pocket. He glanced around the room, thinking everyone was staring at him. An elderly couple sitting adjacent quickly looked away.

"Paper and pen are more ladylike."

She was laughing at him. "Not the same impact."

"Girls aren't as shy as they used to be. Where were you thirty years ago when I needed you?"

"I wasn't born yet. You'll have to make do with me now."

"Would you say my face is crimson, or merely red?"

She cocked her head and stared at him. "Crimson."

They both burst into laughter, and the couple next to them stared darkly and whispered.

"You're sweating, Tyler. Use your new handkerchief."

"I think you've given me a fever."

Seconds passed. They tried to control themselves.

"Do you like horses? She asked abruptly.

"What's to like?"

"Have you ever ridden?"

"I like farms, pastures, but horses themselves; I'd say I'm neutral. I have a Morgan on my farm, left to me by the previous owner."

"You don't ride him?"

"No. We have an agreement. I don't ride him; he doesn't ride me." Ashton mopped his sweating forehead with the napkin.

"He's just there."

"That's right."

"Who cares for him when you're away?"

"One of the neighbors. He mows the fields for the alfalfa."

"Where is your farm?"

"Southwick, not far from Waverley."

"How many acres?"

"Ninety-two. Half in alfalfa, the rest woods. A pond."

"That's a big spread. Do you live there?"

"There's an old frame house. I fixed it up some. Stay there on weekends. I plan to move soon."

"I want to see it."

He nodded. "Sure. I think that can be arranged."

"There are three hundred miles of trails and a stable not far from here where we can rent horses. I checked it out. What do you think?"

"I haven't ridden since I was a boy."

"Good. I reserved two horses. I'll pack breakfast and lunch."

"A conspiracy." He smiled. "I smell a conspiracy."

In the morning, they drove to the stable, arriving at seven o'clock. A patchy fog lay over a swale, muting all color. In the paddock, a teenage stable boy had lined a dozen horses in a row. The first two, Bonny and George, already saddled, were led across the paddock to hitching posts. The boy said the horses were calm and invited them to mount. Whitney attached her backpack to the saddle, while Ashton kept his camera, a 6x7 cm roll film rangefinder, in a bag at his shoulder. He placed a small tripod in a saddlebag.

While other patrons arrived, Whitney and Ashton rode to the adjacent field. Whitney's mare, dun-colored, about fifteen hands, grazed languidly as the boy adjusted the stirrups on Ashton's roan gelding. At the withers, he stood at least sixteen hands. The boy went back to the stable.

While Whitney and Ashton conversed, George dropped, without warning, to the ground, as if pole-axed, then rolled onto his back. Ashton jumped clear of the stirrups just in time. The horse pranced upside-down, a half-ton break-dancer. Whitney clapped her hand to her mouth in shock, but after realizing no harm had been done, her face relaxed in a grin.

"What a way with animals, Dr. Ashton. Must be your cologne!"

"More likely my personality."

The stable boy came over, letting loose a string of imprecations, and struck the horse between the eyes with a crop. The horse jumped to his feet and shook his mane.

"He does that once in a while. Them damn bugs. He won't do it no more. If he does, beat the tar out of that sombitch." The kid brushed off the saddle leather, but smears of green stains were left on the pommel.

"Does he hold grudges? Can I use your stick? Any carrots?"

Ashton mounted, and they reined the horses onto a gravel road. They cantered side by side, their shod hooves clopping below undulating saddles. After two miles, the road ended in a forked, dirt trail. The horses' legs were plastered white from dust cast up from the road. They took the right fork and followed it for ten minutes, coming to an opening in the woods where they needed to ford a creek. Rocks, smooth as hen's eggs, sat amid a sandbar; in places, they were covered with verdant, slick moss. The horses slid down the steep bank, entered the stream, and in passage, stirred up a muddy swirl. Sinking to their pasterns, they sucked through the mud and lunged up the opposite bank. Ashton's horse stumbled, his forelegs buckled to his knees, but he recovered, and they rode on.

At the far side, in an open meadow, they stopped for breakfast. Bonny and George drank from the quick-flowing water. Afterward, Whitney tied their reins to tree branches, and the horses grazed calmly. They whinnied at intervals and pulled at the grass. After a time, without warning, George reared, neighing, and then stood and shook his head. Whitney ran to him and grabbed the halter. She released the rein, and as he reared again, she let him go; after a while, he fell to the ground onto his back. In half a minute, he righted himself. She released the surcingle, removed the saddle, and allowed him to graze untethered.

"Splendid job. Very nice, indeed."

"You could have helped, Tyler."

"That nut-case. He's much bigger than I am. Besides, I don't speak Horse."

"It must not be your personality after all."

"That's a relief."

She opened her backpack and produced hardboiled eggs, bread, two bananas, and a bottle of water. As they ate, Ashton opened a bone-handled knife, inside of which was also a fork and spoon. He gouged out the egg's yolk, flipping it into the woods. Whitney fed the horses two apples and some oats. Reefs of angry clouds had begun to gather, all but obscuring the sun. The day grew dark, the winds, strong. The oats blew from her hand. She returned to Ashton and sat beside him.

She reached inside her backpack, took out a charcoal pencil and sketchpad, and began to draw, periodically looking up at the distant, coalesced trees. The leaves of paper flapped in the wind. After five minutes, she closed the book and stared at her charcoaled fingers.

"Are you going to take any pictures?" Her words were lost on the wind.

"What?"

"Take my picture," she yelled.

"The light is great, but the background could be better. Let's go on."

They saddled and rode on, single file, up and down steep grades along ridges. They forded streams, traversed hard-packed dirt trails, and rode back and forth across switchbacks. An army of beetles had ravaged the forest of pines, whose ochre, bare trunks listed and fell at random, crisscrossed, as on a battlefield. Wispy hemlocks grew interspersed with wind-tilted saplings, black barked, with last year's golden leaves still clinging to splotched, skeletal branches. The sky began to lighten. At intervals along the trail, they stopped; Ashton photographed arches and rock shelters, where waterfalls dropped to mossy ledges.

They approached an abandoned farmstead. Thickets with tall shrubs, their leaves quivering, had replaced formerly green fields. A few goldenrods were trapped in a brindled wasteland of dead briars. Cloven hoof prints of some beast molded the mud. The few outbuildings had long ago lapsed into desuetude; paint had flaked away from the walls that leaned precariously against canted posts and beams.

They stopped and rested. Two mockingbirds flashed white-patched wings and whistled their repertoire. A few sparrows became intimidated, flitted farther and farther away, and left the victors in possession of the field.

"My legs are numb," Ashton said. He dismounted the horse, tied the reins to a branch, and limped to a rock, where he sat. He picked at something stuck to his socks.

He looked up. "I need to raise the stirrups. My legs are in traction."

"Let's rest and finish the food," Whitney said. From her pack, she found focaccia and cheddar, which they devoured; they washed it down with the rest of the bottled water. Ashton got up, went to his horse, and adjusted the stirrups, raising them three inches. By now, it was late afternoon, and they decided to head back before dark. Hoping to save time, they took a supposed shortcut, but soon found themselves lost.

They needed to cross an estuary of the Rudd River, an area swollen to a shallow pool. Whitney fished a map from her purse and studied it.

"I know where we are."

The orange sun was about to fall below a ridge. Stands of windblown grasses swayed in the rippling water. Brooding shadows of giant hands skimmed the surface of the pool, encroached on the bank opposite, and then seized the dark wood.

"Tyler, please take my picture before we go back."

"All right."

Ashton dismounted slowly. They tied their mounts to the same branch, and the horses stood there, nose to nose. He walked around to the other side of her horse.

The light, reflected at the water, danced in concentric rings. The unpredictable force of the wind altered the wave patterns; their crests interfered, diminished, and melted away.

"I'll get in the water if you take it fast." She was removing her jeans.

"What? You're recovering from pneumonia."

"I have a towel, okay?"

She stripped off her clothes, walked into the water, looked back, and stood hands akimbo, perturbed that he did nothing but shake his head. Sunlight glinted on the lineaments of her shoulders as she stood close to the bank.

"I'm waiting. Where do you want me?"

"Kneel by those tuffs of grass, facing north."

"North?" She pointed, and he nodded.

She went into the water and stood in the cold, while he opened the tripod legs and attached the camera to the ball head. She walked to the clumps of tall grass in the foreground and knelt in the chilly water beside them. She and the grass formed silhouettes, shadowed against the sun, and they, together with their mirrored reflections, seemed formed in perfect order, as though they were one.

After a time, she began to shiver.

"Remember, you volunteered," Ashton said.

"Take the picture!"

"Chin down."

"Go on."

"Right arm on right leg. Right. Hold it!"

He pressed the shutter, advanced the film, doubled the exposure, and took a second frame.

"Got it. Now, get out of there."

Whitney ran through the shallows to the bank. They went to the horses, and he retrieved a towel from her saddlebag. She dried herself and dressed hurriedly. Goosebumps broke out in a sandpapery rash on her chest.

"You undress and dress faster than anyone I know."

"Especially with you staring at me. We'd better leave before we get stuck out here."

Cool air descended from the mountaintop in a thick blanket. Mist hung undecided above silvered riffles. In the gathering dark, the horses set a course on hard gravel, and the riders sat their mounts, giving free rein, listening to the nocturne clop, trusting oddly in the instincts of beasts.

Whitney pulled her feet from the stirrups, and her legs bounced against the mare's ribs. Bonny knew the way home. A whisper of wind rose to a gale, and it slapped at their clothes. The air smelled clean, but wet, as before a storm. No sound came from the deep wood; no bird sang.

The wind flogged the trees. Then came a curtain of rain. The sky was black. Somehow, the horses managed to stay out of potholes. By the time they returned, the stable was drowning in a downpour, and in the paddock, raindrops splashed in muddy puddles.

The stable boy had vanished, replaced by a gnome-like man smoking a pipe inside the barn, perched atop a wagon. When they dismounted, he slid off and stood at the entrance, holding the pipe's glowing bowl, and looked with singular amazement at the drenched and mud-spackled horses now foundered in a bog.

"Ordinarily, I'd offer you folks something to drink, but I'll make an exception in y'all's cases."

"We lost track of the time. Sorry. How about a bonus for all the trouble?"

"I was fixing to ask for a fee."

Ashton paid him an extra hundred dollars, and the man seemed mollified. They got in their car, wet as fish, and drove to their lodging through a driving rain. Still wet on arrival, they became soaked again as they ran to the door.

"I'm freezing," Whitney said.

"Shall we clean up and meet across the street for dinner?"

"Sounds like a plan. Meet you here at nine-thirty."

One hour later, they dined in the same place and manner as they had the prior night. The rain had stopped. Ashton wore his usual Oxford shirt and hounds tooth jacket. Painted and perfumed, Whitney was wearing a white décolleté dress and black knee stockings. When they saw each other, they broke out in the smiles of the saved.

"Too bad George and Bonny couldn't come," she said.

"With him scratching his back like that, you have to be careful where you take him."

She sighed.

"What are you thinking?" he said.

She looked at him, then looked away. She rubbed her eyebrow. She seemed to be holding her breath, as though her thoughts were at odds.

"A secret?" he added.

"It's inevitable." She gestured with open palms.

"Okay, it's inevitable. What's inevitable?"

"That I have a clandestine lover."

"I don't want to hear about it."

"Can you guess who it is?"

"It?"

"He."

"No. I don't want to guess."

"You will meet him soon. Tonight, in fact."

"Whoa!"

"You knew I was a siren."

"Was? I can hear you singing right now. I was hoping you were some-one nicer."

She cocked her head at him, and her eyes were serious. "Don't you like me at all?"

"Of course. You're gorgeous. Not just physical beauty, either."

"Well?"

"I'm way too old."

"I am the judge of that, okay?"

"You're too young."

"No."

"You're not going to take off your pants again, are you?"

"What if I'm not wearing any?"

"You seem to have me just where you want me."

"Not yet."

They ordered dinner, and when it came, Ashton picked at the vegetables, cooked almost beyond recognition. Whitney gulped five pills. She bolted her dinner of roast beef, mashed potatoes, and gravy. Occasionally, she coughed. From the depths of her purse, she found an inhaler and sucked on it twice. Afterwards, they both sipped Shiraz.

"It must be nice to eat ten thousand calories a day and not weigh more than a hundred pounds," said Ashton. "Actually, a hundred and five."

"You remember how much I weigh. I'm lucky. I don't have to gag my-self, take laxatives, or anything."

The door opened, and in shambled an old couple. The man took her cane and held her chair. Whitney watched them with sidelong glances. No words passed between them. Silverware clinked. She turned to Ashton, and she smiled.

"I love old couples," she said. "They've stayed the course."

He nodded. After a moment, he said, "Have you talked yet to your father?"

"Yeah. Before I left. He called me and said not to discuss the bank's business with anyone. It might cause him problems."

Ashton raised his eyebrows.

"I'm taking your advice. It's all forgotten. He said he would correct things."

"You might want to disappear for a few days. Take a vacation. In the mountains or something."

"Good idea. Maybe meet someone tall, old, and handsome."

"Not rich?"

"I'm a trust fund girl, my friend. I still don't know much about you."

"Not much to know."

"I don't believe that for a minute."

"Just the usual. School, more school, marriage, work, work, more work, divorce, work, quit. *Voila.*"

"I was thinking about your not wanting a family."

He nodded and said nothing.

"Strange, I want a child, but can't; you can, but won't."

"Life deals some weird hands, doesn't it?"

"Didn't you ever have a minute when you wanted a family?"

"Here we go again." He thought for a moment. "Having a child means acceptance."

"Yes."

"The world becomes your world. Whatever happens, you've endorsed it. You must recant all complaint. Parents become God."

"Parents are God?"

"In the sense they create life. Life that must exist in the world as it is. Not the world you might like it to be."

Her eyes studied the tablecloth. She picked up her fork and put it down again. She crumpled the napkin and put it on the table.

"What are you thinking?" he said.

"I had an identical twin. She died in infancy. It's odd to think about it. I look at her picture sometimes and wonder why I survived, and she didn't."

"You've seen things no one should see."

She smiled sadly. "One of the unfit. The misbegotten."

"No, no. Not you." He looked at her, but said nothing. After several seconds, he added, "Anyway, we shouldn't equate the fit with the best, should we?"

She ran her right hand across the top of her head and then grasped the back of her neck. Her eyes looked down.

"You can't live and understand all at once. Understanding comes gradually," he said. "It's a matter of time."

Whitney offered to pay for dinner, but Ashton insisted. They left the restaurant and walked across the street to the B & B, climbed the staircase, and went down the hallway. She walked in front of him. He studied the way she moved, held her head. They turned a corner and stopped before her door.

A palpable unease tightened Ashton's face, in considering memories of prior consorts. He realized that hormones, secreted by his body's clever cells, knew no quarter. Again, they built in his blood, intent on joining him with another, and they sought to etch away his defenses in an acid of desire. His eyes looked away, vacant, as the foreboding increased. His brain stormed with conflict: elemental urges against tenuous thought.

The hallway was dim and silent. They were alone. She placed the key in the lock, opened the door, and she turned away from the room. Still with her hand on the door, she leaned close to him, closing her eyes. He kissed her. She opened her mouth and pressed against him. Their teeth bumped. He shivered. She let go of the door, and they embraced. Seconds passed in a frisson without a word. With such speed, she had transformed him from refugee, with alien thoughts, to confidante and potential lover. He attempted to speak, but she put a finger on his lips.

"I thought about what you said. Tomorrow. The day after. Or the day after that," she said. And after looking deep into his eyes, she whispered, "No love without fear." She turned, entered her room, and softly closed the door.

At dawn, he lay in bed next to a window. As the hemisphere brightened, objects inside and out shaped liminal shades of gray. Shadows of tree limbs passed over the walls. A shaft of hard light broke through the window, falling on the floor. Sounds of passing cars, honking, and distant voices were interspersed with sleep and sleep's dream. There was a faint knocking at the door, then louder.

"Tyler," she whispered. "Tyler?"

He arose, put on his trousers, and opened the door. She stood already dressed and held in her arms a huge gray and white cat. The cat mewed.

"Good morning. How did you get that thing in here?"

"That thing is Cheshire, my Weegie. I have to warn you. He fights for a place on the bed. He has the heart of a lion."

"What's a Weegie?"

"A Norwegian Forest Cat."

"I'm glad my friend is watching over my dog."

"Oh. Cheshire doesn't mind. Assuming your dog is friendly."

"He's enormous. I didn't know cats got so big."

"Nineteen pounds. He keeps the trolls from trampling the garden. I've ordered breakfast in my room. Come on in when you're ready."

Twenty minutes later, he went to her suite. Oatmeal and juice sat on the table. When they finished, he suggested they explore other places in the forest. They could draw and photograph as they pleased.

"Why not shoot here? I feel like doing something wild."

He smiled, saying nothing. He looked nervously at his watch.

She stood next to the window and began to undress. Sunlight poured through blinds and shone in a striped pattern on her pale skin. Her distorted shadow melted onto the wall. Freckles, bleached by the rays of light, stippled her neck, around which hung a gold chain. She unbuttoned her blouse, exposing small breasts, teardrop shaped, with high nipples. She let the blouse fall. The shafts of light, pulsing and shimmering, skimmed across her breasts. A radio played. Its sounds were faint. There was a man's voice, then sounds of a cello.

Her eyes gleamed, translucent, appearing lit from within. She tossed her clothes to a chair, and then stood naked in laced shoes. She bent to untie them, straightened, and kicked her legs, one after the other. She walked to the window and opened it, exposing her back to his gaze. Slowly, she turned to face him.

Her hair was taken up, gathered, and pinned; he could see escaped nuchal filaments. She stood silently, hands akimbo, one knee bent. Redolent with perfume, the scent of her hair invaded his nose and clung to his memory. She raised one eyebrow. She looked into his eyes. A half-smile formed on her lips. She knew her power, showing little emotion, but arousing more in him. He awakened from the fringe of reverie.

He could not look away. "I'll get my camera," he said.

He sensed a slippage of his attitude from one category to another, from the controlled to the untamed, from the sacred to the profane. She was not subject for art, but object for him. She could want. She could not control her wants. But she would not get what she wanted.

He took double exposures with the camera fixed, with her in the picture and out, producing ghost images. She posed in front of windows, and in the room's corner, and afterwards, modeled prone on the sofa, then sitting in chairs, and before a mirror. Her dance training evinced an amazing body awareness, in which she assumed positions and attitudes, unstudied, both still and in motion. Working quickly, he managed to catch her in a blur of light and form. Dance and dancer merged. She stood before him and performed a graceful plié.

They worked before the sink and claw tub. They returned to the living room, rested, and watched fugitive shards of light slide down the wall. The light's invasion of the room became even, and the shadows withdrew, and with them, their mystery, and the immaterial became material. He needed the shadow; its withdrawal caused him to stop. By noon, he had exposed 100 negatives, 10 rolls.

The series of moments seemed nailed to his memory. A sense of the illicit, the fear of the forbidden, surged, and it stayed.

"Some masterpieces in there," he said, smiling easily.

"I haven't used the tub. Would you like to join me?"

Ashton regarded her without comment. She tossed her head, her smile resplendent.

"I need to get some experience, live for the day," she said.

She moved closer, standing on tiptoes, and they embraced. She opened her triangulate mouth, and they kissed. She ran fingers through his hair. He wrapped his arms around her. The lumbar spine popped, and he felt her back, rib-thin. She led him into the bathroom. They stood silently before the tub. She turned the tap, and as the water splashed onto the porcelain, she came close and pressed against him. She unbuttoned his shirt, unbuckled, unzipped, and prized open his trousers and grasped his risen penis.

"Afterwards?" he said.

She murmured. She turned off the water. She watched as he removed his clothes.

They returned to the bedroom, and she took the cat from the bed and placed him in the open suitcase sitting on a chair. He curled his tail, drew his four limbs underneath his body, and stared unblinking with golden eyes. She closed the curtains and then pulled back the coverlet and sheet.

She knelt and then lay on the bed; Ashton joined her, and their lips opened, tongues met, and legs, chafing on the insides, intertwined and flexed. And their blood throbbed; there were cries and groans, indistinguishable from pain, seemingly unheard, followed by spasms and wet dilation, and afterward, he looked into her flushed face. Her eyes opened and closed, her nostrils flared wide, and she smiled with still closed eyes.

"Are you looking at my eyes?"

She opened her eyes, and he smiled.

Her breath came heavily. At intervals, she coughed. Moisture still on their bodies vaporized in the breeze of an overhead fan. He was suffused with a curious euphoria, caused, he thought, from mere molecules of ephemeral cells, but so close was the feeling to a sense of the transcendent, molecular or not, it was enough. More than enough. Whole years could be forgotten, sloughed off, like yesterday's skin, but he knew that today's events and tomorrow's remembrance would surely help forestall the injuries of time.

She rolled onto her back. He studied her torso. The xiphoid floated upward, caught between flared ribs. Seconds passed on. He ran his finger around her navel and palpated her belly, lingering at the aortic throb. He looked at his watch, counted her pulse for ten seconds, and multiplied by six. Ninety-six per minute.

"What are you doing?"

"Contemplating your navel."

"Do you see the real me anywhere yet?"

"What?"

"Me. The real Whitney Laird. Not just your ideal. Objectified."

He said nothing. He looked at her. Their eyes met. "I know what you mean. Yes. I do see you. I see us." A moment later, he said, "Let this feeling stay."

She touched his chest. "If it goes, I know how make it come back."

"Can you?"

"Yes."

Their speech ebbed to whispers and then fell altogether, lasting minutes, broken only by distant passing voices. Finally, she said, "I'm glad you remembered."

"Remembered?"

"What to do."

"You don't forget. Like an elephant. They say they never forget."

"I've seen the elephant!" She laughed and moved tightly against him. She whispered, "Let's ride the elephant again."

"The elephant is old. Be nice to the old elephant."

There was a space of some seconds.

"What do you want in a woman? Except her body."

"What do I want?"

"Be honest now."

"The same thing as in men."

"What is that?"

"A kind heart."

"Meek and compliant."

"Not at all. There's a big difference."

"Isn't it important to protect yourself? You're vulnerable."

"In this world, lack of guile is no fault. It's salvation."

She traced the outline of his lips with her forefinger.

"What else do you want in a woman?"

He thought for a moment. "A pretty leg. Definitely, a pretty leg."

"No!" She threw a pillow at him. He threw up his hands and caught it.

A horn outside their window began to honk. It intruded on their moment of quiet. They went to the window, and she drew the curtains. A white pick-up truck was parked at the curb. A man pulled on the handle of the driver's side door. Within a minute, he managed to open it and sat inside. When the engine started, the horn stopped, and he drove away.

They walked naked from the window into the bathroom, and she opened the faucets again. They stood looking at each other without modesty. As the water rose, Ashton stepped into the tub and sat at one end. She entered and sat, back to his front. Placing his arms about her waist, he kissed her neck. Her skin was salty. They leaned back without speaking, hearing the water run, and when the tub filled, she closed the valves. After a time, a drop of water fell from the faucet. Then another, and another.

"I'll be right back."

He smiled. "I certainly hope so."

She got out of the tub and walked away. When she returned, she held a wine bottle, a Syrah glass with a broken stem, a waiter's corkscrew, and a box of biscotti. He reached out to help, but as she stepped into the tub and began to sit, her feet squeaked on the tub. Ashton grabbed the bottle. She slipped into the water. For an instant, her head was immersed. Water splashed onto the sash and floor and into Ashton's face and eyes. The box floated and bobbed. She still held the glass. She wiped her eyes and wrung the water from her hair. He picked up the corkscrew and extracted the cork. When she dumped the water from the glass, she giggled, and then he laughed.

"You really came prepared," he said.

"Unfortunately, as you can see, the stem broke during the trip over here. But we can still use it." She looked at a slight cut on her finger. She put it into her mouth.

She kneeled and opened the casement. Shafts of diagonal light brightened the room. Still kneeling, she removed two biscuits while he poured the wine. She sat, leaning against the tub, and said, "Now this is an experience." She closed her eyes, and he watched her lids. After a time, they sat again, back to front. They ate the biscotti and sipped the wine, sharing the one glass. He pressed the broken stem into a soap bar still wrapped in white paper where it sat on the tub's edge.

"I thought it was too late for me," he said.

"Too late?"

"I can't explain."

"Exhilarating, the first time," she said.

"I didn't think it was your first time."

"Why not?"

"The way you act. Your poise."

"Well, it isn't my first time. I'm not a virgin. But it's the first time it is exhilarating, okay?

"I'm glad for you."

"What about you, Tyler?"

"I'm very glad for me."

"I've been with so many men," she said. "Not much exhilaration." She brushed the hair away from her eyes.

She turned around, he looked at her, and she held his gaze.

"Not in a long while, though. I began at sixteen. I didn't think I had the time."

"A wounded bird."

"Does it matter?"

"I'm not just a passing fancy?"

She put her hands to his mouth. "No. I've never felt this before. You must believe me."

"I believe you."

She turned to the front, and after a pause, said, "Could I get pregnant?"

"Does this mean we didn't use any protection?"

She ignored the question. "Dr. Bourke thinks it isn't too likely."

He saw her reflection in a full-length door mirror. She was now looking at the water.

"Don't worry. It's okay." She turned to look in the mirror. "And you're wonderful."

"Not bad for an old coot."

"There you go again. You're not old. Don't talk about your age anymore. It annoys me."

The water temperature had dropped. She shivered, opened and closed the drain, and then ran the hot water until the bath was warm.

"Let's stay in here all afternoon." She rested her head on his shoulder.

"Your skin will fall off. Then where will you be?"

"I don't care."

"Who could understand this unless they were here?"

"Hush."

He sat, thinking thoughts unspoken, until his mind disengaged. The room was warm, the air, wet. A profound quiet settled over them. He closed his eyes. Minutes passed. A tiny teardrop formed at the faucet, grew for some seconds, fell, and pinged in the bath below. Ashton opened his eyes, looked to the spot where it had disappeared into the water, and then glanced back to the source, where another tiny drop was born. After a time, the heat in the tub seeped away. They became cold, climbed out of the tub, and dried off. She opened the drain.

Cheshire slept on the sofa, his head on a foreleg. They left him and went back to the bedroom, got under the sheets, and after some minutes, fell into a deep sleep, untroubled by dreams.

They stayed in bed until the afternoon had rolled on to early evening. Cheshire circled on the bed next to Whitney, stopping twice to gingerly tap his paw against her face. She rose, dressed, fed the cat, returned to the bed, and prodded Ashton in turn. "Rouse yourself, Tyler. We're wasting our lives." While he put on his clothes, she pulled a skein of yarn from her purse and played with Cheshire. She suggested they go across the street for a late dinner.

When they entered the restaurant at eight o'clock, all the patrons were gone, save for two middle-aged men. One smoked, and the other stared hard at them. They took a table in a corner, and a waitress brought them coffee.

"See those guys?" he said. "They're ogling you. Who can blame them?"

"I see them." Her face wore a frown.

The waitress stood at their table and interrupted their conversation. "Hidy. Where you two from?"

"The big city," said Ashton.

"What you all doing? Sightseeing?"

Whitney smiled sweetly. "I get naked, and he takes pictures of me, okay?"

Ashton spit up his coffee and began to cough. The waitress broke into a slow grin. Soon, he was laughing also. The men looked in their direction.

"She's apt to say anything," Ashton told the waitress. His voice cracked. "You can't take her anywhere." The waitress, still grinning, placed her pencil behind her ear and went away. The two men resumed their conversation. "What were you saying?" Ashton's voice had recovered.

"The dark-haired guy looks familiar. I've seen him somewhere. The one looking, well, rodential," she said.

"Rodential?"

"Like a rat or something."

"No such word."

"There should be."

"Don't make fun of someone's looks."

"Whatever."

"Why worry about it? If you've seen him, so what? It's a small world."

"Just paranoia. I did something I shouldn't have. I didn't tell you the whole story."

"Yeah?"

"Remember when I used my Dad's laptop?"

"I remember."

"One e-mail from a man named Moreno mentioned a transfer of ten million dollars."

"You've reached a conclusion, I would wager."

"My Dad's a jerk."

"Oh, boy."

"I sent a reply."

Ashton gestured with his left hand, said nothing, and his eyes looked at the ceiling.

"Yep, I did, all right."

"And just what did you say?"

"I don't recall, exactly."

"Come on."

"'Privy member.'"

"Clever. I'm glad I'm not a member, privy to such knowledge."

"This is serious, Tyler. They're following us. I'm sure of it. We were at the window—remember the truck?"

"That's comforting. They probably took pictures of us together."

She looked into his eyes. "I don't see what they have to gain from that."

The waitress returned to take their order, cutting short their conversation. Neither had looked at the menu, but they did so now while the waitress stood by, displeased. Whitney ordered a roast beef sandwich. Ashton got a broccoli casserole, carrots, and cup of minestrone. The waitress put the pencil behind her ear again and left.

"I like to identify things. Casseroles? Minestrone? You never know what you're eating. It could be anything," she said.

"Eating a cow is no improvement."

"Okay. Where were we?"

"Rodents."

"I'm sure I've seen that guy. Why would they be here? Do you think we should go?"

"You read my mind. Let's eat and leave before they do."

Ashton and Whitney glanced furtively at the men. As though sensing they had been discovered, the men never looked up. Ashton appraised their faces and speculated as to meanness, resolve, and intelligence. The men ate quickly and left the restaurant first, which doubled Whitney's unease. Fifteen minutes later, Ashton paid the bill, and they left the restaurant also.

They passed under the porch light, Ashton in front, and stood there a moment, listening to the sound of their breathing and to the wind's rustling of leaves. When they were sure the two men were gone, they made their way to Whitney's room.

CHAPTER TEN

They arrived in town at ten that evening and took Jasper Road to Whitney's apartment in the Jameson historic district. It stood as one of a fourplex, built in the 1930's, with a brick facing, a stone transom, and a roof of green tile. Her apartment was number three, up the stairs, on the right. They entered through a white wood door. Over stained oak floors rose nine-foot corniced walls, upon which hung a dozen or more of her drawings, lithographs, monoprints, and paintings. A guitar case stood in a corner, and sheet music was scattered on an end table. Bookshelves contained four or five yards of dog-eared paperback novels, literary and otherwise, as well as art texts and monographs.

Cheshire, glad to be home, began to purr, and explored the living room. He crept into to the bedroom and jumped onto the comforter, yawned, and closed his eyes. Another cat, cream-colored, blue-eyed, and black at the feet and ears, strode to Whitney and mewed.

"Erwin! I'm back." The cat rubbed against her leg and began to purr.

A second bedroom had been converted into a studio. Opposite a chest of flat file drawers, a wood easel was squeezed between two windows. Drawings were scattered about the floor. An adjacent tool chest with open drawers displayed tubes of oil and acrylic paints. Sable and hog-bristle brushes and palette knives stood in a jar. Ashton smelled a faint odor of turpentine.

"Make yourself at home. The fridge is fair game."

"Don't mind if I do." He walked to the refrigerator and opened a beer. He carried the can to the west wall and studied her artwork.

"I don't wish to be unkind, but you've lost me on this one." He was studying a distorted figure that seemed to be caught in a cloth. It was titled, "Once."

"You supply the meaning."

He continued to look at it. He held a beer in one hand, the other hand stuck deep in his pocket, rattling change.

"I can't do it for you. That isn't my job," she said.

"What does the title mean?"

"You discover something just once."

"And then?"

"It's remembered."

"What do you get from all this?"

"You mean why do I paint?" She paced back and forth from painting to painting, talking slowly, searching for the right words. "I have to do something. I've found that if I start with a hundred drawings, throw away ninety of them, and study just the best, it helps me to know who I am. What is left is me. Those drawings I use as models for paintings."

"So that you know you were here. Discovery. Is that it?"

"It's a process. I don't what to be pretentious, but painting feeds the soul. Even if I don't sell anything."

"Your work does seem to have a signature style."

"Do you want to buy one?" She smiled.

"I did already."

"How about a second one?"

"All right. 'Once.' We'll learn to live with each other."

"It's yours. A gift."

"Are you sure?"

In answer, she went to the wall, took down the painting, and handed it to him.

There was movement in the doorway. The cat skirted the room, his tail up. He was rubbing himself on the door edge. He moved on and then stopped at the sofa, reached up with both forelegs, and clawed the fabric. She screamed, "No." He stopped clawing, went to a doormat, and stared, as though conducting some thought experiment. He licked his foreleg.

"Erwin! It's time for sweeping," she announced to the cat. "Sweeping! Sweeping!"

The cat went to her and lay on the floor. Whitney pulled out of the closet a stick vacuum cleaner, turned it on, and ran the brush gently over the cat's head, around the black-edged ears, the neck, and the back and legs. The cat mewed. "Turn over, turn over," she said. He refused to move, and Whitney turned him onto his back, where he lay with feet up, forelegs bent, looking ridiculous. She then vacuumed him on the underside. When she turned the vacuum off, they could hear the cat humming louder.

"Astonishing! He's not afraid of the vacuum at all." Ashton leaned the painting against the couch.

"No, he used to hide, but now he likes it."

"How many cats do you have?"

"Just two."

"Don't they fight?"

"No. They ignore each other."

"It's your turn!" She ran after Ashton with the vacuum. The cat ran off.

"No, I'm clean," he said, grinning. She came close and kissed him.

"Let's make a film. I have a video camera."

"A film?"

"You'll have the leading role, Tyler. Pivotal, I'd say."

"What do I have to do?"

"It's easy, you write the dialogue."

"What will you do?"

"I'll be the director."

She slipped her hand under his belt.

"Directors don't do that sort of thing. Auteurs, maybe."

"The producer, then."

"No."

"The grip!"

"That's it. I'm the gaffer!"

"What if we break out the wine?"

"No."

"Music will put you in the mood. We can dance." She touched his arm.

"I always made an awkward dancer."

"A mask. A masquerade ball."

He rolled his eyes. His face began to flush.

"I can make paper-mache out of brown bags and paper towels."

"Takes too long."

"Okay. I can draw and paint on lunch bags. Let's do it."

"You can draw if you like.

"Okay. I'll start drawing."

Whitney produced two lunch-sized, brown paper bags. Using markers and pastel sticks, she drew a face on one and then the other. The first had cutouts for the eyes and mouth, blond hair, and Geisha lips. The second had openings for just the eyes. There were glasses. The tongue protruded like a Maori dancer.

"What do you think?"

"Very nice. Lascivious."

"Try it on for a dress rehearsal." She put the sack on his head. She went to the mirror and studied her puckish face.

She went to the closet, got her video camera, placed it on the dresser, and looked through the viewfinder. She went back into the living room and put her mask on. They gaped at her workmanship and lapsed into a fit of giggles.

"I've misplaced my frontal lobe. Have you seen it?" He replaced his mask, walked to the mirror, and gazed at his new face, tilted a bit.

"You had it removed in medical school."

"Oh, yes. They did such a good job, I forgot about it."

Whitney switched on the stereo, playing music he had not heard before—primal, chant-like. They undressed, both wearing their absurd disguises. She rubbed oil on her skin. The eye of the camera stared over the tiny dresser tripod.

She danced and mimed, a mummer, sitting him in a chair while the camera watched. She circled, and he pulled in an attraction, like charged particles. He sat in the chair, feeling something akin to embarrassment, but after a time, the limbic gates opened, and he became enchanted. Dance, dancer, and music merged in an apotheosis of beauty. It seemed a dream. She removed her mask, came close, and then removed his.

"We don't need to hide. No one is watching," she said.

"Do you always tell the truth?"

She thought for a moment. "Yes. No. Maybe."

She resumed her dance. He sat in the chair, a person outside himself—watching her, watching them. It was as if he were two: the subject or object of action, the other a non-participant. As the seconds passed, his detachment faded, replaced with simple joy. He found what he had sought. It was there, faithful, waiting, all along, like sparks from a blacksmith's hammer.

"I hope you remember your anatomy," she said.

"My anatomy? Oh, yes."

He laughed.

"We aren't wrong," she said. "Don't feel guilty."

"I'm becoming quite a voluptuary in my dotage."

"Stop!"

They slept well, and in the morning, Whitney prepared breakfast. She fixed egg whites and toast for him, whole eggs for herself. She wore a white bathrobe and he, having showered and shaved, put on yesterday's clothes. She seemed not in the least embarrassed. He looked diffident, lost in thought.

"What's going on in that mind of yours?" she said.

"An ascetic and a libertine. That's what we are."

"You're the libertine; I'm the ascetic."

"How do you figure that?"

"I don't figure anything, really. But this is what I know. You are only with me. I am only with you," she said.

He looked at her. His face was unreadable.

"Always," she said.

"I never knew love." He looked down.

She whispered in his ear, "Me neither."

She went to him, and they embraced, and then she went back to her seat. The silence of minutes was unbroken except for the clinking of plates and glasses.

His attention shifted to her hands. "Where did you get those rings?"

Whitney held up her right hand. Three rings.

"I have a whole collection."

"As you know, I don't wear one. Never been one for jewelry."

"I have a wonderful idea. Let's get matching rings!"

"Do I have to?"

"I know a custom jeweler. She does very nice stuff. She made this one."

She held up her hand, pointing to a silver ring.

"Well—"

She went to the telephone, dialed, and spoke to her friend, saying, "We'll be there in an hour," then hung up.

In an hour, they were at the jeweler's house. She lived in an apartment north of town, over a small shop where her husband sold some of the items and made some as well.

They went upstairs; Whitney greeted her, and introduced her to Ashton. They looked at some of the jeweler's patterns, perhaps fifty different styles. Something caught her eye.

"Can I see this?" She pointed to a pendant under the case. The jeweler opened it and removed the item. She held it between two fingers, and then handed it to Ashton.

It was gold, large, and heavy, with an onyx, flat stone, into which was etched a stylized archer holding a gold, recurve bow, pointing up forty-five degrees. There were two golden arrows, fletched with red feathers, at full draw.

"Beautiful," Whitney said. "Two arrows."

"It's one of my older designs, but it's the only piece left."

Ashton asked about making one with two archers, but the jeweler said there was not enough space on the stone. He examined the necklaces and selected one, and the jeweler joined the pendant and chain. Ashton fastened the piece around Whitney's neck. She broke into a grin, and she grabbed onto his arm and thanked him. She wanted to buy him something, but he said jewelry was not his passion.

"What is your passion, Doctor?"

"If you don't know now, it's doubtful I can tell you."

When Whitney left the jeweler's house, her face shaped into an expression of matchless delight.

CHAPTER ELEVEN

Whitney noticed Claire's absence from the bank three days running; a matronly woman, festooned with jewelry, had taken her place.

"Is something wrong with Claire?" Whitney asked the woman. "We were supposed to have lunch on Friday."

"She went back to Michigan."

"To Chicago? That's where she's from."

"Wherever."

"When was that?"

"I think over the weekend."

"She didn't say anything to me." Whitney gave the woman her brightest smile. "I'm Whitney Laird. What's your name?"

"Daria."

"Well, Daria, I would like to speak to Mr. Coulter."

The woman nodded, with no change of expression. "He's eating lunch in his office. I'll ask him. Have a seat."

She walked behind her desk and into Coulter's office. Whitney could see them talking through the large glass window. He sat at his desk, slumped over a cardboard box, working on a fifteen-inch pepperoni pizza. Light flickered through the outside window as a breeze swayed the birches outside. He looked up and looked through the window, saw Whitney, and nodded to her. The secretary escorted her into his office.

He swiveled in his chair, stood, and walked around his desk, wiping his fingers with a paper napkin. He was a tall man, six-feet-four, or five, and although slightly overweight, he appeared to possess great physical strength. He had dark hair and a mustache. He spoke with the open vowel accent of the upper mid-west.

"Hello, Whitney, please come on in."

The office smelled of an odd mixture of coffee and fresh pizza. With a theatrical gesture, he motioned for her to sit.

"I was just wondering what happened to Claire. We usually go to lunch on Fridays."

"Care for a slice?" He grabbed a wedge, bent down, bit into it, and tore off a jagged piece, which dripped red sauce onto his chin. He snapped at it, dog-like, and then quickly used the napkin over his mouth. He briefly held up his palm.

"No, thank you." She looked away.

"Claire had some kind of family emergency, I believe. She was needed back home. Hopefully, everything will sort itself out."

"I'm sorry to hear it."

"Yes. Something about her mother."

Whitney let a moment pass. "When is she due back?"

"I'm not sure. She said her mother is ill. Her heart. Claire's on extended leave."

"She left this week?"

He chomped and chewed, attempting to speak. One finger pointed upward.

"Four, or maybe five, days ago."

"It's odd she didn't say anything to me. We're good friends."

"She's had a difficult life, you know. Lots of family problems."

"Has she sold her house?"

"Sure you don't want a piece?"

"No, thanks."

"Her house? I wouldn't know about that."

"No forwarding address?"

"Her family is from Chicago."

"So I guess you'll be in contact with her," Whitney said. "Please tell her I asked about her. Tell her I'm concerned."

"She'll call, I assume. That's about all I know." He turned his attention to what remained of his pizza, letting her know she was dismissed.

Instead of going to lunch, Whitney drove to Claire's suburban house. The grass needed mowing. There was no sign of Claire or her car. The only vehicle close by was a silver panel truck having the name Johnson Brothers Electrical painted on the side; it was parked across the street. She walked up the sidewalk, approached the house, and looked into one living room window. It was dim, but she saw Claire's furniture. She rang the doorbell, and then knocked and waited. She turned around and leaned for a moment on a pillar.

Whitney returned to her apartment. She retrieved the key to her deposit box, Claire's padlock key, then drove to the bank and entered the vault. She and Jeannie opened the door of her deposit box.

She took it into a stall, opened it, and took out Claire's small container and unlocked it. Inside were two bundles of US currency in various denominations, as well as a journal. There were three keys, two large, and one small. She held a bundle of bills, not braking the seal, and fanned them, trying not to think where all this was leading.

She picked up the journal. Claire had recorded, in perfect cursive, names, addresses, and bank account numbers of persons residing in six countries, in Europe, Mexico, in the Caribbean, and in the USA. Passwords or codes of some sort were underlined in red. Brendan Coulter and Juan Moreno were listed among them. She turned the page and found a pink, folded letter addressed to her. She read the letter and put everything back, except the keys, and left the vault. She completed her workday.

On her way home, she visited Oriental Carpets and Antiques. Scores of oriental rugs were stacked in bundles, arranged by size. Several ten by twelve-foot or larger carpets adorned the walls. A few pieces of antique furniture sat on the carpets against two of the walls. She examined some of the six by eight rugs. An employee, Mr. Arturo Lopez, asked if he could be of assistance. He recognized her from the bank; it was he who made the deposits. He mentioned this fact, and she smiled and said that she did remember him.

He said, "This rug is an original, hand-made, look at the knot count. Natural dyes, made in Qom, very beautiful."

"I'm sorry, I can't afford it."

Whitney browsed for a few minutes, thanked Mr. Lopez, then left and returned to her car. She glanced down an alley. There was a white pick-up truck. She walked to it, looked at the license plate, and memorized the number: 83649. She was glad the owner of the truck was not in the store. Or was he?

Dinner consisted of linguini with mushroom sauce. She went to the cupboard, opened four bottles, poured pills from each into the palm of her hand, threw the pills into her mouth, and swallowed them with orange juice. She finished her meal. She took out her inhalers, and using one at a time, exhaled, pressed the button, and inhaled deeply. Afterward, she bent over, coughing, and gagged once. She extended her hands and watched coarse tremors in her fingers. After a few minutes, she lay on the sofa and drifted into a fitful sleep.

She awakened in three hours. It was half-past eight. In five minutes, she rose, dressed, found her backpack, flashlight, and keys, and went to her car. She drove toward Claire's house in the dark. The panel truck was still there, but parked on the opposite side of the street. She drove on, turned left at the next street, and left again at the next block. She estimated the distance to the house and parked. Approaching from the rear, she passed through one yard, and then the other, and skulked to the back door. One of Claire's keys opened the lock. She went inside.

Cleaving to walls, ducking under sashes, she made her way to the staircase, and sneaked upstairs to the first room on the right, a bedroom. She glimpsed out the window. The van was not visible. She went to the room's northeast corner, used her flashlight, and pulled back the carpet, exposing what looked like normal, hardwood boards. She went to the closet and discovered it full of clothes. She went downstairs, got a chef's knife, returned, and pried up a section of the floor.

She removed a small portmanteau and, holding the light with her teeth, reviewed its contents. There were dozens of pages listing wire transfers—transactions to and from numerous offshore shell corporations in Grand Cayman, Bahamas, and Antigua. Russian, Swiss, and South American banks were implicated. In Mexico, a Mr. Juan Moreno was chairman of some corporation, with himself listed in various accounts as the nominee signatory.

There was a stack of compact disks. Next to the portmanteau were two ledgers, which appeared to be separate sets of books for the same transactions.

She gathered up the papers, CD's, and ledgers, put them into the bag, and replaced the flooring and carpet. She descended the staircase, walked down the hall, and looked out the front window. There was the van. After putting the knife back, she slipped out the back door, jogged across the yards in darkness, and got into her car.

In all that time she saw no one, including the two men concealed inside the van, filming through a mirrored window with an infrared camera and 400mm lens.

She made it home without incident, fixed herself a turkey sandwich, and poured a glass of milk, took two more pills, and then fished her inhalers from the bathroom drawer and used them. She undressed, put on pajamas, sat in bed, and read the papers again and again. She studied the entries involving her own bank. Eight entities wired money to and received money from overseas. She recognized two of the depositors, one J. X. Dunsenon, a supposed gold and jewelry merchant, and A. Lopez, owner of the carpet store. Monies exceeding $100,000, accruing in the various businesses, were then pooled in a master account amounting to 7.2 million dollars. That sum was wired, in parcels, to a Guadalajaran bank, and then to two Bahamian banks. Transfers occurred about every two to four weeks. There were photocopies of signatures; among them were those of Juan Moreno and Brendan Coulter.

At quarter-past three, she fell·asleep with the light still on.

CHAPTER TWELVE

Taking the road Ashton had suggested, Whitney drove her Volkswagen Cabrio to the turn-off at St. Ann's Church. The top was down, the windows up. The tape deck played Dire Straights' "Brothers in Arms," followed by Bob Dylan's "Forever Young," and then songs by REM and U2. She turned right onto Sedgewick Lane, a chip-sealed asphalt road, scarcely wide enough for two cars.

Sections of stone fence wove around huge burr oaks and black walnut trees. Half a mile down the road, she came to a ninety-degree turn and stopped the car. On the right was a brick entrance, the color of burnt sienna. A small limestone plaque inserted in the brickwork had the word "Palisade" carved in it, and below that, in smaller type, "232 Sedgewick Lane." She got out of the car, went to the gate, and unlatched it; it swung open gently, as gravity pulled it downhill.

The gravel lane turned right, went across a knoll, and wound downhill again, skirting an impenetrable wood that bordered the road for two hundred yards. A thirty or forty-acre undulating field grew alfalfa, about one foot tall, deep green with blue flowers.

Running along the side of the road, a four-board fence, creosote black, surrounded a barn. It stood adjacent to a twenty-acre pasture. Beside the fence, a stallion stood alone in fescue and clover. About a hundred yards in the distance, she saw a saltbox house, painted off-white.

She turned sharply left and began to ascend the long hill. Below on the right was a pond, more than fifty yards long, shaped like a butter bean. A wooden pier jutted from one end, and cattails grew along the pond's western border. On a hillside above the water, an orchard of perhaps two hundred trees stood arrayed on a contour grid, the trees separated in each direction by five or six yards. Blooms, like wispy, white clouds, gave shape to the trees, which together formed a subtle beauty, and the tableau, by its very geometry, seemed to impose order midway between the wild wood and the groomed lawn.

When she gained the hill's crest, she stopped. White dust skimmed across the road. She looked down to the pond, thirty yards below. A snapping turtle sat atop a rock at the water's surface; its carapace, big as a dinner plate, gleamed in the sun. From the north came a throb of an engine, and she looked around. Ashton was riding an ancient red and gray tractor on the hillside opposite, and she drove around the house and across the field to where he worked. She parked and got out of the car. She walked a few yards. A brood of strange chickens with deformed beaks shifted and pecked at the ground around her, at intervals flapping their sparsely feathered wings. She gingerly backed away.

He was drilling holes with an auger attached to the power take-off. Pieces of metal, like bolts, had been welded to the auger blade. It dug a ragged hole. Ashton put his gloved hand to the brim of a charcoal-colored fedora. He watched Whitney with eyes obscured by aviator sunglasses. The hat brim cut the light on his face and formed a black shadow. He looked like he was wearing a mask. She walked over to him.

"Hi. What are you up to, Tyler?"

"Planting more trees."

"Need help?"

"Yeah, sure."

"What kind are they?"

"Dwarf apple."

He got down from the tractor, removed his gloves, and leaned on the tractor. He bent his right leg. His boot rested against the rear tire. She faced him, wearing overalls, hands thrust into her pockets.

"What's wrong with those chickens?"

"They were on the short list for bird heaven when I found them at the packing plant. They do seem improved. Their feathers are growing back."

Her expression was incredulous. "How about those over there, the ones with the wattles?"

"Guineas. Watch birds. Ferocious little buggers."

"One is laying an egg on your car."

He raised his eyebrows and looked toward the barn. The dog came up and barked.

She held out her hand to pet the dog. "Is he friendly?"

"Piper? She helps the burglars carry the furniture to the truck. She's noisy, but doesn't mess with the birds."

"It looks like you have an orchard already." She played with the dog. Piper's tail wagged. She jumped up with her paws on Whitney's shoulders. The dog licked her face.

"Yep, the one you saw, and a second one, now mostly gone."

"Gone where?"

"Last year was bad news. I brought in sixteen beehives, and the bees infected the orchard. Fireblight. They did their little waggle dance on my dream. Not to be outdone, as you can tell, I'm determined to succeed."

She nodded and then tilted her head.

"It's a bacterial disease. Spreads down from the blossom. It took me most of two months to prune it out. I had to cut down half the orchard."

"It will come back."

"I think I nailed it with sprays of streptomycin."

"Okay. Let's plant."

"The trees are heeled-in over there." He pointed to a mound of dirt about twenty yards up the hill. "I've drilled about fifty holes, and I have two hundred rootstocks."

"What are you going to do with all these?"

"I'm not going to do anything."

"No, really."

"They're just here. Just to see."

"Just here to see. Okay."

"Maybe, I'll have a small pick-your-own operation. I don't have a lot of money in it. At worst, I can feed a few deer."

Whitney went to the mounded dirt, with the saplings stuck at an angle, pulled up a spading fork, and dug up four, bare-rooted trees. A vole squeaked, scuttled away, and trembled under a clump of fescue.

She took the trees to Ashton, who was spading loose loam out of one hole.

"Thanks. It takes seven years for them to bear. I guess I'm being a bit nostalgic."

"Why do you say that?"

"My father was a plant breeder, a horticulture professor. He taught me all of this."

With a trowel, Ashton scored the sides of the hole, and, at the bottom, tamped the dirt. He placed the roots into it, replaced the dirt around the collar with a spade, and packed the dirt with his boots. He pruned away two branches, forming too narrow an angle with the trunk, and finally, wrapped the tree with a crinkled paper. He watered it with a blue fertilizer solution. They planted the remaining trees, two hours of steady activity, and afterward, they admired their work.

"Time to rest," Ashton said.

"I'm really thirsty."

"There's tea in the refrigerator. I'll put away the tractor and tools."

Whitney walked to the house while Ashton, spade and shovel across his lap, drove the tractor through the door opening and into a two-story pole barn. He stepped onto a packed dirt floor and hung the tools in neat rows against the east wall. The air smelled of hay, mixed with manure. He left the barn and walked to the house, where Whitney had poured iced teas.

"Let's sit outside."

They went to the porch, its roof supported by six wood pillars. The heat was tropical, unusually so. They sat in faux wicker chairs, separated by a small, wood table, and after a time, as might a child, Whitney drew her knees to her chest, where she rested her chin and wrapped her arms around her legs. Her shoes fell to the floor. She looked at her toes. From her purse, she retrieved a clear nail polish, and began to paint her toenails. The air reeked of solvent. The low eye of the sun cast a copper glow to the western sky, and a tongue of light gleamed on the balustrade.

She walked to the porch's edge, leaned over the railing, and looked for some time.

"This one is still moving, but it's lost its head."

Ashton went over to where she pointed and watched two insects, one with a triangular head and the other with none, commingling.

"What a stud," he said. "Spurred on to greater efforts, I suppose."

They walked back to their seats and drank tea. The sounds of frogs croaking came from the direction of the pond.

"Frog symphony," Ashton said. "Doubtless, some mating ritual. An orgy or something. They've been carrying on for days, like drunks."

The Morgan ambled along the black fence and walked into the barn through the back door.

"Do you just leave him out there all alone?"

"What am I supposed to do with him? He goes in and out as he pleases."

"As you said, he's just here, like the trees," she said. "I'm not criticizing. I wish I had a place like this for my horse."

"I didn't know you had one."

"Annabelle. I board her at Webster's."

"I have a free stall. You're welcome to have her wander around here, if you like. Plenty of room."

She laughed. "You're serious."

"Morgan could use company."

"Why do you call him Morgan?"

"It was supposed to be temporary, until I thought of something more descriptive. That was a while back. He doesn't seem offended."

She turned an index finger against her temple. "You're crazy."

"That's a given." He smiled. "And you're a little strange yourself, my dear."

"Not as strange as you, Tyler." She stuck out her tongue.

They waited until the gloaming sky gave way to darkness. Whitney began to slap at her forearms and scratch at invisible wounds. Ashton entered the house and returned with repellant.

"No mosquitoes this early, but you can apply this anyway, whatever they are."

After a while, in humid, soft focus, attended by wispy clouds, a half-moon climbed the sky and cued the coyotes congregating in the numinous wood. They yapped and howled incantations like aboriginal bards.

"Listen. Listen to them," she said.

"Here, you can still feel the mystery. This is what people need."

"Imagine you were a year old," she said. "It's all pure sensation." She gave a meaningful look, and then added, "You'd better build a coop for those chickens."

The night was alive.

"If you can't feel anything here, you don't have a pulse." Ashton leaned back in the chair, fingers laced behind his head.

They sat until it grew late, then they went inside. He slumped on the sofa, and she joined him.

"You printed one of the pictures!" She pointed to a matted and mounted black and white photo sitting on top of a bookshelf.

"Two, actually." I'll get the other one. He returned from the bedroom and placed the two photos side by side.

"Wow! I love that one!" She motioned toward the scene of still water. She was kneeling with the tall grass, silhouetted against a setting sun. The other picture showed a figure standing in the corner of a room, near full-length windows. Her arm was up, partially covering her face, seeming to gleam in the light. It was called *Amaranth*.

"These are awesome," she said. "Do you have any others?"

"Of you?"

"No, I mean other photos. Well—yes, of me, okay?"

"I printed two others. Several portfolio cases of other stuff. Plus some on the walls."

"Can I see them?"

"Sure."

He went down a short hallway into a room and returned with a black case that he opened on the coffee table. He removed twenty-four matted, silver gelatin prints.

She began to look at them. "Where did you take these?"

"Europe, American West, some here. I used to think you had to find subjects in exotic places, but now I find them everywhere."

"You should publish them. Make a book."

"I once looked into doing that. I'll have to tell you about it sometime."

There were prints of fog-laden Venice in winter, of Provence and Tuscany, of ruins in Greece and Turkey, of Norwegian suns shining on the horizon, of full moons balanced among backlit clouds. There were nudes set against landscape, small figures, comfortably clothed in their skins. Others were lost in implacable deserts or exposed against Old Testament skies.

"Tell me about the publishing."

"Oh, yes, the publishing." But he said nothing, only smiled.

"Well?"

"It's not a pretty story. I sought the advice of an Englishman, the curator of the photography section of a British museum. Long story. He looked at twenty-four prints and said they were 'splendidly' printed. Then he pointed to three of them, saying they reminded him of pieces done 'during the Pictorial Period. I fear the subject is exhausted.' I asked him if he made photographs, and if so, of what, and he said he did, of machine tools and tumbleweeds."

"Who cares? In the art world, we see that kind of thing all the time. Artists need a point of departure, sometimes, just anything to be different. This is superb work. Go somewhere else. The next one will be better."

"I might."

He reached for his wallet and began removing cards, first from one section, then another. He dumped them all on the table.

She rested her chin on a closed hand.

"I'm reminded of something a gallery owner told me after seeing some of my nudes. Ah, here it is."

He handed her a business card, printed with the name, Tyler Brooks Ashton, and below it, Bigot Pornographer.

"My photography didn't conform to her theories, I suppose."

Whitney's eyes squeezed shut in laughter until the tears ran. She got up and walked around the sofa, waving the card around, and holding her belly with her other hand, and then fell into the sofa again. "Bigot Pornographer. You're too much." Her smile lingered.

"The poor woman harangued me for photographing only white women—nude. Like a schoolmarm. Thought she was some moral arbiter. I sent her an invitation to the opening, but she didn't come."

She wiped her face and eyes. "How incredibly stupid! One of the sob sisters, I guess. Artists don't need rules."

"She wasn't model material, I'm afraid. Actually, I can almost understand her. She was rebelling against the tyranny of nature."

"That's a paradox. I do know something about genes."

"A paradox, then."

"You must add the words sexist and racist, too." She grinned.

"Good point. I'll order a new batch."

"I want a picture with me and the moon."

"You're on. We'll set it up tomorrow."

They sat quietly while Ashton gathered the photos and returned them to their box. Whitney crossed her legs and kicked them. She finished her drink and stared at the empty glass.

"What are you thinking?" he said, studying her face. "Lost your best friend?"

"You won't understand."

"Try me."

"I hate to bring this up."

"It's all right. Whatever it is. Just say it."

"I found out my father is a crook."

"Really?"

"I have the evidence, the money transfers."

He rubbed his fingers across his mouth and regarded her with a solemn face. "You'd better be careful."

"And Claire is missing."

"There must be some simple explanation."

"They say she went home to Chicago. But I called her parents at home. She isn't there, and they haven't heard from her for weeks."

He said nothing.

"I'm starting to despise him."

"What will you do, Whitney?"

"Maybe I should tell the bank regulators. Without giving my name."

"If you piss against the wind, you get wet. Old Ashton family proverb."

"Not if you're under a poncho."

"The best poncho is the one you have with you when the pissing starts. Where is yours?"

She stuck out her tongue. "'You're my poncho,' she said."

"Don't bet the ranch on it."

The next afternoon, close to dusk, under a smoky sky, they walked east, and wound down the gravel road, where the land sloped away to the woods. A cloud passed in the wind, and its shadow, as they turned into it, fell upon them, erasing their own. The cloud and its shadow moved away as they left the road, and they ambled through a remote field until they came to a limestone shelf where masons once had quarried rock.

They climbed a knoll. In the distance was the object of their quest, an outcropping of gray stone. Large pieces of it had broken away and fallen in a mound, resembling a stage. They walked on, their shadows sometimes merging, always in front, grown long in the afternoon light, longer than themselves.

Dozens of grasshoppers sprang before them. One stuck to Whitney's sleeve. It looked at her with its jeweled, compound facets, and as she grabbed it about the spiracles, it spat in revolt. A brown stain wet her blouse. She flicked it away. "You're not a nice bug," she said. She looked at her fingers.

They sat on stones. Neither spoke. They listened to the wind. Driven from the west, it quickened, and as they waited for the sun to descend into the earth, boiling cloudbanks formed and reformed on a seamless sky.

The moon rose above the mound, and Whitney, seeing her cue, clambered to the top; she wrapped a cloth taken from the dining table around herself and formed it into a cowl. In the half-light, she stood, arms outstretched, like some phantom, free of the earth. Ashton bent over the tripod, his back to the shrinking sun, his clothes flapping about him as he struggled against the wind to make the ten pictures. Man and machine, rigid; shutter slow, shutter fast. The clouds flew by, swirling, and within seconds were gone, and the moon continued to rise as if powered by its own will.

The next morning, after breakfast, Whitney prepared a picnic lunch. They went to the outbuilding where Ashton stored his 1967 Austin Healey 3000. From a spigot abutting the horse trough, he filled a twenty-liter jerry can. He carried it to the Healey, opened its trunk, and, using two bungee cords, strapped the can inside.

"What's with the can?" Whitney said.

"Water."

"If you drink all that, you'll get sick." She laughed.

"There's trouble with the car's cooling system, a leak somewhere. The radiator, I think. I've got a guy looking for a new one." He leaned over and pointed to the temperature gauge. "We need to fill it if it gets too hot. Watch the needle."

He put down the car's ragged top, struggling with it, and finally snapped on the cover. They jumped in, and he attempted to start the engine, but it would not crank. He cleaned the battery cables and tried the starter again. The fuel pump ticked, the engine sputtered, coughed, and then came to life; black smoke curled up from the exhaust pipe. Whitney, too, began coughing.

"Sorry about all the smoke."

"Don't we get to wear scarves?"

"No."

"Goggles, then?"

They pulled out, and Ashton drove slowly over the half-mile road, keeping close to its edge. As they passed the pond, a small flock of wild turkeys, a jake and four hens, foraged among the milkweed. When she placed her hand on his leg, he put his arm around her shoulder. From time to time, he abandoned the steering wheel to shift gears, and once, as he turned the corner on Sedgewick, the car veered toward the fence.

"Use both hands," she said.

"I have to drive with one," he said, smiling. "Sorry."

When he got to the pavement, he opened up the engine, ran through the gears, and they barreled along country roads in overdrive, until they reached Webster's Stud. By that time, heat from the engine poured through the firewall. They were streaming sweat in spite of the wind.

They pulled up outside the stable. Whitney entered, saw Annabelle standing in the third stall, and called her by name. The horse spoke no greeting. She saddled her and fit the bit, bridle, and reins. Ashton walked around the barn and peered at the other mares. Whitney mounted, wearing jodhpurs and cavalry-style, knee-length boots, and rode through the barn doors and into the sunlight.

A wood fence in sore need of repair wrapped around a dirt track. Whitney walked Annabelle at first, then increased the pace to a canter, and finally to a full-tilt gallop. Ashton, again wearing sunglasses and a fedora, stood at the fence, drinking bottled water and watching her. She pulled up to him.

"Do you want to ride her? Or just look cool?"

"Look cool."

"I'm going over there." She pointed and thundered off to an adjacent field, passing through a white, open gate. Ashton followed at an ever-increasing distance. Six or eight jumps were arranged as a practice course for steeplechase. She took Annabelle over the course three times; she and the horse launched over the jumps harum-scarum. Ashton was impressed. Just as he was thinking how adroit she was, the horse balked, twisted to the side, and Whitney catapulted over the jump. She was lost to view. Ashton vaulted a fence and ran to her. She was already on her feet and smiling sheepishly. Her blouse was smeared with grass stains, and on her pants was a large mud patch. Annabelle had run off, but had stopped after thirty yards.

"I haven't performed that trick in a while."

"Don't you think you might need brain protection?"

She blushed. "I should have been able to control her." She shook her head.

She went around the hedge, took Annabelle by the reins, and they walked back though the gate to the stable.

She put Annabelle in the barn, removed her saddle, tied the reins to a column, and brushed her. Bathing was next. She talked as if both she and the horse were children. Ashton walked around for thirty minutes, looking at the house, stables, and fenced fields, and when he returned, she was finishing up, and they went to a table under some trees and ate lunch.

Later, as they were driving back to the farm, Ashton pulled over and pointed to the needle on the temperature gauge. He got out, opened the hood, and using his shirt to shield his hand, turned the radiator cap. It began to hiss and spurt, and he quit turning. After a few seconds, it stopped, and he opened it. Steam fogged upward. He wiped his glasses, and then got the can. Water gurgled into the radiator. He replaced the cap, lowered the hood, and got back in his seat.

"I love this car!" she said.

"I found it four years ago and restored it. Or rather, had it restored. When I was about your age, I had one, and I should never have sold it."

"Just look! It's so sensuous."

"But very temperamental. Like a beautiful woman."

"No." She shook her head.

"You can drive it if you're careful."

"Really, Tyler? I do have a couple of errands."

"Take it if you want. I'll give my insurance guy a call, just in case."

They made it back without the engine overheating. She went to the trunk for the jerry can and topped off the radiator. He entered the house and called the agent. When he returned to the car, Whitney was sitting in the driver's seat. She shifted the gears. He explained how the overdrive worked, and then he gave her the keys.

"Don't wreck my beautiful lady!"

"You don't trust me."

"I trust you. You're the lady I'm concerned about."

"I'll be careful."

They said their goodbyes, and she drove away. From the porch, he watched her go down the sinewy lane; the car formed a lead point of white dust covering the limestone ribbon. Near the woods, the car yawed and hopped on the gravel. It bottomed on the undercarriage, veered off the road, then back on again. He shook his head as she disappeared around the bend. The exhaust note remained for a time, and then it, too, vanished.

When she got to the main road, she turned left, toward town, starting a twenty-four-mile drive along Highway 87. About midway, a white pick-up fell in behind her. She slowed. It came close. A horizontal, telescoped rifle hung in the back of the cab. She increased her speed, lengthening the distance. After two miles, she spied a gas station, drove in, and parked. She entered, bought a Coke, and when she returned to the car, the truck was gone.

She sat in the car, drank half the Coke, got out, and threw the can in the garbage. Still no truck. Satisfied, she continued her journey. But two blocks down, on a side street, a white pick-up sat behind a stop sign. She turned left, went around the block, and when she returned, the white truck was still there. The driver flicked the ash of a cigarette out of the partially open window. Smoke curls dispersed in the wind.

She turned left again, pulled up alongside him, and stopped. She turned her finger like a propeller, and he rolled down his window. Dark hair stuck out below a cap that read, "Smith & Wesson." He wore sunglasses. There was a tattoo of barbwire surrounding his biceps. She did not recognize him.

"Tell me. Have you ever been awake all night in a hospital bed, wondering if you would live 'til morning?"

He stared at her for a long moment. "Can't say that I have, Miss."

"If you get the chance, you should try it, okay?"

"Why is that?"

"You wouldn't be afraid of people like you, ever again."

"Thanks for the advice, young lady," he said. Then he added in a hoarse, tobacco whisper, "Maybe you should be."

She drove away slowly and looked over her shoulder, trying to read the license number, but managed to see only the first two numbers—eight and three. The truck began moving, but it did not follow her. She pulled to the side of the road and sat there until she stopped shaking. Ten minutes passed before she turned around and drove back to the farm. She found Ashton sitting at the pond's pier. When they embraced, she was shaking again. Her voice sounded thin and hoarse when she told him about the man in the truck.

"Maybe you should stay here," he said, "For a while, at least."

"I wasn't afraid at the time, but I am now."

He hugged her as they sat side by side, dangling their legs over the water. A shock of hair fell over her eye, and she brushed it away.

"That really got to you, didn't it? Are you all right?"

"I'm okay."

"We'd better call the police," he said.

"I don't want to drag you into this."

"Looks like I'm already in it."

"I don't want to call them yet."

"Why not?"

"I think I need to know more. Have more evidence."

"Don't wait too long."

"I don't know what to do. But they won't bother you."

"Maybe. I can't defend us here, you know. Surrounded by these woods."

"I don't need defending, okay?"

"Do you have a gun?"

"No. Of course not. I don't know how to shoot."

"I can show you."

"I don't want to learn. I hate guns."

"Sometimes a gun can be your friend. This might be one of those times."

They went to the house, into the bedroom, where a metal gun case had been bolted between two studs in the closet wall. Ashton unlocked the case and removed one of two Colt .45 automatics, the smaller one, a "Lightweight Officer's Model." He took hearing protectors and two magazines loaded with hardball into the kitchen. He found an empty Coke can in the pantry.

They went outside; he threw the can on the ground, and stepped off seven yards. He reviewed with her the pistol's manual of arms. It was always loaded, a round always chambered, the safety on, in "cocked and locked" mode. To unload, take the magazine out first, pull back the slide, remove the cartridge, press-check it again, make sure the chamber is empty. He seated the magazine, racked the slide, and applied the safety. He put on the earmuffs, turned a dial, and adjusted the amplitude.

"Plug your ears," he said. She stuck index fingers into both canals.

He depressed the safety and fired at the can, hitting it; it hopped. When it hit the ground, he double-tapped. The can hopped wildly again. He snapped up the safety, stuck the gun in his belt, put the muffs over her ears, the gun into her hands, and refined her two-handed grip.

The safety came off. Her finger squeezed around the uptake. She held the gun over the target at forty-five degrees, and lowered it. Ashton opened his mouth, was about to say something, when suddenly the gun discharged, putting a bullet into the woods. It cracked against a tree. She turned and offered the gun to him, as though it were a live grenade. He raised his hands, palms forward.

"Not bad for a first shot. Keep your finger outside the trigger guard until you're ready to shoot. Let's give it another try."

"That's it. No more."

"It's for your own protection."

"No colon, no colitis. Guns are evil." Her face turned impish.

"No, they're not. Only some of the people who use them."

She held the pistol with two fingers of each hand. "I'm sorry Tyler; I don't need to be rescued, okay?"

"Rescue yourself, then."

Ashton took the pistol, snapped up the safety, and stuck it under his belt in the small of his back. He picked up the can. She was ahead of him by ten yards as they walked back to the house.

"I'll talk to Michael Amberley tomorrow. He's my attorney. We went to college together. He'll know what to do."

"I want to go with you," she said, forcing a smile.

CHAPTER THIRTEEN

They met at Amberley's office the next afternoon. Downtown, on a side street, the office had been converted from an old house. Amberley had shared the space with his partner for some twenty years. The receptionist greeted them and offered them coffee; they thanked her, but refused. They sat together in what had been the living room. In less than a minute, Amberley emerged from a side room, and said with a smile, "An emergency visit to a lawyer usually isn't happy news. What can I do for you?"

Whitney told him what she had discovered about Juan Moreno, her suspicions regarding her father, and Brendan Coulter.

"I've heard of Moreno. A wheeler-dealer—a retired South American judge. Mexican, I think. He's got a big horse farm in Sutter County, Caballo Manchado, it's called, and he owns a bunch of property here, downtown, including the Grayson Hotel. Been here a few years now."

She related being followed, possibly stalked, by one or two people in a white pick-up. Ashton recalled that a white truck's alarm went off when they were at Wycliffe. Amberley indicated that it was probably intentional, a ruse to get people to come to the window for photographs.

"Also, a friend, and colleague, is missing," Whitney said. "At the bank." She told him about Claire.

"I think you need to make the police aware of this."

Whitney looked at Ashton. He raised his eyes and fingered the corners of his mouth.

"Four years ago, when my house was burglarized," he said, "the police were more interested in filling out forms than solving the case. Do you think the FBI would be better? Or the DEA?"

"From the sound of it, you don't have enough evidence to get them involved, Tyler." Amberley shook his head.

"What about Claire?" asked Whitney.

"Report that to the police, too."

Ashton nodded. "I guess you're right."

"What's the next step?" Whitney asked.

"You have to make a formal complaint."

"If my dad's not guilty, I don't want the police involved, but I know he is." She fidgeted in her chair and brushed her hair behind her ear.

"What about reprisals? Retaliation?" Ashton asked. "What do we really know about this guy?"

"You're in a difficult spot. You could find things unpleasant," Amberley answered. "At a minimum, you should file a missing person's report and notify the police about the stalking."

"And not about the bank?"

"If there's a connection, perhaps you should alert the police. But right now, you're mainly interested in your safety. We could hire a detective, a man of our own. Find out the extent of their property holdings, check into his past, and see if you're followed."

"One detective can do all that?" Whitney asked.

"You'd be surprised what a good PI can do. I can recommend a few."

"All right. What do you think?" Ashton asked, turning to Whitney.

"Okay. We have to do something." She rummaged through her handbag and handed him a piece of paper. "This may be the license plate number. I got the first two numbers, 83, and at the rug store, there was a white truck with the number 83649."

"I would suggest a very smart guy who has worked for me twelve years. He's a good money hound. Former police officer. We'll search public records, vehicle licensure, deeds, anything else that turns up."

He opened a drawer in his desk, rummaged around, pulled out a folder, leafed through it, and handed Whitney a photograph. "David Mortenson. If you see him around, don't worry about it." He handed her two of Mortenson's business cards. "I'll fill him in on the necessary details. He may want to talk to you. Don't get too specific if he does."

"All right."

"Give me the names again."

"Brendan Coulter, Juan Moreno." She spelled them for Amberley as he wrote them down.

"What's your father's name?"

"Geoffrey Laird."

"Are you going to report Claire missing, Whitney?" Amberley asked.

"Yes. As soon as I leave here."

"You two should lie low for a few days. I'll get back to you as soon as we find out something."

"Okay," Whitney said, nodding. She smiled at Ashton. "I feel a little better now. At least we're doing something."

"One more thing, Tyler. I saved the best until last. I'm not supposed to know this, but I saw Black at lunch. Clement wants to talk about dismissal."

"Excellent!" Ashton grinned.

"Dismissal with prejudice, if you agree not to file any malicious prosecution countersuits," Amberley added.

"What does 'with prejudice' mean, exactly?"

"After this decision, it cannot be brought up again."

"All right."

"Somebody sued you?" Whitney said, frowning, clearly concerned.

"Yeah. It's been going on three years now. What a relief it's over."

"Are you going back to work then?"

"No, no. My farm needs me now. And I need it."

They left the office, and Ashton drove Whitney to the police station. She inquired about reporting a missing person and was given forms to fill out. She was told someone would contact her the next day. They returned to the farm, but in the afternoon, an officer called with questions. Whitney decided to go back to the station.

Ashton walked outside with her and watched as she drove away in the Cabrio. He ambled west, skirting the woods until he had walked about one hundred and fifty paces. He stopped and looked back. Circling one hundred and twenty degrees, hugging the wood line, he never strayed more than two hundred yards. Piper followed him as he went to the other side. He studied the serpentine lane, abutting half a mile of forest, and considered the possibility that someone with a 12X telescope might be watching him.

He and Piper walked around until twilight, and then they returned to the house. Ashton fixed and ate dinner—a beer and a sandwich. He developed the most recent negatives, hung them in the darkroom to dry, and then ran through a wasteland of television channels before switching off the set. Back in the darkroom, he worked on one negative for three hours, and titled the print, *Risen Moon*. At quarter past one, he went to bed.

At 0345, pounding on the front door awakened him. Piper growled and stood, hackles up. Ashton climbed out of bed and into a pair of jeans, picked up the .45 from the side table, and walked with the dog to the living room window. He looked outside. A white pick-up truck was in the driveway. Two men stood on the porch. He went to the door and listened. There was no sound except the dog's low growl. He opened the door. The two men had separated and were standing on either side of the porch. He snapped off the pistol's safety, which made an unmistakable sound in the otherwise still night. He held the gun at his side, looking straight ahead, trying to watch the men's four hands.

"My name is Aaron Cox, and this is my brother-in-law, Lester Towne. We live down the road about two miles. We lost track of our coon dog over here, somewhere. I think he treed a coon, off in your north woods, and we was looking to get it back, but we didn't want to be nosing around without you knowing and all."

Cox attempted a crooked smile. He had a leathery face, weathered by years spent outside. The other man held his hands together in front, as if he didn't know quite what to do. He seemed embarrassed, uneasy. As Cox leaned closer, Ashton glanced at their clothes and shoes. They did look like farmers or coon hunters. They bore no visible weapons.

Piper snapped and barked, an act of aggression of which Ashton had thought her incapable. Her lips curled back, her teeth were bared, and she advanced toward the men with a low growl. Ashton grabbed her fur at the haunch, dragged her back, and got hold of her collar. She stood on hind legs, her jaw snapping. He restrained her as best he could. Both men retreated a few steps. The one at the rear lost his footing on the first step, but he recovered before falling.

"All right," Ashton said. "Find your hound, but don't hurt the raccoon."

"Thank you. Sorry for the trouble and all."

"Aren't you Dr. Ashton?"

"That's right."

"You worked on my Amy ten or twelve years ago. Diabetes. When she was six, I think. They said you saved her life. I never did thank you. So I will now."

"What were your names again?"

"I'm Aaron Cox."

"Lester Towne."

"Down the road, you say?"

"Down by Lincoln Crossroads."

"I see. How is she doing now?"

"Just fine. Going to college next year."

He snapped up the safety. "Well, I hope you find your dog."

The men got into their truck and turned around in the driveway. Ashton memorized the license number. He searched for a pad in the kitchen, and, not finding one, wrote the number on his hand. He watched the men park on the gravel road near the entrance to the farm. Then he went to the refrigerator and poured a glass of orange juice. He took it to the living room and sat in a chair by the window, allowing a clear view of the front yard. He drank some of the juice, then went back to the kitchen and added a jigger of vodka.

After twenty minutes, the lights of the truck began to move. The truck approached St. Ann's Road, turned right, and went a distance of several hundred yards. Its lights were finally lost in the darkness. Dawn found Ashton still sitting there, still awake. Beside him, Piper lay asleep, head on paws. On three occasions, she uttered a series of muffled barks. Her lids half opened. A hind leg moved as though she were running.

He dressed and then drove the two miles to Lincoln Crossroads. He found a mailbox with the name Aaron P. Cox printed on it. A white truck was parked in the driveway. The license numbers matched. There were no eights or threes. He went back to his place, put his gun away, and collapsed in bed, with Piper on the floor beside him.

CHAPTER FOURTEEN

At ten that morning, at the bank, Geoffrey Laird, Brendan Coulter, and Juan Moreno sat around a table in a conference room. Moreno had called the meeting, but its agenda was unknown. Moreno's words danced across his tongue as he raced from one subject to another. He was in a noisy, excitable mood. His high-pitched voice gave vent to frequent bouts of giggles, as if illuminating everyone with amazed discovery. Laird and Coulter listened intently, waiting for the meeting's true purpose. Moreno was given to long and discursive speeches. You needed patience.

Coulter resembled a big predator. His dog eyes had a way of fixing a stare, missed little, and reflected nothing. He exuded animal cunning; his confidence was supreme. One sensed he had few doubts and fewer scruples. He dominated people because he knew a secret: most men lacked conviction, and the rest were too civilized to fight. Both types were easy to bait and bleed. He knew when to cajole and when to threaten. If one failed, use the other.

Laird sat at the head of the table. Moreno produced a cigarette from a crushed pack in his breast pocket and searched his trousers for a lighter. Coulter was quick to light it with his own silver lighter.

"No smoking inside the bank—policy, sorry, Judge," Laird said.

"Well Geoffrey, I'm not as smart as you are, but I do know policies sometimes must admit exceptions." His laughter lasted a long time. "Without a smoke, you might find me unpleasant."

Laird sighed. "All right. We'll make an exception."

Tobacco stains coated Moreno's thumbnail and forefinger. Aromatic clouds lingered; smoke penetrated their clothes. Moreno talked with the cigarette held between his teeth or lips. As it burned to a nubbin, his beard seemed to smolder.

"What about the reply to this e-mail?" Moreno handed Laird a transcript.

"Excuse me?"

"It did come from you."

Laird began reading, shook his head, and looked up in puzzlement.

The email said, "Wire transfer, Banque Duvall, 5,000,000.00. Tuesday, deposit 3,700,000.00 in 35754890023." The reply said, "Privy member."

"I didn't send this," Laird said.

Moreno regarded him without warmth.

"What do you suppose that means, e-mails you did not send, but coming from you, Geoffrey?"

"I'll look into it. Be back in a second."

Laird left the room, was gone less than a minute, and returned with his laptop. He put it on the table, opened it, and clicked e-mail.

"No one has access."

"What about your wife?"

"My wife? She just had a baby. She almost died."

"You have a daughter. She works at the bank as a teller?"

"It's a temporary situation for her. She's an artist." He sighed. "Or wants to be."

"But she does work here."

"Yes. But she wouldn't read my e-mails. She knows nothing."

"I don't know about your daughter, but my daughter *would* do such a thing. She's not too pleased with me just now." Moreno chortled, but his eyes were not amused.

"Could she have used your laptop?" Coulter said.

Laird knitted his brow as he stared at the screen. "It's possible she used it once or twice."

"Kids these days know the technology. They can perform miracles." He shook his head. "I think there's been a serious breech of security, señor."

"There's nothing here. I'll ask her. I know she wouldn't cause me any problems."

Coulter said, "I'm not sure she's all that innocent."

Laird's face reddened. "What are you driving at?

"She was asking an awful lot of questions about Claire. I tried to put her off."

"They're friends." Laird raised his voice. "What I'm telling you is that Whitney would never act against me. It's not in her nature. I know my own daughter."

"She's a teller," Coulter said. "She processes deposits. Maybe she discovered something."

"She is also my blood, and how much can a person know from an e-mail, even if she did read it?"

"This game is high stakes. We need a guarantee." Moreno blew a smoke ring. "I'm prepared to be generous."

"Where are you going with this?"

"We must be secure. Me, you, Coulter here—we could be ruined. You Americans have a saying, 'CYA.'"

"'Cover your ass,' so?"

"Geoffrey, I am not sure about your daughter." He chuckled. "You see, we have been watching."

"Watching?"

"Watching. Yes. I haven't gotten where I am by being careless. We cannot have loose ends. Clean everything. I've decided to move along. One door closes. Another will open."

"What do you mean?"

"There is also a certain doctor, a Dr. Ashton." Moreno leered. "Did you know they are having an affair?"

"Damn you—" Laird stood. Coulter did likewise, and Moreno said, "Sit down." They both sat.

"Calm down, Geoffrey. You are one of us. I am sure we can work this out. You told me your daughter was sick—a breathing problem—is that not so?"

"Leave my daughter out of this."

"I don't want to see anything happen to her," Moreno went on. "I think I know a way. It is your mistake. It must be absorbed."

"Absorbed?"

"Persuade Dr. Ashton and your daughter to open accounts. Split your cut with them, fifty-fifty. Who could refuse such largesse? Otherwise, who could believe they won't go to the police? Only we know. Let's keep it this way. No one in Miami needs to know the details. I'll handle it. Then we close the books. This is the last chapter, señor."

Coulter waved a hand dismissively. "Why should we do that? We're not finished."

"You want me to tell my daughter?" Laird said. "Tell her that her father launders money? Demand she take some of it? That is absurd! Besides, you don't know her. She won't do it."

"Perhaps if she considered the alternative," said Coulter.

"Leave my daughter alone!"

"I'm not sure that's possible."

Moreno waved his hands like a referee. After a few moments, he said, "Did I tell you how I came to this occupation?"

Laird shook his head.

"My father owned land in Argentina. We had a ranch—more than three thousand hectares. My elder brother, Miguel, would inherit the ranch. It is the custom. I needed to find a profession. I studied for the law."

Laird and Coulter listened with ill-disguised annoyance.

"I passed the necessary exams and was admitted to the bar. I was successful, made money whenever a lot of money changed hands. I was there to siphon. I became rich. I knew people, important people, who suggested me for a judgeship. I became a judge. Then came the military coup. I was removed, along with others. I wasn't their favorite, you see. I would not bend. I saw many things I interpreted as bad. Thousands of protestors, some not protestors, disappeared; good people, detained by the army. Nobody helped them. Justice was not served."

Laird's lips turned down. He exchanged a glance with Coulter.

"The new government saw no need for me, or I for them. I left the country and moved to Mexico, where I practiced law. I had clients in the drug trade. They had the most money, also the most need of lawyers. The jury decides the case, no? I am an advocate. This is the system. As soon as I could, I became a citizen. Through 'miraculous' influence, I became a judge there also."

"You see, morality is often a contrivance. We make up the law as we go. The world remains a mystery to us, does it not? People act in accordance with their needs. Survival. Security. Wealth makes both. Where money is concerned, sentiment is lost."

"Get to the point."

"Please. Allow me to continue. I was having problems with my health, and I decided to leave Mexico. Leisure was good for a time, very pleasant, but then I grew bored. Mind numbing, complete boredom, very depressing. I got an offer to work for this organization, as counsel. Life became exciting again. There was danger, the forbidden. It was more fun than being a judge. You see, we never stop wanting, Geoffrey. Control is the main thing."

Laird eyed him warily. "You wouldn't harm my daughter, would you?"

"I am one man among many, Geoffrey. Everyone can be replaced. Eventually, everyone is. Me, you, your daughter. But I wouldn't consider such a thing unless the threat was sure to harm us. Which, of course, it will not be."

"Geez," said Coulter. "We just moved here three years ago."

Moreno spread his arms in a friendly gesture. "You see, I can speak for all of us, but there are others in Miami who may see money or pride at stake."

"I was getting out after this deal," Laird said. His eyes looked away.

"So you can," Moreno said. "Everyone wants to leave, including me. You get her to take the money. We leave."

Laird seemed anxious. "What if I split the money with her, but she didn't sign for it? She might agree to that."

"Her name must appear on the account. Leave the money in it however long she wants," Moreno said.

Laird looked down.

"You said your daughter's life was fragile," Moreno said. "Putting myself in her place, I wouldn't want more problems from persons such as us."

Coulter leaned forward. "You said she won't live a long life anyway."

"Is that a threat?" Laird's eyes bore holes into Coulter. Coulter's eyebrows raised, but he returned the stare.

Moreno held his arm out over the table between them. "Geoffrey, I did not finish my story. Have you ever wondered why a lawyer, a judge, a man respected in two countries, is now in your country running a drugs and laundering money?"

"Yes, it has crossed my mind."

"The threat of violence can be very seductive—fear of being caught, the skill to avoid it. The passion for power, for money. Call it lust, if it pleases you. Pride in our power. Our success. These things drive us forward, do they not? Life would be intolerably dull without a gamble, no? What is sport, but an antidote to numbing boredom? No conflict? We will make it up."

"What about honor and respect?"

There is respect. There is esteem—what others think of you. But the law is something else; it is meant to coerce. The ones with the power to change. I am not impeded, breaking the law. It is not a dishonorable activity. Who makes the law, after all? The majority seek their own interests, their own lusts. To curb the power of the strong."

"Every real man decides what law his will be. We don't force people to take cocaine. Some want it legalized. Remember prohibition? Men made that law. Not so long ago, there were slaves, right here in America! Men made that law, too, no? Ten million native people were killed. And that was legal. So it is, always. Before the white man came, the Indians killed each other. Montezuma was not a victim. No. He was just a weaker Cortez. You see, Geoffrey, the law is just words, which only appear to be right."

"One other thing," said Moreno. He stared hard at Laird. "This Dr. Ashton—we have been studying him, along with your daughter. She is very beautiful. As I said, she's been seeing him, living with him. If he decides to interfere, we have a problem."

"My daughter's not having an affair with her doctor. He's thirty years older than she is. Doctors don't have affairs with their patients."

"You haven't been listening to me. We have pictures. See for yourself."

Laird reviewed the images. Two people stood behind a window. It was a close-up of Whitney and Ashton, partially concealed, naked. Laird swallowed and continued to stare. "How long have you known this?" he asked at last. The two men ignored the question.

"What do you know about him?" Moreno said.

"He practices at the university. I met him once. Several times, he's treated my daughter. He assisted in the delivery of my baby."

"You have a saying, 'the Big House,'" Moreno drawled. "I'd like to avoid that. How about you?"

"Leave her out of this. She doesn't know anything; she wouldn't turn against her own father."

"I don't think she likes you that much. What did you do to hurt her?"

"I didn't do anything to her."

"You left her mother and married a young woman, not much older than she is."

"Whitney has everything. I've given her everything."

"It looks like she needs something else."

A trace of displeasure darkened Laird's features. He put his palms on the table and pushed his chair back.

"All right. Do what is necessary. What you must." Laird sighed. He tugged at his collar, as if choking. "I just want out. I've paid almost everything back. Before the audit. I want to end this. I have a new wife and child to think of."

"I sympathize. Your share is what, two million? Offer them half that. Leaves you with one million. It was your carelessness, señor."

"When is there another shipment?"

"Let us hope the currency speculation goes well, eh?" Moreno said. "You will think of something. Set up a time I can meet with her. Include the doctor. Make it a public place."

At half past-eight, Whitney's phone rang.

"Hello?" Seconds lapsed.

"Hello, Whitney. I need to talk to you."

"Dad?"

"I've got some bad news," he said. "At the bank—you did discover something." His speech was slurred.

"Discover something? Like what, Dad?"

"It's very difficult for me to talk about this." He paused.

"I'm listening."

"I always wanted you to be proud of me."

Whitney waited, refusing to make it easier for him.

"I don't ask how they get the money, but I help them with it. Help them move it around."

"They call it laundering, Dad."

"I didn't think it would be so bad. Just 'til I got back on my feet. That was the whole idea. It was an emergency measure."

"Dad, why am I always being punished for things I didn't do?"

"You sent that e-mail, didn't you? These men I'm involved with, they're no gentlemen. That's for sure. They worry about prison. We all could end up behind bars. Millions are at stake. They want to talk to you and Dr. Ashton."

She held the phone away from her ear and put it back. "What about Dr. Ashton?"

"They've been watching. They want assurances."

"They have been watching?"

"They want to meet with you both."

"Are you crazy? No way am I going to do that. Do you think I would tell Tyler a bunch of criminals want to meet us?"

"You won't be hurt in any way. He gave his word. You must hear what he has to say."

"Who is he? What does he want?"

"A deal. Talk to him. Please. Otherwise he could be extremely dangerous."

After a pause, she said, "It's Juan Moreno, isn't it? He's the one. I know it's him."

"The horse park, downtown, nine tomorrow morning. Sit on one of the benches."

"Goodbye, Dad." She slammed the receiver into its cradle.

CHAPTER FIFTEEN

Moreno went outside, walked one block east to his favorite tobacco store, and bought a box of Nicaraguan hand-rolled cigars. He stood outside the door and fired up a smoke. He watched as a mendicant sat propped in a moving, battery-powered wheelchair. An elderly woman, warped and skeletal, carrying produce in a paper sack, passed the man by. She paused, turned, and tore a banana from a stalk, and saying nothing, handed it to him. The man thanked the old woman, calling her "Madge."

Moreno set forth along the pavement, stopped next to the chair, regarding the man as if in a quandary. Moreno put his fingers to his mouth; his eyes were lowered. The man turned his head and seemed to stare past him. He canted his head, as do the blind, and held out a porcelain cup. Moreno, as he walked past the man, pulled out a handful of twenty-dollar bills and handed them to him. The man called after him, saying, "God bless you," and Moreno, without looking back, held up his hand in a gesture no one saw.

Whitney drove to McGraw's bakery, bought a large coffee and bagel, and then parked her car one block away from the horse park. She walked to a bench and waited. At exactly nine, a man in a gray suit approached and inquired whether he might sit next to her.

"Juan Moreno," he said, with a slight bow. "Pleased to make your acquaintance."

"Okay."

He sat heavily, with a slight wince. "Is Dr. Ashton coming?"

"No. It's not his concern. I didn't tell him about my father's call."

"I do need to talk to him."

"He doesn't know anything. Leave him out of it."

"Did your father tell you why I am here?"

"Yes."

Moreno spoke slowly, choosing his words carefully. "Unfortunately, you and your friend Dr. Ashton have stumbled on our enterprise. That is bad for us. Not so good for you, either. I want to make sure nothing bad happens to us." He seemed almost avuncular, as if relating terrible family news.

"Again, Dr. Ashton has nothing to do with this." She sipped her coffee.

"Forgive me for showing you these photos, but we have to assume he does know." He reached into his coat and produced the pictures. She looked at them.

"So? You're a dirty old man, too?"

"I think we should stay focused here, Miss Laird. We want you to receive, shall we say, a windfall. An amount I'm sure you will find agreeable. All you need to do is open two accounts; the money will be deposited in two names. Nothing more."

"I don't need the money."

"I'm afraid we must insist. Otherwise, how can I be sure you won't harm us? It's in our mutual best interest."

"What if I don't? Are you going to kill me?" she said sarcastically.

He smiled. "That's not an option for me, of course. But there is a saying where I come from—'pesos or pistolas.' Think about your friend, your father. Think of their best interests. You get half a million, so does the doctor. Give it away, if you like. I myself have given over five million dollars to charity."

"What are you doing in the meantime?"

He ignored the question. "I'm moving on soon. But it takes time to disengage. To relocate."

Her gimlet stare bore into his eyes. "I'll think about it."

"I want to press upon you the importance of your decision."

"Yeah, you've done that."

"When you've reached your decision, call this number." He wrote the number on a card and handed it to her. "We will not meet in person again. Let me know within two days."

"I have no idea how to explain this to Dr. Ashton. I really want to leave him out of it." There was a moment of silence. "What if I take all the money? Isn't that enough?"

"You say he doesn't know?"

"He knows nothing."

"We should ask him, I think. Where is he now?"

"I don't know where he is. It's just best if you leave him out of this."

"Two days," Moreno said. "You must get back to me."

He rose with difficulty, finding it necessary to brace himself, hands on thighs. Finally, he held out his hand; Whitney hesitated before shaking it.

She watched him walk away, before rising herself, and went in the opposite direction.

She stayed in the apartment all afternoon, and in the evening at half-past six, she called the number Moreno gave her. He answered.

"I can't take any money. It wouldn't be right. But I promise I won't tell anyone. I won't rat on my father. Dr. Ashton doesn't know anything. I just can't involve him."

"I'm sorry to hear your decision."

"Aren't my assurances enough?"

"I won't accept this as your final word. Please think more on it."

"I've made my decision, Mr. Moreno."

He made a clucking sound. "See this from my perspective. I'm trying to protect myself, your father, you. Also, there are others, far away, who do not know you. They might not have my patience. Help me out here."

"Apparently my word isn't good enough."

"For me, yes, but you know how the world is. Do me this great favor. Throw me a bone. Accept our offer. It would be better for everyone. Is that so terrible?"

"I don't want any trouble."

"All the more reason to accept. Think about it a bit more, and call me back. I sense you want what is best. If not for yourself, do it for the doctor."

"I wouldn't send my father to jail. Goodbye."

"Think on it and call me back. But I need your answer soon."

CHAPTER SIXTEEN

As planned, she met Ashton at Amberley's office. Amberley's secretary led her to the room where Ashton sat alone at a long conference table. She kissed his cheek and slid into the chair next to him.

"You look worried," he said.

"I'm scared. I need to explain some things."

He nodded. "Go ahead."

"I told you about my father. His friends are big league dope peddlers. Dad washes the money. They know I know, and they think you know. I just met with this Moreno guy, who says we have to take part of my father's cut to implicate ourselves. To assure them we won't talk."

"We have to take bribes?"

"I told him you weren't involved."

"Did that satisfy him?"

She looked at her shoes and tapped them together. "I don't know."

"Does he seem calm or agitated?"

"He seemed almost apologetic. He didn't made direct threats, and he wasn't angry. I don't think he's violent."

"Maybe it's time for the police. We might not be able to avoid bringing them into it."

She sat quietly for a moment. "And send my father to jail? I don't like my dad much, but I don't think I can do that."

"First you wanted to, now you don't."

"I don't know what to do. I'm really confused."

"You said the scope was international. You could get hurt, Whitney."

"I've thought of that."

"You couldn't live at the farm."

"Why not?"

"It's too exposed."

"What can we do then?"

He smiled and shrugged. "Looks like a year of living dangerously."

"I got you into this, Tyler. I'll think of something."

"Let's say you did take the money. You could leave it in the account, and after the storm blows over, you could report it to the authorities, or just give it away. You'd satisfy them and protect your father."

"I can't accept bribes."

"I just don't want anything bad to happen."

"He doesn't seem violent," she said.

"But can you trust him? Come on!"

"I have to do something, Tyler, and he's demanding an answer."

"Some things don't work out the way we want. Plans fail. Sometimes we have to compromise." He leaned back in his chair and put his ankle on his knee. "Let me tell you a story."

"All right."

"When I graduated from college, I was drafted into the Army. I thought about going to Canada, but I didn't. I became a medic. Better to suffer injustice, than do injustice. Soon, I found myself in Viet Nam in a helicopter, a modified Huey, picking up the wounded. We flew them to MASH units. There was a pilot and co-pilot, sometimes a gunner, two medics, sometimes a nurse."

"I had flown eight or ten missions. On my last mission, we were ambushed when we landed. The other medic was killed. We were taking heavy fire. I wasn't thinking, just reacting. I picked up the corporal's M-16 and fired a burst at two people firing at us. They were less than ten yards away."

"My God, Tyler—"

"I killed those two people. They were just kids." He looked into her eyes.

"What else could you do?"

"I could have gone to Canada and never been in that jungle."

"What does this have to do with us, now?"

"Don't get into the war. Don't take sides. Do your work. Stay out of it." He smiled. "In other words, go to Canada."

"But it's not that easy. They want us to take money."

"Both of us?"

"They want you to take half of it. That buys your silence, too."

"Whatever we do may be difficult."

"Not taking sides is taking sides."

"Why make more problems for ourselves? Money in and of itself isn't evil."

"You sound like you want to take the money!"

"I was a medic because I was against killing, but I ended up killing anyway. Taking the money might be our way of going to Canada."

"I haven't done anything wrong. I don't deserve this. Taking the money is not an option."

"Somehow, you need to get out of this, Whitney. You can't control these people. They run a cartel. Do you really believe they will leave you alone if you don't accept their bribe?"

"I can't stand my father for what he's done," she said softly. "I won't let him hurt me anymore." She sighed, got up, walked to the window, and folded her arms tightly across her chest.

"If you want to go to the DEA or the FBI, all right. If you want to take the money, all right. Otherwise I'm out."

She whirled to face him. "What do you mean, you're out?"

"This is a fight you can't win, Whitney. Not alone. Something will be lost whatever you do."

She turned around. "Don't you want to help me?"

"You're living too dangerously. I see nothing but trouble." He looked away.

"I won't bother you anymore." She walked to the door, opened it, and turned to look back. Ashton sat glumly, his eyes on the table.

"I'm not worried about myself," she said. "But I couldn't live with myself if something bad happened to you."

Ashton looked at her and said nothing.

She nodded and sighed. "I have to go."

"I'm leaving for Wycliffe in the morning. You're welcome to come, if you like."

"No, I'll see you when you get back. How long will you be gone?"

"Two days."

"Be careful."

She looked at her double arrow pendant, took it from around her neck, and handed it to him. "Keep this for me for a while. Until we get through this." There was sadness in her eyes. She smiled slightly as she walked to the door.

"When you don't know what to do, do the thing least harmful. Let it sort itself out," he said to her back. She hesitated and said, without turning to him, "I'll consider your advice. But I'm not sure I want to go to Canada."

"All right."

She closed the door behind her, went to her car, and drove away. Ashton stood at the window and watched—his face emotionless.

Amberley met her on the way out. He smiled, was about to speak, but she just nodded and walked by. He waved to his secretary who pointed to the room where Ashton sat, and he went in.

"She seemed upset, Tyler."

"She's very upset. Did you find out anything?"

"I spoke with our man this morning. Moreno's house, hotel, and apartment building are owned by one entity, Grayson Enterprises, registered in the Bahamas. Shell corporation. I can't find what it is they do. Coulter's house is in his own name."

"Anything else?"

"Laird has money problems. A friend, a bankruptcy attorney, thinks he's on the brink."

"Drugs?"

"I think so."

Ashton nodded. "That's what I was afraid of," he said.

CHAPTER SEVENTEEN

It began to rain, gently at first, followed by a downpour. It rained most of the morning and then let up. In the late afternoon, Ashton changed his mind. He would go to Wycliffe. He got Piper and his gear and made the journey in his truck. Another squall moved in. The storm surged. Raindrops bounced on the street. He drove to Pott's Creek Motel, got a room, put food and water out for the dog, then headed for Quinn's Place.

A pink neon light flickered, dim as a dot, but it grew in size and brightness. He parked, got out, and entered, wet to the skin. His hair was slick and plastered. The Fergusons were playing pool. She waved.

A local, four-piece bluegrass band was slated to play. Three male musicians, all middle-aged, played banjo, mandolin, and fiddle; a young woman sang and strummed a guitar. Pleased with their musicianship, Ashton listened to the entire set. Adrian and Nell Ferguson came over, and he bought drinks all around. They listened to the set, talked a while, and then went back to playing pool. Ashton stayed another two hours, hoping the storm would pass, but it settled in, and the second set, because of the rain, could scarcely be heard. The Fergusons came over and kept him company.

Lightning bolts flashed, the sky flickered, and rumbling concussions of thunder soon followed. As the storm raged, patrons ran out, one by one. Finally, only the Fergusons and Ashton remained, along with the fiddle player and Quinn. Adrian went to the window and stared out at the storm; he appeared to debate what to do. Raindrops drummed against the windowpanes, the wind howled, and when the lightening blinked again, the water glowed and ran over the curb. The torrent flooded the sidewalk. Ashton walked over to them.

"Look at that!" said Adrian, shaking his head.

"I'd better be going," Ashton said. "It's not going to stop."

"I'll think we'll hang on a bit longer. It'll have to let up soon."

"All right. Maybe I'll see you tomorrow."

Ashton ran out amid the downpour, got in his truck, and drove toward the motel. The rain hammered the top, and the windows fogged over. Straining to see, he wiped the condensate off the windshield. He parked the truck and walked down a short sidewalk to his room.

He fumbled with the key ring, put the key in the lock, and began to turn the doorknob. Someone waited, hidden behind a corner. In the near darkness, a stocky man advanced quietly and approached Ashton as he pushed open the door. Ashton turned as the man, holding a baton, struck him above the left eye. He tottered for a second, put out his hands as if to catch himself, and crumpled to the sidewalk. Muscles contracted, back arched, limbs stiffened. He jerked in a series of spasms. After a few seconds, the rigidity relented, and he lay limp, bleeding from a head wound, eyes half open.

A low growl came from inside the room. The man slammed the door and took the key. Piper kept barking. The man placed the baton under his belt and dragged Ashton across a small patch of grass and onto the parking lot. He stopped between two parked cars, leaving Ashton in a puddle while he opened the trunk. He looked around the parking lot, then grabbed Ashton around the chest and heaved him onto the spare tire. Ashton's legs stuck out, so the man folded them inside and closed the trunk lid. He looked around again before climbing into the car and headed in the direction opposite the bar.

After a minute or so, Ashton began to awaken. He put his hand to his forehead and felt a wet lump. It took several seconds to realize he was inside a trunk. He could not recall how he came to be there, but however that had happened, the situation was bad, maybe even terrible. He considered his options and finally positioned himself to kick out the taillight, but when he did, it only popped forward an inch. After another minute, the car stopped, and Ashton heard a train clack and clatter pass. He groped around for a latch, but did not find one. He did find a lug wrench. When the car started again, the gravel pinged against the rocker panels and Ashton began to count the turns, and then the car pulled up slowly and stopped.

Ashton gripped the lug wrench. The trunk lid opened, and he tried to dive out, but the man with the baton struck him twice on the head.

When Ashton emerged from his stupor, he was taped to a chair, in his underwear, sitting in the center of an empty room. A single light shone in the hallway.

His head ached, and the room seemed to move and tilt. He heard a high-pitched, continuous roar in his left ear; when he opened his eyes, there were double images, superimposed, out of register. A man with glasses, dressed in dark trousers and a sport shirt, stood above him. He held a collapsible metal baton, which he kept telescoping in and out. Another figure stood obscured by shadow. When Ashton's head bobbed forward, the baton tapped his shoulder.

"Dr. Ashton, listen very carefully to what I have to say. If you cooperate, you can save yourself further trouble." Ashton said nothing. He did not recognize the voice.

"We need to know what you know." The man stood over Ashton, slapping the baton in his palm. A tall man emerged from the shadows and sat on a sofa, his eyes fixed on Ashton.

Time seemed to slow. Ashton fought to remain alert. Sweat beaded on his face and dripped from his nose. He could not remember how he came to be in the room.

"Think about your options, Doctor."

"Options?"

"That's right."

"I'll ask George."

"Who is George?"

"My accountant."

"I'm talking about the girl."

"The girl."

"Whitney Laird."

"What about her?"

"What did she tell you? We need to know what she told you."

Ashton blacked out. He awakened to muzzy labors of his mind.

"Rodent."

The man slapped Ashton in the face.

"Wake up," the man said.

"Rodential."

"What did she tell you? We have to know what she told you."

"I feel sick," said Ashton. "The room is spinning."

The man in the corner got up and walked around the room. "He's squirrelly. You knocked him silly."

"Don't worry, Coulter. I know how to deal with him."

The younger man went to the kitchen, filled a pan with water, returned, and threw the entire contents into Ashton's chest and face. "Wake up, Doc. We're losing patience here." Ashton moaned, but said nothing.

The man entered the bathroom, took a hand towel from the holder, refilled the pan, and returned. He threw the towel over Ashton's face and grasped his jaw while he poured water on the towel. Ashton lurched, twisted, and made guttural noises. There was a choking cough, a seal-like bark, but the man continued to pour water. When he released Ashton's head and removed the towel, Ashton gasped and wheezed—his eyes wide, mouth agape. The man was beginning to come into focus.

"Let's try again. You have to do better, Doc."

Ashton cleared his throat, tried to speak, but his words came in squeaks.

"I'm losing patience with you, man.

"Bathroom," Ashton managed, in a whisper. He began to shake as an animal fear sat on his face.

"What?"

"I have to use the bathroom," he said.

"Looks like you already took care a that." He pointed with his finger.

Ashton looked at the dark stain on the front of his shorts.

"I have to go."

"Pretend you're in the bathroom."

"I can't."

"What did Whitney Laird tell you?"

"She discovered something wrong at the bank, but I don't know what."

"Do you want the towel again?"

"If I knew anything else, I would tell you."

The older man, his voice deep, took over the questioning. "Did she report her suspicions to anyone?"

"I have to use the bathroom."

"Dr. Ashton, mutual cooperation is called for here. You help us, and I promise nothing will happen to you."

"I'm going to vomit."

"I can cut him a little, Coulter."

The younger man pulled a black knife from his pocket and with one hand snapped open the serrated blade. Grinning with pleasure, he nicked

Ashton's forehead with the point. A drop of blood formed at the cut and rolled down beside Ashton's right eye.

Coulter said, "Let him go to the bathroom. He's going to throw up all over the damned place."

The younger man cut the tape on Ashton's arms and wrists, re-taping the wrists in front, while Coulter trained a short-barreled pistol on Ashton's chest. He ordered Ashton to stand, and from behind, he sliced through the tape at his ankles.

"Don't be too long. I'm waiting with the scalpel. I'm the doctor, now."

Ashton stood, seemed to lose his balance, but then recovered. He shuffled to his clothes. He took his pants and walked toward the bathroom. "Leave those here. You can put them on when you come out."

He entered the bathroom. His mind raced over any words that might appease these men. There was a window, but it was too small to crawl through. He lifted the toilet lid at one end, but then lowered it. He feigned vomiting, flushed the toilet, and returned to the living room, taking notice of the outside door and an adjacent picture window. A pillowed sofa was set against a wall, and Coulter sat the far end, gripping the baton like a baseball bat. The younger man held the gun and the knife.

"Your pants." The man pointed. "Put them on if you want."

Ashton stood, not moving, and turned toward where his pants lay on the floor. With a feigned limp, he reeled toward his assailant, and he gave the man a shove. The man hit the wall hard, and fell sideways. The gun went off, and a bullet drilled through the ceiling. Plaster fragments and dust blew out. Coulter rose to his feet, but he did not advance.

The younger man struggled to rise, waving the gun. With desperate speed, Ashton grabbed a pillow from the sofa, held it to his face and chest, ran to the window, and crashed through the glass, shattering it into knives. Orange flame leapt a second time, another huge blast. A bullet followed him out the window and whistled passed his head as he fell. He landed on his back on top of the taxus shrubs, amid glass shards.

He rolled off the shrubs, got up, stood on glass, and cut the bottom of his left foot. He let loose a cry and staggered into the woods behind the house, running as fast as he could. His ears were ringing again. Vertigo came and went. With each blink, orange clouds seemed to billow in his eyes.

After running madly for two hundred yards, he paused, squatted in the wet field, and listened like a fugitive eluding hounds. He groped for his foot in the blind night. There were voices and two cones of flashlights. He failed to quell his heavy breathing, and became certain they heard him. They quartered thirty yards away, and moved in a zigzag direction, but then they veered off and disappeared.

He remained perfectly still for minutes, and when he sensed he was alone, he crawled through a thicket that cut and scraped his skin. He reached a clearing.

The rain continued to drop from the black sky. He shivered until trembling took over. He squatted in wet leaves. The shaking remitted after some minutes, only to return in dread prospect of the wet towel if he were caught. He tried to check his body for cuts. There was sticky wetness in places on the right arm and leg, in addition to the gash on his foot and the wound above his eye. He strove to clear his mind. Could this really be happening? He seemed in a fugue.

With his remaining strength, he crawled over swampy ground until he came to an impasse, an embankment before a swollen stream. Along the riparian weeds, he crept forth and scrambled upon a large tree root. He saw diffused streaks of flashlights crossing in a distant fog. He lurched forward drunkenly, lost his footing, and pitched headlong into the stream with a splash. He fought through the cold water and lunged at the bank opposite, only to slide back, mud-covered and grass-stained. In a third attempt, he managed to ascend the bank, but then collapsed.

Like a beached fish drowning in air, he lay on the ground and gasped. Once again, he summoned his strength and snaked on his belly or crawled on all fours until he reached an escarpment. He came to a huge corrugated pipe, having retained at its bottom pestilential ooze; he thought mightily about entering the black void, but finally did. Breathing a malignant air, he crawled, polluted, in the dark, twenty yards to the pipe's end. It opened upon an esplanade. There was a bit of light glimmering through the mist.

The ground was freshly mowed and sweet smelling. Bales of alfalfa dotted the field surrounded by woods. He spied a rusted, bent fence, slumped against the wires, and there he dripped with water and sweat. Sawing the tape against a post did nothing but rub his wrists raw. He was shaking again. He pressed his bound hands against his knees and moved air in slow, deep breaths.

He was on the move again after a brief respite. He stayed within the wood line. Five hundred yards ahead, he clambered over the fence, falling to the other side. He got up and limped on, finally emerging from the dark wood. A large barn and adjacent frame house stood at the clearing's edge, scarcely illuminated by a light hanging on a pole. He came to a second fence. He stopped. He considered whether he should enter the barn and stood indecisively, wiping the rain from his face. The tape made the cut worse, and there was blood all over his hands and arms. His assailant had had a baton and used a Glock. Maybe they were police. He had to keep moving.

He climbed the fence, crossed the field, and went to the barn. There was no lock and no dog. A dozen chickens crowded against the door and squabbled as he passed among them. Across an untidy wall, farm tools hung on nails: fork, spade, adze, axe, scythe, sickle. He removed the double-bit axe. After testing its edge, he held it between his legs, and with a sawing motion, cut the tape. His eyes slowly adjusted to the faint light, but not soon enough. Gingerly feeling his way through the barn's interior, he knocked a two-gallon bucket from a stool. It fell, clattering to the floor.

He waited. No one came. As he made his search, he found gray coveralls, too short for his torso, but they would suffice, even though they chafed at his groin. He put them on, scarcely concealing a subversive glee. The barn was sultry in spite of the storm, and the coveralls made the heat almost unbearable.

He came upon a small room and opened the door. Inside were sacks of fertilizers and chemicals. He pulled a light string, squinting when the sixty-watt bulb glowed. He looked at his hands and arms. More than just blood—there was a rusty stain from the tunnel. A gallon jar of insecticide stood in a corner. He found an empty bottle, poured four ounces into it, placed the bottle in his pocket, and returned the container. He leaned the axe against the wall, picked up the sickle, and made whooshing cuts, slashing the air.

He turned off the light and lurched outside, crossed the field, and hid in the woods. His skin bore the stench of sulfurous mire, and it began to sicken him. He vomited. He crept back to the barn. A hand water pump stood nearby, poised over a concrete trough, half buried in soil. Debris lay at the far end—dead leaves, a few boards, and three inches of dark water. He tried the pump, it squeaked open, and the water began with a trickle—rusty brown, which cleared after a minute.

He leaned the sickle against the trough and removed his coveralls. He palmed water over his head and hair. He stuck his foot under the water and tried to clean it. He hesitated, looked around, hunched over the pump, and sluiced water onto his chest, legs, and back, washing himself as best he could. He began to shiver, smelled the coveralls, and put them back on anyway.

The rain had begun to slacken. A thick, evil steam seemed to settle in its place.

He took the sickle, walked back to the wood line, and waited for a long moment. When no one came, he left the sickle leaning against the fence and approached the farmhouse door. He knocked. He knocked again. On the porch floor was an oval patch of white and gray feathers, some tinged with red, and a few bits of bone. Ashton averted his eyes. He raked back his wet, plastered hair, while he knocked again on the door with his other hand. No one came.

Off to the side lay a nearly concealed gray cat with a big ruff. The cat's eyes opened, eyes yellow and glowing—unrepentant eyes, as a lion's—seemingly reconstituted as some primordial force, silent and terrible. It arose, advanced out of the fog, and stopped. After a few seconds, its attitude changed in equal portion. The cat mewed, walked over to him, rubbed at his pant leg, and then purred. Ashton bent down and rubbed the cat's fur at the angle of the jaw. It cocked its head.

From behind a window curtain, he saw the face of a young woman, a brunette, with hair brushed behind her ears. She appeared at the window-panes of the door, wearing a nightgown and holding in both hands a yellow plastic gun. She looked to be in her mid- to late twenties. She had fine features, a large cranial vault, a pointed chin, and huge, brown eyes.

"Who's there?" she said in a high, muffled voice.

"I'm sorry. This is an emergency. Could I use your phone?"

The door opened about four inches. The gaudy gun barrel protruded. A thin voice, sounding like a child's, said, "It's not fair. It's not fair."

"Excuse me?"

"It's not fair."

"Do you have a telephone I could use?" He gestured with his hand to his ear.

The door opened wider. The woman stood under the transom, still clasping the big water gun with both hands.

"Don't come no closer."

"Please, can you call the state police? I've been attacked. They're trying to hurt me."

"Go away."

"Please call the police."

"It's not fair. Hurt." She glanced toward her right and waited, pointing her gun toward the corner of the porch. The cat slinked. The woman sprayed jets in its direction. It bounded under the porch.

"It's not fair."

"What's going on here?" A man appeared in the doorway, standing in a white nightshirt. One hand held the door handle. The other was behind his back.

"Could you please call the state police?" Ashton held out both hands like a supplicant. "Two men attacked me."

"I've got me a gun. Keep your distance."

An older woman, clad in a housecoat, with gray hair long and streaming, slipped in next to the man. Her hand was clasped at her throat.

"What is it, Efrem?"

"I'm Dr. Tyler Ashton." Ashton's eyes pleaded with her. "I've been assaulted, robbed. They're after me—out there in the woods." He pointed.

"Stay on the porch. Don't come a step closer. You got any ID?"

"They took my wallet. Could you call please call the state police?"

"Stay here."

The rain had dissolved to a fine mist. Ashton sat on the porch steps, breathing in the wet air. The night made little sound, except for the periodic tunes of tree frogs croaking their invisible presence.

In but a moment, the man and older woman walked onto the porch. The man held a top-break S&W, nickeled and chipped. He said he was sorry about the gun, but he had to take precautions, "There being no law and all."

"I'm sorry to cause you any trouble."

The man studied Ashton's face. "Them sons of bitches."

The woman went into the house and returned with a telephone and a phone book. She turned on the porch light.

"Here."

"Thank you, ma'am."

Ashton fumbled through the first pages, and he found the listing for the state police, but he could not make out the numbers. His vision was blurred; double images came and went.

"Can't you make it out?" she asked.

"I'm having trouble."

"I'll do it."

She dialed the number and described what had happened. She spelled out the directions to the farm.

After she hung up, she asked, "Where's your clothes?"

"They took them. I borrowed the coveralls from the barn. I hope that's okay. I didn't know what else to do."

He did not mention that he also took the insecticide and sickle.

"Looks like you're in more a need than us."

"Thank you. I wonder if I could make one other call to my attorney?"

"You go right ahead." She handed him the phone again.

Their daughter sat on the porch next to Ashton while he talked to Amberley.

"Hurt," she said. With the water gun on her lap, she reached up and touched Ashton's forehead. He turned to her. A drop of his blood glistened on her finger.

He touched the cut. With his other hand, he discovered an egg-sized welt on the back of his head. There was a crusty area where the blood had dried.

"I can clean up them wounds," said the woman. "It'll sting right smart."

He nodded. "I'd appreciate it."

She returned with a bowl of warm water, soaped the half-inch cut in his right eyebrow, washed his face, and soaked his clot-matted hair. After the rinse with hot water, the two cuts opened again and bled. He held a pressure dressing on his forehead while she sponged his arms.

"What happened to your eyes?"

He shook his head. "I don't know."

"Wait." She went inside and came out with a mirror.

He looked at himself. The sclerae were bloodshot, his eyes—red orbs with blue centers. Pin-dot hemorrhages covered his face in a red rash.

"They choked me," he said.

"Looky here." Her fingernails pulled a glass sliver from his scalp. "We're the Pattersons," she said as she worked on him. "Efrem, my husband, Kali, my daughter—and I'm Martha."

She offered him a hot bath and dry, clean clothes, arranged for him on the towel rack. He refused, but relented when Efrem said he would stand guard on the porch. When Ashton returned twenty minutes later, he sat on the steps, and the daughter came close and sat next to him. She still held the water gun, and she began to rock back and forth, plucking at the hem of her gown. Martha bandaged one of his cuts. Kali watched her mother.

"So you're Kali?" Ashton asked her.

"Kali." She pronounced it "Cay-lee."

"That's a very pretty name."

"What?"

"Kali. The sound of it."

"Thank you."

The cat appeared at the side of the porch. Kali held her gun to her eye and fired several streams. The cat, seemingly experienced at these outbursts, shot behind a shrub.

"It's not fair." Seconds later, "It's just a game."

"I'd like one of those," Ashton said. "Where did you get it?"

"Ma give it to me."

"Can I see it?"

"It's all just a game. It's not fair."

She handed it to him. He practiced squirting water. She giggled, thrusting her head back, guileless as a child. Now that the mist had cleared, her gaze was suddenly caught up in the dome of the star-strewn night. "Look. Big!"

She buried her hands in her pockets, looked down, sideways, again squealing with glee. Ashton stared at the random constellations for a long moment and wondered at the unseen deeps waiting behind them, ineffable and dimensionless, as if everything, stars, earth, man, woman, cat, had grown out of an unconscious dust.

"Wow," he said.

"Wow!" she said, mimicking him.

She reached for her water gun. "It's just a game."

The cat emerged from under the bush, sat next to Ashton, and then purred. She laughed and petted the cat's tail. It mewed.

"What's your cat's name?"

"Carver. Ma named him."

"That's a pretty name."

When the state police arrived, Ashton told his story and said he would sign a statement. He got into the police car after thanking the Pattersons effusively, and Kali, still clutching her gun, gave him a hug. He asked the officer to wait, got out of the car, and walked back to the porch where Mrs. Patterson stood.

He whispered, "I'd like to get Kali a gift. What would she like?"

"That's nice, but that won't be necessary. We can't take something for doing what's proper and all."

"I'd really like to get her something."

"It wouldn't be right, now."

"It's not payment. I accepted a gift. And I'd like to give a gift."

She looked down, saying nothing.

"I'm not used to such kindness, Mrs. Patterson. I'd really like to get her something."

Mrs. Patterson folded her arms and looked away, fidgeting.

"Her doll's pretty much wore out," she said. She pointed to a small, torn doll, missing both eyes, lying twisted on a chair.

"Perfect. A rag doll. Thank you for everything." His smile showed lots of teeth. He turned to leave.

"Goodbye. Take care of yourself. Say goodbye to the doctor, Kali."

"Goodbye, Doctor."

"Bye, Kali," he said.

He asked the officer to stop at the mailbox, borrowed a pen and paper from him, and copied the Pattersons' address. They drove away and searched for an hour before Ashton identified the building where he was assaulted. It was a rental vacation lodge. The officer drew his pistol and turned on his three-cell flashlight. The door was unlocked. He entered first. Ashton was a step behind him. The house was deserted. They listened to the silence. Ashton shuddered. The doors and rooms were dusted for fingerprints. Photographs. Tire impressions. Ashton watched, clasping the poison bottle with his hand in the pocket of someone else's clothes.

Two detectives arrived, and so did two more uniformed officers. They searched the woods within a perimeter of thirty yards. Ashton's pants were found hanging on a limb. The wallet was missing, but in a few minutes, an officer found it under a bush. The money was gone. They dusted again for prints, and finding none, gave it back to him. As the search continued, Ashton found his shirt wadded on the ground. A spot of blood stained the collar. Shoes and socks were not to be found. The officers took the clothes as evidence.

They wanted to take him to the hospital for an examination and treatment, but Ashton said that, as a doctor, he knew he would be fine. The officers debated the issue. They finally determined he could go home if he would submit to having photographs taken and would initial an amended statement. Ashton agreed, signed, and initialed the statement; the forensic photographer took twelve pictures.

The police drove Ashton back to the motel. His truck was outside his room. They got the clerk to open the door, and they went inside. Piper jumped up, her paws on Ashton's chest, and then she sniffed the officer suspiciously. The officer offered to get anything Ashton needed and gave him a number to call. Ashton thanked him. The policeman left.

Ashton went to his truck and opened it. The pistol was still where he had put it, inside the glove compartment. He stuck it in his pants, returned to his room, and got his suitcase. When he and Piper drove off, the dashboard clock read 5:17 AM. His vision was still blurry, and his stomach roiled. After ten miles, nausea got the better of him, and he stopped at a roadside park, leaned out the door, and vomited. Piper whined, he smiled at her, and they both exited the car. They walked together into the dark wood where Ashton leaned back against a tree, as though giving due thought to something of great moment.

Still on St. Ann's Road, he dimmed the car lights, turned onto Sedgewick, and crept along until he got to the gate where he parked. He opened the gate, walked to the woods' edge, and followed the path up to the house with Piper at his heels. He entered and conducted a slow, thorough search. Everything was in order. He stripped and sat on the floor of the shower stall with water raining down on him until it began to cool. Piper sat outside and put her nose to the glass. A soggy bandage slid off Ashton's face. When the water was too cold for comfort, he got out of the shower. He examined his cuts. Except for the scalp wound, he closed them with sterile butterfly tapes. He then dressed.

With a cordless drill taken from a toolbox, he bored holes through the ground floor window sashes and fused them with two-inch wood screws. At last, he walked to the guest bedroom, locked the door, placed a chair behind it, and went to bed, clutching the gun. Piper lay at the foot of the bed, her head toward the door. He sank into an exhausted sleep, troubled by savage dreams.

CHAPTER EIGHTEEN

In late morning, Ashton drove back to town, arriving at his house just before noon. A church bell rang. He drank a glass of cold water in the kitchen and phoned Whitney. No answer. He talked to the machine as though it were alive. He fixed breakfast, but he had no appetite, so he threw the food away. He called Whitney again. Still, no answer.

His head was pounding. In the mirror, he studied his face, and then drove to the university emergency department. One facial wound got six stitches, even though the wound was twelve hours old. The cut on his foot got three. Maybe they would not get infected.

At half-past one, he went to a toy store, Cundiffs. He explored the aisles, attracting some curious stares, and came to shelves of stuffed animals and dolls. Rag dolls large and small stared at him with huge, crystalline eyes. He settled on the biggest one, about three feet tall, and carried it across the street to a neighborhood store. They wrapped and boxed it. He added the borrowed clothes, along with a note that said, "I hope you like it, Kali, and thank you, Mr. And Mrs. Patterson, for all your help." He paid for the shipping and handling. With a slight limp, he went to the car and returned to his farm.

When Whitney finally returned his call, he described the events of the night. She reached the farm in a short time. They clung to each other in a fierce embrace. The blinds were closed. He kept the cocked and locked .45 stuck in his pants at the small of his back. She discovered it and pulled it out, holding it between a thumb and forefinger, as though she had a dead rat by the tail. He took it from her and put it on the table.

"Your eyes! My God, Tyler, what did they do to you?"

"Everything will heal. I'll be fine."

"What about the rest of you?" She gingerly touched his face.

"Just a few scrapes and cuts. A bump on the head."

"Now, I am really afraid. We have to go to the police."

"Let's take a drive and talk."

He picked up the gun, stuck it under his belt, and walked to the door. He turned the knob, but hesitated, went to the window instead, and peered out. Satisfied, he opened the door, and they went to the BMW. He drove through the gravel driveway much faster than usual; when they hit the blacktop, the tires screeched and hopped. He headed to a restored Shaker village, once a nineteenth-century home to several hundred people, now a tourist spot.

He kept looking in the rear view mirror. For some miles, there was no traffic. They stopped at a roadside store and bought bottled water. Then he put down the top, and they drove on.

"We need to talk to my father, okay?"

He turned and studied her face. "Will that help?"

"We must get the straight story out of him. He owes me that—if he has a shred of decency left."

"We can call the police, too, but—"

"But what?"

"These guys can't be persuaded. Only appeased or coerced. They're no gentlemen. That is a fact. I would be hard to mount an effective defense, police, or no. As I told you, the farm is surrounded by acres of woods. They could get to us."

They drove down the sinuous road, cut through rolling pastures, and after twenty minutes, they entered the gate to the Shaker village and parked. There were few cars in the lot. He opened the glove compartment, fumbled around for a spare magazine, and then shifted the gun to rest under his belt at the back. He covered it with his shirttail.

"Do you really have to carry that here? Are things that bad?"

"They're that bad."

They exited the car and climbed a gentle incline, still on the blacktop, until they reached a gravel walkway. Twenty or so buildings were arrayed in simple squares, wearing fresh coats of white paint. They entered a family dwelling, preserved as a museum. Light shone through windows, illuminating a hat and four inverted, ladder-back chairs that hung on wall pegs. A grandfather clock stood in a corner. Its hands were still.

They entered the ministry dining room. Place settings for six were set on a table for diners who had vanished a hundred years ago. There was a contiguous bake room with a fireplace built into the wall at waist height. Its coals glowed and delicious smells of hot bread filled the room. A woman in period dress removed the loaves with a huge wooden spatula.

They looked in the bedrooms, segregated by sex, where simple beds were lined in rows. There was nothing in excess, as though nothing could be added, nothing subtracted, everything neat, everything clean.

They walked side by side over the gravel paths, studying the buildings. A café was open at the path's end, and they entered and ordered coffee. She smiled at him and ran fingers over his bruised face.

"Well, are we going to confront my father?" she said.

"If that's what you want."

"I don't think we have a choice."

He nodded. "You may be right."

"We'll go tomorrow morning, then."

They arrived at the bank at nine the next morning. A young woman resembling a prom queen was opening the front door. They went inside. Whitney guided him to her father's expansive office. His secretary, Ms. Fritz, gave her a cheerful greeting and gestured them to follow her. Simultaneously, Laird saw his daughter and Ashton and asked them to come into his office. A large oil painting, depicting a bullfight, hung on the rear wall. The doomed bull, with fierce eyes, bled from the shoulder and stood before a shrunken killer dressed in gold.

"This is a surprise." He had a half smile. "What brings you two here?" His eyes stared with unusual intensity. He looked at Ashton. "What happened to you?"

"I think you know why we're here," Whitney said. "Kidnapping, torture. Attempted murder."

"Attempted murder?" Laird's eyes widened. A frown replaced the smile.

"Just look at Tyler's face," she said. "He didn't cut himself shaving, did he?"

"When did this happen?"

"Two nights ago," she said.

"Do you know who they were?" Laird said, directing the question to Ashton, who looked away from the painting and regarded Laird with some skepticism.

Before he could answer, Whitney said, "You're despicable! Pretending you know nothing about it."

"Control yourself, now. Don't talk to me in that tone of voice."

"You know who they are!"

"I have no idea what you're talking about."

"I know what you're doing, Dad. This isn't just laundering."

"What are you saying?"

"I don't care about you or what you do, as long as it doesn't spill onto us," Ashton said. "But it has. That's the problem."

"I don't take your meaning, sir."

Whitney said, "Stop it! What happened to Claire? Do you really think you can get away with this? The off-shore banks, the money, Coulter, Moreno. Torturing people? You're up to your eyeballs in everything!"

Ashton noticed a photograph hanging among the certificates on a wall opposite a window. He walked over to it. He looked at the people pretending to smile at a camera lens.

"This guy." He tapped on the glass. "He was there. The big one on the left."

Whitney walked over, looked at the photo. "It's Coulter, Claire's boss."

Mr. Laird was silent. He stared at his desk, his hands tented under his chin.

"What have they done?"

"What have you done?" Whitney said. "You can't hide from this."

Laird glared at her. "This seems to be a case of the pot calling the kettle black."

"What do you mean?"

Laird opened his drawer, pulled out an envelope, and threw it on his desk. Photographs spilled out and fanned like cards. Whitney scooped them up and slowly leafed through them. Ashton walked up behind her and looked over her shoulder. Suddenly, she threw the photos into her father's face. He wheeled backward in shock. The phone caddy, sitting on his desk, she picked up and threw, missing his head by inches; the caddy struck the wall and sprang open, spewing its pages across his desk and chair.

"I hate you. You're despicable!"

Laird jumped up, ran around his desk, and slapped her with the open palm of his hand. Whitney recoiled. Her mouth opened in astonishment.

She was speechless. Ashton stepped forward. "Easy, both of you. This isn't solving anything." Laird stepped back a few steps and returned to his seat.

"Don't lay a hand on her again," Ashton said.

Laird slumped in his chair, his face pale. He placed his fingers under his chin, his elbow on the desk. Whitney looked away, and then she felt her hot cheek, now colored with a red handprint. Ashton moved closer to her and put his arm around her shoulder.

"I was desperate to escape financial disaster," Laird said slowly, lifting his head, whispering the words. "I got out of one hole and fell into a bigger one. I'm sorry. I'm so sorry. I'll leave you alone." He paused and looked up. "But I don't know if they will. It's a big organization. It's out of control."

"They offered us a bribe," Whitney said. "A million dollars! But I'm not a criminal. I'll never take any money!"

"I didn't dream this could happen. All I wanted was to repay my debts, and then I would be out. No one would get hurt. You have to believe me."

"You've never cared about anything or anyone except yourself!"

"Don't fight them, Whitney. Take the money," Laird said, sheepishly. His countenance was altogether changed. "You don't have to spend it. You take it, and they'll leave you alone. It's the only way."

She crossed her arms in front of her body, and then she extended them quickly downward in a scissors motion. "I won't be bribed, Dad, period."

"You can't say you haven't been warned."

"If anything happens to Whitney, you'll pay," Ashton said. "I'll make sure of it. You won't be able to run far enough."

"Let's go, Tyler."

They turned and walked away, leaving Geoffrey Laird sitting at his desk, holding his head in his hands.

CHAPTER NINETEEN

There was clamoring in Ashton's brain. Part shouted action, part advised restraint. The drive to be good, so deeply ingrained, was fixed to normal times. Given sufficient impetus, as in his present extremity, he was capable of the opposite. Hostility awakened. Feelings were stronger than thoughts, and he wondered whether he was the author of either. He considered the paradox that he could apply loathsome tactics to effect righteous goals, but he had weighed his options. He would strike first. The tactics were justified. Brute determination washed over him.

He prepared himself in the evening at eight o'clock. It was expected to rain. He dressed in a green jumpsuit, worn over his street clothes. After tucking in the trousers, he laced up a pair of boots. From the gun case in the bedroom closet, he selected the Colt National Match, and then reconsidered. He settled on the Officer's Model.

Wearing latex gloves, he loaded two seven-round magazines and three eight-round ones, placed one in the gun, chambered a round, engaged the safety, released the magazine, put the gun under his belt while adding a round, tapped it against his forearm, inserted and clicked it into the gun. He put the pistol on a shelf and removed his gloves. He selected an open top holster, worn inside the pants, put the gun in it, unzipped the jumpsuit, and clipped it to his belt.

He went to the kitchen and injected two milliliters of the purloined insecticide into two jumbo-sized frankfurters, just in case he ran into dogs. The meat went into plastic bags, then into a backpack. He started a fire in the woodstove, added more wood, and turned the damper down.

He sat in a chair. After a few minutes, he got up, went to the backpack, opened it, took out the poisoned meat, and threw it in the stove. He couldn't kill any dogs. From the medicine cabinet in the bathroom, he removed sixteen yellow capsules and retrieved a bottle labeled pentobarbital, and inserted them, two each, into the four halves of the wieners.

He looked in the phone book. At 4:30 p.m., he left the house in his 4x4 pick-up truck. He headed in the direction of Moreno's farm, Caballo Manchado, in Sutter County, about twenty miles away. Thirty minutes later, he had passed Moreno's farm twice and finally parked his truck a mile away on the shoulder of a gravel lane. Satisfied that it would arouse no suspicion, he took his pack and locked the door. He walked across the lane, climbed a four-board wood fence, and headed across the fields in the direction of the estate.

About halfway there, he slid into a ravine to a swale of snarled briars, and at its end, fought through a stand of arm-sized sassafras. He walked up a hill into a hardwood forest. A bomb of wild turkeys exploded and tore through the woods. A few leaves fluttered to the ground. All became quiet again.

When he reached the crest of the forested ridge and climbed over a fence, he emerged from the wood and looked down on Caballo Manchado. Black board fences wove through pastures where thoroughbreds grazed among a few Herefords. Across another fence in a near pasture, two spotted yearlings reared and nickered. In the distance, the mansion stood like a painting, framed among the dense woodlands.

He sat next to the fence for some minutes, studying the bucolic scene. It was quiet, with only a breath of wind. He jumped a fence next to a paved, single lane and put on his ski mask. He advanced through a field for two hundred yards, approached the house, reached the front door, and rang the bell. Two surveillance cameras were bolted under the eaves. No one came to the door. On his new cell phone, he called Moreno's number, and he heard the phone ring. Still no answer.

The deep barking of large dogs came muffled from somewhere inside. He removed the backpack and took out the wieners, leaving two halves of them at the far side of the garage. He nestled up against the house behind the pieris shrubs, prepared for a long vigil, and rested his head on the pack. He removed the mask.

He waited for three hours, and the night sky had yet to cloud and obscure the glitter of stars.

In the distance, headlights glimmered. He crouched behind the shrubs and drew the Colt. The lights moved from the county road into the driveway as the Mercedes wound its way up to the house. The garage door opened, and the car entered the left bay. The door began to fall. At three feet from closing, Ashton rolled under it on the right side, farthest from the car, shielded by the pick-up truck that occupied the right space. He depressed the safety, keeping his finger outside the trigger guard. His hands were gloved with orthopedic latex, washed free of dust.

The engine stopped, and the car door opened. As Moreno came around the back, Ashton sprang upright with the .45 and placed the front sight on Moreno's chest. The man recoiled, wide-eyed, and grunted something in Spanish.

"Do what I say, and you'll be fine. Turn off the alarm. If anyone calls or shows up, you're dead." Moreno went to the lighted keypad and punched in the code. It beeped, four times.

"Face forward, hands up, lean on the wall," Ashton said. "Legs spread." He kicked Moreno's legs backward, one at a time, so that he and the wall formed a triangle with the floor. He put the automatic next to the back of Moreno's head.

"If you move, I'll pull the trigger."

Ashton pulled out a syringe with a 24-gauge needle, removed the cap with his teeth, and stabbed it through Moreno's trousers and into his right thigh. He injected the syringe's contents and then removed the needle. In two or three seconds, Moreno's head slumped, and his legs gave way. Ashton flipped up the safety. He grabbed Moreno's belt from behind, preventing him from crashing to the floor. He eased him to the concrete, where he lay in a stuporous heap.

Dogs barked inside the house. One threw itself against the door. He opened the door a couple of inches and tossed the sedative-laced meat. He slammed it shut. After a time, the dogs stopped barking. He waited fifteen minutes, opened the door a crack, then three or four inches, and looked. One Rottweiler lay on its side. The other sat his haunches, but seeing Ashton, it lunged and snapped, its lips curled, teeth bared. Ashton closed the door and sat on the concrete for five more minutes. The dog quit barking, whimpered, and he heard a rhythmic scratching against a wall.

He went back to Moreno and felt his pulse. He opened the garage door again, went outside, got the franks and the pack, returned, and closed the garage door. He opened the side door to the house, whereupon the dog again began to bark. He flipped in more meat and waited. After twenty minutes, hearing nothing, he opened the door and found both dogs unconscious. He dragged them into the laundry room and closed the door.

He grabbed Moreno's legs and wrestled him up two steps. The head bobbed over the treads. He dragged him across the tile floor and sat him in a kitchen chair. Moreno's head and chest slumped over the table. Ashton searched the hallway and the kitchen for hidden cameras, found none, and closed the doors to the dining room.

With duct tape, he restrained Moreno's hands, chest, and legs. From his backpack, he got a canula, IV tubing, and two liters of intravenous fluid. He placed a rubber band around Moreno's head above both ears and selected a plump scalp vein. He inserted the tiny catheter, cut the band, removed the stylette, advanced the catheter, taped it in place, and attached it to the bag of fluid. He taped the bag to the door and ran it wide open. It didn't run fast enough, so he taped it to the ceiling.

The phone caddy sat on the counter; Ashton threw it into his backpack. He went to the living room. Two photo albums were lodged on a shelf of the tea table. As he waited for Moreno to awaken, he leafed through the photographs. There were thirty pages of old sepia, faded prints of a man and woman in their early twenties. Pictures of a baby—a smiling infant with his parents—pictures of that baby as a toddler, pre-schooler, pre-adolescent, a teen-ager. There was a house. Then a much grander house. Graduation pictures. A man dressed in black robes, the man with four others in similar garb, sitting on a judicial bench. Color photos of a beautiful young girl, the same girl graduating, and the girl at some university. The girl in a chef's outfit.

Ashton closed the albums and walked into the first floor bedroom. There was a king-sized bed, a television, a bookcase, and an armoire. He looked in the closet and switched on the light. An HK MP-5 submachine gun and a CZ Skorpion machine pistol, both loaded, were wrapped in oilskin and propped in the corner.

He found two pill bottles on the nightstand and bent over to read the labels. One was for diazepam. The other was for amitriptylene. A bottle of vodka sat on the table, half consumed. There was a flashlight, a book on stock options and futures, and a *New York Times* crossword puzzle, filled out in ink. He discovered a laptop computer and went through the hard drive, studying the names of banks and transactions. About half of it was in Spanish. Passwords limited access.

He returned to the kitchen and removed his ski mask. Moreno was groggy, but awake.

"Who are you?" Moreno said with a groan. "What do you want?"

Ashton looked at him, but said nothing.

"I know you." Moreno's chin drifted forward for a moment, and then he seemed more alert. "You're the doctor."

Ashton nodded. "I couldn't wait for you choose the time and place for our meeting, so I decided to take the initiative."

"What do you want?"

"Where are the surveillance tapes?"

"Why should I tell you anything?"

"Because I'll hurt you if you don't."

Moreno motioned with a turn of his head. "The bookcase."

"Who is looking at them now?"

"Nobody."

Ashton went to the bookcase, removed the tapes from two recorders, and placed them in his pack.

"Okay. Let's talk."

"Talk?"

"I came here to be informed."

"All I want is security. I'm offering money."

Ashton walked up close to Moreno. "What about this?" He pointed to his face. "Do you have an explanation?"

Moreno stared, and then looked away. "No. I did not order that."

"Is that the best you can do?"

"You're mistaken. I've done nothing to harm you."

"A man will do anything, given the right circumstances. Don't you agree? We need the right motivation. A suitable history."

"What?"

"I shall do whatever is necessary. That's what I'm saying."

"I don't understand."

"Do you think I've come down from these thousands of generations because I am weak? Do you think you have a monopoly on force?"

"I really could use a smoke, Dr. Ashton. There's a pack in the drawer."

Ashton removed a cigarette and lighter, stuck the unfiltered Camel in Moreno's mouth, and lit it.

"You are more like me than you know." Moreno talked with the cigarette between his lips. He squinted and held his head away from the smoke as it curled into his eyes.

"I'm listening."

"The winner writes the history. We're both winners. We get what we want."

"I don't buy the parallel. I'd prefer not to kick or be kicked. But kick unto others before they kick unto you. I'll go that far."

"You would make a good judge."

"Who judges the judges?" said Ashton.

"We do. We are the problem solvers."

"Good. Solve my problem. That's what I came here for."

"I'm sure we can work something out."

Ashton waited for him to go on.

"What is this plastic?" Moreno tilted and rotated his head.

"You might encounter some problems with your heart. Fortunate for me the medical schools dispensed with the Hippocratic Oath some time ago. Things change."

Moreno's eyes were wide. His mouth opened, the cigarette dipped, the ash fell into his beard. Moreno shook his head; the ash dropped onto his pant leg. Ashton raised his eyebrows and smiled. Moreno finally said, "No."

"I found your medicine, Mr. Moreno. Hearing any voices? Any hallucinations? Maybe you'd like to take the whole enchilada."

Ashton produced a syringe and a small glass bottle. He showed them to Moreno.

"If you don't like pills, how about an injection?"

"No. All right."

"How did you meet Laird?" He moved his chair in front of Moreno and sat inches away.

Moreno's fingers trembled. Spittle gathered in the corners of his mouth.

He said in a shaky voice, "Why do you want to know about Laird?"

"Just answer the question. Don't try my patience."

"Laird found out. He was going to file a suspicious activity report. But what he really wanted was a piece of the action. I was forced to offer him a deal."

"A piece of what action?"

"He gets ten percent, as a facilitator. To make sure no one asks any questions."

"Money selling drugs."

"That's right."

"Take me through the process."

"We collect and sort the cash. When we have enough, we fly it out of the country, or we deposit the cash here, wire it to other banks, the Bahamas, maybe, or somewhere else. We move it around, combine it. Then it all comes back here."

"You have accounts here?"

"I have businesses. We run cash through them."

"Be specific."

"Jewelry store. Antiques and Oriental Carpets, a restaurant. A movie theatre. Profits are put into my account. Couriers deposit the money."

"Laird discovered it, and you bribed him?"

"That's correct."

"You could have gotten rid of him. Why didn't you?"

"I made inquiries before using his bank. To find the person most likely to help us. He was the perfect fit—ambitious, willing, and desperate. Besides, getting rid of people is extremely dangerous. It creates more problems than it solves. I'm a businessman, not a killer. He has been a big help. He writes letters of introduction for our foreign accounts. He can be trusted; we don't have to look elsewhere."

"Why all these foreign accounts?"

"No taxes. Bank secrecy. Our money moves so many times, it's clean."

"What about the e-mail that Whitney found about incoming money?"

"Something else. Money wired from another bank to be used to buy real estate."

"Is that how you got this farm?"

"Laird lent me the money from collateral I had in Mexico."

"What else does he do?"

"Different things. He is on various bank boards. Has inside information on various corporations. Our people bought options on a stock. When the stock tanked, we made lots of money. So did he. Kickbacks."

"How much?"

"Maybe three or four million."

"Who else is involved in your operation?"

"I report to a man in Miami on a need-to-know basis. There's no one else."

"How about here?"

"The couriers, four of them. They don't know anything. Just get paid. And we have a regular pilot."

"Who are these people who kidnapped me?"

"I don't know about any kidnapping."

Ashton regarded him with cold, unblinking eyes. "Why should I believe that?"

"I did not order a kidnapping. I know nothing about it."

"What did you order?"

"I offered money to the girl. To you also."

"In exchange for silence."

"Insurance, until we close. Then you do what you want."

"It's too bad you don't know these people. Maybe you need more medication." Ashton removed the syringe and bottle from his pocket. Moreno's mouth sagged, his eyes flew open, and sweat beaded on his forehead. "I'd tell you if I knew. I'll receive a call here, sometime this weekend."

"Who's calling you?"

"Brendan Coulter. The couriers, a man on the police force."

"I know Coulter. He works at the bank."

"Yes. He runs the day-to-day business. He's the COO."

"And he's part of your group?"

"Yes."

"What does he look like?"

"Tall. Maybe a little overweight. Dark hair."

"All right. The police must be involved here. I've met one of them already. Buzz cut. Stocky."

"There is one. Ferris Salizar. Short, a weight-lifter type."

"Tell me something, Mr. Moreno. Why did you get into all this?"

"I was a lawyer in Buenos Aires. Then in Mexico City. When I became a judge, I began to see things differently. I lost conviction. I saw many people getting rich. Favors were bought. Why shouldn't I be one of the smart ones? Why shouldn't you? He paused and puffed on his cigarette. But I wasn't so smart at first."

"Go on."

"There was a case involving the brother of a big boss. They offered money to find the technicality. I said no.

"The prosecutor made mistakes that weakened the plaintiff's case. True, the mistakes helped the defense, but my job was to be honest, no? I refused to take money from the defendant's brother. But during the trial, I found a briefcase in my car, a hundred thousand dollars in small denomination bills. I would have been in trouble had I not accepted the gift. I accepted it."

"I was about your age, what—mid-fifties? Work was a chore. I was going to retire. Having money gave me a taste for more."

"When did you start working for them?"

"The next year. They needed people to run their American businesses— someone educated, English speaking. Accounting mainly. That was four years ago. Dr. Ashton, you now face the same decision. If you're unwilling to take our insurance policy, they will get to you. They are not like us. They have no sentiments. They see only money or stubborn pride. You cannot reason with them."

"Not like us, eh? I imagine not. They're drug lords."

"Drugs satisfy a need. No one forces people. I take drugs for my mood." He smiled for the first time. "I'm addicted to pleasure."

"And I'm not addicted to pain. You people have a lot to answer for."

"I have not hurt you."

"No? Who do you think caused these injuries?"

"It wasn't me."

An interlude elapsed with no words passing between them.

"Let me tell you a story," Ashton said. "I'll be brief. In the interest of time. In the late eighteen hundreds, a girl of three was kidnapped from her farm in Ohio by gypsies. When her father discovered she was missing, he got on his horse with his Winchester '73, and searched two days with no sleep, until he found her. She hadn't been harmed. He would have killed them if she had been. That girl lived to be a very old lady. She was my grandmother. My great-grandfather didn't go to the police. He took care of it himself. Now, after all these years I'm here. My great-grandfather's heir. I'm perfectly willing to take care of business my own way."

"I understand."

"Here's what I propose," Ashton said after a long silence. "Neither Whitney Laird, nor I, will take one cent from you. I'm willing to let you live if you can convince others we're no threat. We shall remain silent, and you will do nothing to harm us. Can you find a way to do that?"

"You have my word."

"Can you do it, Mr. Moreno?"

"Yes, I can keep that bargain."

"If you don't—if we're threatened or harmed—I'll go after you. Next time, I won't be so nice."

Ashton picked up the photo album and scrapbook. "You have parents, brothers and sisters, grown children. Is this your grandchild?"

"No. My niece."

"I'm going to leave now. Talk is cheap. Believe me; I have a will sufficient to cause you great regret. I mean what I say."

"I'm not in position to argue."

"Just remember that. I'm taking the albums, computer, and phone caddy."

"I need the albums, computer."

"I need them more. A person never knows when he might befall some terrible, freak accident."

Ashton removed the catheter. He placed it, the tubing, and IV fluids in his pack. To these he added the computer, albums, phone caddy, and soda can. He went to the laundry; the dogs were coming out of their drugged sleep. When he approached, they struggled to get up. He dragged them inside the garage and closed the door, and then he returned to the kitchen.

"I hope not to see you again," Ashton said.

"That is best."

He opened a lockback, serrated knife. He removed the duct tape, aiming his pistol at Moreno. He backed away, wadded the tape, and threw it into his pack.

"Where are the other surveillance cameras?"

"I don't have any others."

When Ashton left the house, it was one in the morning. He ran down the driveway to the main road and turned left onto the highway. A light rain was falling. He saw no cars and continued jogging along the roadside. The distance was longer to his truck, sticking to the highway—perhaps by a mile, but by avoiding the thickets and woods, it was faster.

He made it to the truck in twelve minutes and quickly removed his jumpsuit, boots, and gloves, and stuffed them into a garbage bag. He drove in the direction of Moreno's house in order to avoid the police, who might come from town, went past Caballo Manchado for seven miles, where he stopped next to an abandoned shack. He went inside and hid the albums behind two loose boards, then drove toward home.

There were no police cars on Sedgewick Lane. As soon as he entered, he walked to the woodstove, opened the damper, and added more wood. The fire flared.

He searched his pack for metal items and removed the stylette and catheter needle. He cut off the pack buckle, and then placed the pack and its contents, along with his clothes, into the fire. The fire roared and devoured the traces of the evening's deeds.

He showered, dressed again, and returned to the truck. He drove to town, discarded the metal items in a landfill, and afterward, stopped at a self-serve car wash and cleaned the truck inside and out. He vacuumed it three times. On his way back to his farm, he considered stories to give if the police came, and decided to tell them Moreno had invited him to meet about buying a horse. If there were more questions, he would avoid further comment without Amberley's presence.

He went back to the farm. From his closet, he removed his father's L. C. Smith 12-gauge double from a canvas case, snapped together the stock and barrels, and fitted the fore-end. He loaded the gun with old number 1 buckshot, the only size he had. He taped a small flashlight to the fore-end and paced the house in semidarkness, testing the on/off button. He decided to sleep in the living room on the sofa, with the shotgun on the floor beside him, and the Colt under a cushion. No one disturbed the evening's peace, and after three hours, he fell into an uneasy sleep.

At dawn, he ran the vacuum for one hour, sucked up the cool ashes from the stove and the dust and fibers in the carpets, and scrubbed the vacuum. He drove across town and tossed the ashes in a dumpster. His evening's work was complete.

CHAPTER TWENTY

Ashton rose at mid-morning, dressed, and fixed breakfast. He glanced and then stared at the telephone. Had someone bugged his phone? He inverted it, studied the base plate, and opened the back with a screwdriver. There was nothing suspicious looking, and he considered the possibility that caution was giving way to paranoia. He called Whitney, and told her to meet him at Amberley's office at eleven o'clock.

The secretary ushered them into the lawyer's office. Amberley offered them coffee. Whitney took a cup, but Ashton declined. They related in detail their confrontation with Geoffrey Laird. Ashton reviewed the events of his kidnapping, in sequence, but kept silent on the matter of his invasion of Moreno's home.

"They really did a number on your face," Amberley said.

"Yes, they did. Not to mention my mind."

"What did the police say and do?"

"Since I didn't give them all the facts, they speculated it was an unknown assailant. A crime of opportunity. The primary motive was robbery."

"You didn't tell them about our concerns? Moreno?"

"No. I didn't mention that."

"Why not?"

"The less they know the better."

"You stumbled on a hornet's nest. This is big, international," said Amberley.

"So, do we have to go to the FBI?" Whitney said.

"I see no other way," Amberley answered.

Ashton looked at them both and slowly shook hid head. "Delay before error," he said.

"Amberley frowned at him. "What do you mean, Tyler?"

"There could be unintended consequences if we do that."

"Like what?" said Whitney.

"Cops solve crimes; they don't prevent them. Do you think they're going to protect us? If one of us is killed, they won't lose any sleep."

"Now you're changing your mind!"

"We're exposed any way you look at it. We might have to go into hiding. I'd have to leave or sell the farm. Whitney, you wouldn't be safe."

He got up, went to the window, and stared out.

"Then what do we do? We have to do something."

He turned. "We wait. We lie low. We let time sort it all out. It always has. It always will."

"I refuse to take bribes. We've discussed this, Tyler."

"I'm in complete agreement, but whatever we do, it's bad. We're choosing among evils."

"How can we let them walk all over us?"

"Time and silence."

"I hate them," Whitney said.

Ashton walked back to his chair. "I haven't told you everything yet. Consistency, as you will see, is not always my strong suit. The fact is, I had a chat with Moreno last night, and he agreed to leave us alone."

"What?"

"Why didn't you tell us?" asked Amberley.

"And why did he agree to that?" Whitney added.

"Let's say I made him see my point of view."

"Well, are you going tell us the whole story?" Whitney said, as she and Amberley leaned forward in their seats.

"I met him at his house. It's best if you don't know the details. But I did persuade him to stop."

"You threatened him, didn't you?" she asked.

"Some people might see it that way. Not exactly a fact. Just one man's opinion about a fact. Right, Michael? I'd rather call it the art of gentle persuasion."

"You actually did that? I'm speechless."

"An angry man will do most anything. Strange, when he was defenseless, my anger left, and I completely lost my resolve. Like the wind had changed direction. I couldn't act. I hope he didn't see it."

"Will he keep his word?" said Amberley. "The law never favors the aggressor. You have seriously damaged your case. What would a jury think?"

"No evidence, no jury."

"Forensics can always place you at the scene, you know."

"I wouldn't want that to happen." He raised his eyebrows. "And I've made every effort to make sure it doesn't. If they find something, I'll tell them I was in his house, but at his invitation."

"Moreno may have friends in the police. Or downtown."

"This is ridiculous," Whitney said. "It's crazy. This is total lunacy!"

"You're getting paranoid. I know the feeling. But if we're careful, and most of all, if we don't go running to the FBI, I think we'll be all right."

Whitney got up without saying a word and left the room. The outer door opened and slammed. Ashton looked at Amberley and raised his eyebrows. A moment later, she returned with an artist's portfolio case.

"Here's the evidence from Claire. The account numbers, transfers, names, places, dates." She opened the case and pulled out the papers, wrapped in a rubber band, and laid them on the table. She closed her portfolio and handed it to Amberley. "Maybe you could keep these for us. I'm afraid to carry them in my trunk."

"Can we put them in your safe, Michael? For now?"

Amberley nodded. "Yeah, I can keep them for you."

Ashton thumbed through the pages, his eyes flicking quickly from page to page. When he finished, he handed the roll to Amberley.

For a moment, all three were silent.

"What now?" Whitney asked, finally.

"It's a waiting game. We'll see whether Moreno calls off the dogs." Ashton turned to her. "If you'll feel safer, you can stay with me."

"I'll think about it, Tyler. Right now, I'm so confused."

The meeting ended. When Whitney went home, she picked up her mail. There was a letter from Claire, mailed from Chicago. It had no return address. She tore the end of the envelope, blew it open, and pulled out a sheet filled with Claire's scrawl. Claire had feared for her life. She had driven to Chicago. She was in hiding. She asked Whitney to destroy the contents of the box, except for the money, which Whitney could hold for her. She would write again.

CHAPTER TWENTY-ONE

When Whitney finished reading the letter, she thumbed through the telephone directory, looking for the number of her family's Presbyterian church. She had not attended church for more than three years, but she did know the pastor well. She put her finger on the number. Cheshire wandered in and rubbed against the refrigerator. She sat with her head bowed for a minute and then picked up the phone. Pastor Edwards was not in, but the secretary gave her an appointment to see him at two o'clock.

She arrived downtown, thirty minutes early, and strode half a block to the large, stone edifice with its cross-shaped ground plan. The side door at the east transept was locked, so she cut around across the yard to front door, entered, and walked through the vaulted nave, where the light streamed prismatic from stained glass windows. She headed for the ministerial offices and opened a door next to a side chapel.

"Hello! I've come to see Pastor Edwards."

The secretary looked up from her computer. "Sit over there," she said, and returned to a pile of papers with a sigh.

"Sit over there, please," Whitney said, glancing at the woman.

The middle-aged woman looked up over reading glasses. "Excuse me?"

"Sit over there, please." The secretary looked askance at the young woman's sandals and jeans and seemed to be struggling for a clever response.

"Please," she said finally. Her mouth curled in a frown.

"Thank you."

When Edwards arrived, the secretary rose from her chair and walked into his office. She spoke to him in what was intended to be a whisper, but her voice carried. A moment later, the pastor stood at the door of his office and smiled at Whitney.

"Please come in," said Edwards. "Have a seat, Ms. Laird." He had a kind face.

"I appreciate you seeing me."

He started to close the office door, thought better of it, and left it open. Whitney waited until he sat behind his desk and then went to the door, gave the secretary a long stare, and closed the door.

"I hope you don't mind," she said. "This needs to be private."

"I understand. How can I be of help?" He smiled. "I haven't seen you at church for quite some time."

"This will remain confidential?" she said, ignoring his comment.

"Of course." He hesitated. "Except for extreme circumstances."

"Such as?"

"Let's say someone was going to harm himself or harm someone else."

"Okay. Nothing like that." She was quiet a few seconds. Finally, she began.

"Do you believe in rewards and punishments, Pastor?" she asked.

The minister hesitated. "Well, yes, of course."

"Perhaps you can tell me why I'm being punished."

"What do you mean?"

"I have done nothing wrong."

"You mean your illness."

"In part."

Pastor Edwards leaned back in his chair. He took off his glasses and drew a deep breath.

"I've struggled with this question for some time. Are you familiar with the Book of Job?"

There was no response. He looked at her, and she, back.

"Yeah, I've read it. I studied it in a Western lit course at the university."

"Some things just seem to happen. We can't always know the reasons why."

"As I remember, God allows Job's children to be killed and then later gives him new ones, right? Not a good example in my case, okay? Maybe for my father, but not me. I'm not Job. I'm Job's child!"

Edwards put his hands on the desk and leaned back from the force of her words. "I don't think God kills the innocent. No, no. But he can't do it all. He can't do everything for everyone all the time. We would have no freedom. I think he's there to help us. To give solace."

"Then it's all just mischance? Bad luck? A sperm lottery?"

The pastor's eyes widened, and he blushed. He tented his hands under his chin.

"The world can be unfair. We know this. But something is here, rather than nothing. Some things are providential, but not all things. It's not perfect, but still it's good."

A calm look settled on his face. Whitney folded her hands across her chest, waiting for him to continue, and when his silence went on too long, she said, "I'm really here to discuss another issue, if I may."

"I'm here to listen. And to help, if I can."

"I'm not making this up, okay? Through my work at my father's bank, I discovered a money-laundering ring. No joke. I told someone else about it, a close friend. Unfortunately, at least two of the people involved now know that we know. There are threats. And bribes. It's a huge mess."

Edwards rubbed his palms together and began to blink nervously. "Did you contact the police?"

"Do you think I should? I have to tell you, my father's involved. He's part of it."

"Geoffrey? That makes it very difficult for you."

"I know he's caught in a trap. I don't think he meant things to go this far."

"Nonetheless, crimes have been committed, and they should be reported. You mustn't be a party to it."

"But it's not just my father. It's my friend—he could be in great danger."

"In what way?"

"These men will do anything to protect themselves. They're operating a drug cartel. Major money is involved."

"I see."

"What would you do, Pastor Edwards?"

"If there are crimes, threats, and bribes, you must get help. Help from the authorities. I don't see another way."

"But aren't you supposed to honor your father and mother?"

"If you're in danger, you must report it. If someone can be harmed. It's your first duty."

"It's as simple as that?"

"You must have faith."

"Faith."

"Reason can take you only so far. Then, you must have faith."

"Reason and then faith."

"Yes. It's the only way."

She lapsed into silence, and Pastor Edwards made no attempt to break it.

"Faith is a difficult concept for me just now," she said at last.

"We are all tested. We have doubts. But we can't remain neutral forever. Eventually we have to choose."

"If everything stems from God, why worry about choosing anything?"

"Whatever happens is meant to be. Is that what you're saying?"

"Why don't we just wait? My friend says we should wait to see what happens."

"You do have free will. Not choosing is choosing. You must have faith that good will be rewarded, sin punished."

"Like a big ledger or something."

"Faith is what matters. We can't understand all of the world's motives and ironies."

"What I do will affect my friend. That's for sure. He doesn't want me to say anything."

"Think how you will feel if you accept this money and things still go bad."

"I will not take any money."

"I say you should let the police handle it. It's their job. How could that be wrong?"

"My friend's life may well be destroyed. At least he thinks so." She bit her lower lip.

"Destroyed?"

"To save himself, he might have to pull up roots and start another life."

"We have to do what is right."

"That's easy to say, sitting here in church."

He did not respond, but leaned forward, elbows on the desk. "I don't have perfect vision. But I think it will work out." He shifted in his chair and cleared his throat. He stared at the floor.

"Okay. Thank you so much for seeing me, Pastor Edwards. You've helped me a great deal." They rose, shook hands, and he walked her to the door, inviting her to call him in a few days for a visit. He was relieved to see her go.

It was raining when she returned home. She dialed Michael Amberley's number. The receptionist answered, and after an interminable wait, he came on the line. She asked if she could have the evidence in his safe. When she learned he had given it to Ashton, she slammed the phone down and went to the refrigerator for a beer.

She called Ashton, but couldn't reach him at either residence. She drove to his apartment, and then traveled the thirty miles to his farm. By the time she arrived, a hard rain was falling. She traversed the gravel road up the hill into the driveway, and parked next to closed garage doors. She knocked at the front door, and he instantly appeared, smiling.

"Come in, Whitney. I didn't expect you."

She strode into the living room.

"Something's different about you," she said. "You seem so happy."

He nodded and smiled. "The university has offered me a part-time job. Attending physician on weekends, the ER, two twelve-hour shifts. That would give me the weekdays off. I'm thinking about doing it."

She pursed her lips and tilted her head. "You're a walking contradiction. I thought you didn't want to be on both ends of a leash."

"Did I say that? I guess I say a lot of things."

"You do, Tyler, a man of many words."

"Wouldn't you like to sit down?"

"I prefer to stand." She continued to look at him. "I just had a talk with Amberley."

"What about?" His smile faded.

"What do you think?"

"I don't like guessing games," he said.

"The records are not in his safe. He gave them to you."

"Yes, I asked for them."

"Why?"

"I didn't want anything to happen to him or to you."

"So you took them."

He nodded.

"Where are they?"

"Locked away."

"Give them to me."

"What are you planning to do?"

"I'm going to the police."

His eyes were downcast. He said nothing.

She raised her voice. "Well?"

"I can't get to them just now."

"Yes, you can."

"I buried them in a container."

"Well, dig it up."

"I'd need the tractor and auger. It's too muddy now."

"You did this on purpose! I want those records. And I want them now!"

"I'm sorry, I can't do that."

"If you don't give them to me, I'll go to the bank."

"They've sanitized everything by now. Changed codes and keys. Besides, you couldn't get in there, anyway."

"You're ruining everything!" She balled her hands into fists and held them straight down at her sides.

"Whitney."

He walked to the window and motioned her to join him. Rain cascaded on the panes. He pointed. "The records are in the new orchard. Deep below one of the trees. Along with some other stuff."

"Which tree?"

"Third row, third tree."

"I have to make things right. I want those papers. I'll be back to get them."

She swiveled, walked to the door, opened and closed it, got into her car, and roared off down the driveway, turned the corner and slid off the road. She yawed through the S-shaped curve, bottomed twice, and turned onto the highway, where he lost her from sight.

Before she went to bed, she sat at her desk and looked in the mirror. She opened the drawer, grabbed the scissors and comb, took her hair down, and began to cut. When she had finished, most of her hair was in the wastebasket. What remained was sheared into a tousled bob. She was a new Whitney Laird.

CHAPTER TWENTY-TWO

On the first floor of the Grayson Hotel, the Dressage Bar occupied a space opposite the main restaurant. Two patrons sat at the counter watching a small television. A pall of smoke made visible an oblique shaft of light, which came from a side window and brightened the entrance door. Coulter was ensconced in a padded chair away from the bar. He sat in shadow and gazed at the door. He held a martini glass, fidgeted, and kicked a leg.

At half-past three, Moreno walked in, went to the bartender, and ordered a gin martini. His affect was flat, his mood somber. The bartender, a woman of middle years, grinned and inquired as to his health, and he reciprocated with a muffled, terse phrase. He joined Coulter, who stood at his approach.

"I needed to talk to you," Coulter said, with no preliminaries. Moreno nodded with a sigh. He lowered himself into a chair.

"I'm here," he said.

"The doctor won't trouble us anymore."

"Why do you say that?"

"I talked some sense into him."

"You think so?"

"You should have seen the look on his face."

"Tell me something I don't already know."

"What?"

"He paid me a visit, in my garage, Friday night. I saw what you did." Moreno angled his head and pointed his gnarled finger in a contrapuntal gesture.

Coulter's jaw dropped. "That son of a bitch. He went to you?"

Moreno raised his hand in a dismissive wave. "I'm sick of your stunts. Not everyone is predictable, like you." He fixed Coulter's eyes in a stare, and after a few seconds, Coulter looked away.

"The guy has guts, that's for sure. Jeez, Moreno, I didn't think—"

"That's right, you didn't think. I won't tolerate insubordination."

Coulter continued to stare at his drink. His mouth turned down.

"Why the hell did you do such a stupid thing?"

Coulter looked up with shifting eyes. "I was sure he would cave. You had other things on your mind. I thought I was helping."

"What do you mean? Other concerns? What is more important than what I am doing?"

"I just tried to scare him. He jumped through the glass window. Into the damned woods. At night, in the rain, without his clothes!"

"You made a mess of things, mister. I tried to use reason. Now he is afraid. And mad. Violence does that. Get it? You've made him dangerous."

Coulter said nothing.

"I was buying time. People study their possibilities. They cannot decide. Violence shortens our time. They might counter-attack. What else might they be planning, eh?"

"I didn't think he'd escape. I never dreamed he'd go to you."

Moreno leaned forward and then back again. "You didn't think he'd escape." He reached for a cigar. "This is your last chance. No more mistakes. Basta!"

Coulter's face tensed. To avert Moreno's eyes, he held up and rotated his glass.

"They're definitely forces to be reckoned with."

"What do you want me to do?" Coulter said.

There was silence as Moreno lit the cigar. He rolled smoke in his mouth. Coulter sat impassively.

"Our options are few. We can believe they will not go to the police. That a daughter will not harm her father, or a lover, his love. We can continue the pay-off. We can eliminate the threat."

"Whatever you say. It's your call. You're the boss."

"Or, we can just leave sooner. The urge to do something is great, not just to stand there. Sometimes it's better just to stand there."

"I don't understand."

"Sell the real estate. Start today. Get whatever price you can for a quick sale. Suspend shipments. Close the stores. Clean the computers."

"Sell the farm, too? And the horses?"

"Yes."

Coulter nodded, amazed. "Should we get help from Miami? Do you want me to call?"

Moreno ignored the question. "You Americans have a saying, 'Cut your losses, and let your winnings run.' Never add money to a losing bet. We're cutting our losses, and we're doing it today. It's difficult, but it must be done."

"What if we staged an accident? A car wreck?"

"What would we do with Geoffrey? Get rid of him, too?"

"If we did it right, he wouldn't be the wiser."

Moreno seemed to study a spot on the rear wall. "Any accident or disappearance would cause great scrutiny. Of this, I am sure. We will close and relocate. There will be other victories." He stared at him and said, "Do it."

Coulter sighed. "Whatever you say."

Moreno blew a smoke ring. "You screwed up, bad. Now make it right. This is your last chance."

He nodded. "Understood."

Moreno rose, turned, and left the bar. Coulter upended his martini glass and walked out immediately afterward. When home, he called a number in Miami. The man he called was named Raul.

CHAPTER TWENTY-THREE

Whitney awoke the next morning to the cats' mewing, her summons to feed them. It was eight-thirty, time to get up anyway. She considered fixing breakfast, opened the refrigerator, and decided against it. She showered, dressed, jogged the half-mile to the deli, and ordered coffee and a bagel with lox and cream cheese, bought a newspaper, and sat at a wrought iron table. She was about finished when an SUV stopped at the curbside; out of the truck stepped Brendan Coulter. He approached her table with a smile.

"May I join you?"

Her mouth turned down in displeasure. "Something on your mind?"

"Have you heard from Claire?" He pulled out the chair and sat.

"I haven't seen her." She thought herself clever in substituting a technical truth for a lie.

"I'm sure she'll turn up eventually."

"Think so?" She stared at him until he looked away.

"Listen, let's cut to the chase here. It's too bad you found out, but you did. This presents certain problems for us." He pulled out a handkerchief and blew his nose.

"Certain problems?"

"Dr. Ashton, for example. What a shame he was dragged into it. He's making things more and more difficult."

"Where are you going with this?"

"I understand he stubbed his toe."

"You've got some nerve. Coming here and—"

"Look, Whitney, we're through playing games. Moreno offered one million, in cash, deposited in your father's bank, divided between you and Ashton. You said no. We've changed our mind. We can leave him out of it. Totally. We know he wouldn't do anything to hurt you. If you don't care about yourself, you'd better care about him. I've been authorized to transfer one million dollars to you alone."

"To shut up. Go away." she said.

Coulter stood. "Let me know your answer within twelve hours. Don't discuss this with anyone. Don't contact me by e-mail. Use the telephone. Call this number. Land line." He wrote on a card.

She said nothing, but took the card. He nodded grimly, as if she had said something, and walked away.

She alternately sat and paced in her living room for more than three hours. She looked at her paintings. She played her guitar. Finally, she called Coulter at the bank and said she would take the money. He agreed Ashton would be left out of it. She wanted the money transferred by wire, but Coulter did not want anything traced to him. He said he had the cash ready in hundred dollar bills; he and Moreno were in the process of closing their operation, and they were moving on. It would take them a few weeks to disengage entirely because of the property sales. Whitney hesitated. At last, she agreed to meet him in a public place; they settled on the horse park downtown, next to the library.

She phoned Ashton at his two residences, but there was no answer. She tried again. Still nothing.

Cheshire wandered in, circled the room, and appeared behind Whitney, and then he rubbed his face on her leg. She picked him up, and he sat, purring, on her lap. After a few minutes, she put him down and searched her purse for David Mortenson's phone number. She finally found it and dialed. He answered his cell phone while driving. They talked for two minutes. She walked to the window and looked out, as though pondering something of great consequence.

She called Ashton's numbers again and cradled the phone without speaking. She went to her computer, and composed an e-mail:

> dearest tyler,
>
> i've decided to accept their offer. there's not enough benefit in refusing, and a lot to lose. i am going to canada. you are in the clear. repeat. you don't need to do anything. i'm meeting someone at the bronze park downtown at seven to pick-up a package. call me when you get back. sorry about the other day. i couldn't get in touch with you, so i called our detective friend. he doesn't know the real reason for the meeting or about the package. i'm afraid i

did stretch the truth a bit. He will watch me with his camera from the library second floor window. you know, two can play at this surveillance stuff. i wouldn't want him to know anything more or get any closer. in case there's a problem, he won't get into any legal trouble. but i'll be okay. There are lots of people around. They wouldn't dare do anything, especially if I mention I'm being observed. See you soon.

love,

whitney

She waited all afternoon, but there was no reply. She called his two houses nine times. At six, she went out for dinner.

Ashton carried his tripod and camera bag into the living room and placed them on the floor. He let Piper outside; a few minutes later, he called her back in. He checked Whitney's message at six forty-five and looked at the screen with incredulity. Why did she need to meet them by herself, now, even in a public place downtown? He sat at the screen, wiped sweat from his brow, and ran fingers across his lips.

In large letters, he replied, "*Do NOT go! I'll choose the place and time.* He called her apartment. There was no answer.

CHAPTER TWENTY-FOUR

He ran to the bedroom, entered the closet, and turned on the light. He slid the clothes on their hangers away from the gun case and opened it. He settled on his Colt. The National Match was loaded. He grabbed a stack of six magazines loaded with hardball, put them in his pockets, and took out a holster. He put the Officer's Model .45 in the holster and clipped it to his left side. He pulled a lace from a shoe, formed a two-inch loop, and knotted the loose ends to his belt. He stuck the match pistol barrel through the loop, Mexican carry, inside the pants, cross draw. He picked up a jacket on his way out the door.

He sped away in his truck, hoping he hadn't delayed too long. He circumnavigated the driveway, drove past the orchard and down the hill, skirting the pond on the left. He made the S-shaped bend at high speed, and the truck slid in a detour through the alfalfa field for twenty yards until he slid onto the gravel again.

As he reached the bottomland, two silver eyes gleamed for an instant, then disappeared, and his lights fell on a running doe, bounding, white tail up. A spotted fawn followed her. Ashton bounced through the opening in the woods, left the road, fishtailing for a second, but righted the truck, shot through the gate, and screeched onto Sedgewick Lane.

He sped to town, to the park where life-sized bronze horses and colts ran in a narrow field. There were dozens of people milling around. He searched the park. The parking lot was empty except for two cars, and they were not Whitney's.

An elderly couple he had seen twice before sat on a bench next to the sidewalk.

"Excuse me; I am wondering whether you might have seen a young woman here a few minutes ago? About this tall." He gestured. "Blonde hair, slim." His eyes implored them for answers. "Meeting a big man?"

The gentleman looked at his companion. "There was someone like that, yes."

The woman nodded. "They left about thirty minutes ago, I'd say."

"They seemed to be in a big hurry," the man said. "Didn't stay long."

"Did they go together?"

"No, I don't think so. I'm not sure." The man looked again at the lady.

"Separately," said the woman. She pointed to a spot about twenty yards away. "She was parked right there."

"Thanks," Ashton said over his shoulder, as he ran to his truck. He looked at the library second-floor windows, but saw no one there.

Ashton passed the Grayson Hotel and then drove to Whitney's apartment. Her car was parked in the lot behind the complex. He ran up the stairs and knocked on the door. She did not respond. He knocked again. He tried to turn the doorknob, but it was locked. He paced in the hallway some moments before using a credit card to try to slip the lock.

"Damnation," he said in an incongruous whisper. He drew his pistol, and then kicked the door at the level of the lock. The doorjamb splintered, but the deadbolt held. At the second kick, the door flew open and banged against the wall, and then it bounced back, where he stopped it with the pistol frame. He walked inside. Whitney's purse was on the floor. Her lipstick and compact had spilled out. There was a crushed inhaler under an overturned chair. He searched the apartment, but found nothing. He picked up the purse and found her keys. When he ran out into the hallway, he noticed an unfamiliar woman's partially concealed face staring wide-eyed through a crack in her doorway. The door closed, and the bolt latched.

Ashton descended the staircase four steps at a time and went to the parking lot. He looked into Whitney's car, and then opened its trunk.

He returned to his truck, sped to Caballo Manchado, and approached the front gate, lights off. It was locked. He activated the four-wheel drive, backed up, drove onto the grass, turned right, and advanced about twenty yards through the shrubs, crashing through the four-board fence. He drove across the fields in near darkness until he came to a stone fence; he parked the truck in a swale. He tossed his jacket on the seat, found the toolbox behind the front seat, opened it, and took out a pair of bolt cutters.

He exited the truck and drew the match pistol. The starlit night was hot, the air a moist precursor of storms. The air quivered with cicadas, buckling their tymbals, clicking like castanets. A few fireflies on the ground, and some in the air, flashed. An owl hooted, and Ashton looked to his right, startled. A pair of binocular eyes, huge and yellow, stared at him, embedded in a head that rotated ninety degrees. It flew from the limb, its wings beating noiselessly against the sky. Ashton moved on.

He saw no one as he approached the house. No dogs barked. There were four vehicles in the driveway—a white pick-up truck, a Mercedes, an SUV, and another sedan. He looked into the cars. Nothing. He circled the house and peered into the ground floor windows. He neither saw nor heard anyone. He tried the doors, but they were locked. He found the telephone lines, cut them both with the bolt cutters, and then stuck the bolt cutters into his belt. He wondered about cell phones. He returned to the back of the house where he saw a distant light about sixty yards away.

Using the darkness as cover, he advanced and hid behind trees as he approached the light. It came from a large barn, blackened with creosote paint and filled with staves of hanging tobacco in tiers. To the left of the barn, a security lamp on a pole cast pooled light in a white circle. As he approached, he heard voices; a female voice said something garbled, and then a sharp, "No!"

The barn doors, front and rear, were open; a slight breeze passed through. The pungent smell of tobacco hung in the air. He tossed away the bolt cutters, went around to the back, and crept through the open sliding doors. The tobacco smell intensified; what was pleasant from a distance became cloyingly sweet. He fell to his knees, crawled under the staves, and positioned himself behind alfalfa bales. He slowly stuck his head up.

He saw Coulter and two other men, one of whom held a pistol and had a submachine gun slung over his shoulder. The third man was restraining Whitney. Her hands were pinned behind her. Her hair was short and mussed. She was struggling with the man who had used the baton on him.

"I said I would, didn't I? Haven't I done what you asked?"

"Sorry," said Coulter, "but we had a change of plan."

He turned to the man with the pistol. "Put that away." The man placed his gun in a holster on his right side and walked over to a square alfalfa bale. He produced a knife and cut the jute twine from it, securing a length of about four feet. He returned to the light where the other man was holding her.

Coulter shook his head. "Use that plastic bag." He pointed.

"No," said Whitney. She began kicking with both feet. Her shoes flew off. She screamed. The man gripped her around the waist as she arched and twisted in his arms.

"I'm going back to the house," said Coulter. "Laird showed up. I'll need to deal with him."

Whitney saw her father first and screamed, "What the hell is going on? Stop them! I agreed to everything you asked."

Laird rushed in, panting, red-faced. Coulter was a mere step behind him.

Ashton placed his match pistol on the alfalfa bail. Which man should he target first? He flicked the safety, leveled the sights on the man with the bag. Once again, it was Viet Nam: the brain directing his hand to squeeze a trigger. When chance favored him, he would shoot. He fought to control his hand's tremor. In near darkness, with Whitney's wriggling, it was hard to align the sights. The man dropped the plastic bag. He was closer, quartering toward Ashton. Seven yards. There was a moment when he stood still.

Huge was the flash and percussion. Ashton's ears rang. The man was no longer before the sights. The corral doors opened; mayhem set loose. Ashton tried to fix the front blade on the second man, but he disappeared through the open door. He fired twice more anyway, blasting holes in the barn wall. Laird disappeared. Whitney screamed and trembled. Her hands were upraised. Ashton sprinted toward her.

"Let's go." He pulled Whitney to his side.

She stopped screaming when she saw him. She searched for her shoes.

"Forget those."

He looked at the man he had just shot. The 230-grain slug had punched a half-inch hole in his temple. A piece of the skull opposite the entry wound was blown off. There was a shudder. He made guttural noises; fingers twitched. The eyes bulged in astonishment.

Whitney screamed again.

"Be quiet. We've got to move."

He grabbed her hand and led her under staves of tobacco, which crackled as they brushed by them. They went through the back door. No one waited to ambush them. They fled in the blind night. She fell, groaned, and was slow to get up. A medley of muffled curses and shouts came from beyond the barn. Ashton stuck his pistol inside his waistband. He looked about, saw no one following, picked her up, and in a fireman's carry, hoisted her body over his shoulder. The pistol fell out of his pants. With his right hand, he grabbed it and ran across the meadow toward his truck.

Several yards distant, he saw two dark shapes in front and to one side of him. He changed direction and descended a hillside about a hundred yards until a marshy area with a large pond at one end stopped them. The marsh was choked with cattails. He was exhausted, and put Whitney down. They splashed into the water.

"They were going to kill me," she said in a whisper.

"We're not out of this yet."

"I can walk."

She saw flashes of light and heard staccato gunfire coming from somewhere on the hill. Ashton's voice was cut off. Bullets ripped and splashed around them. He lay on the swampy ground among the reeds and would not get up.

"Tyler!"

"Get down!"

She knelt on the wet soil, grabbed him under the arms, and helped him sit up. "Are you okay?"

He ignored her question. "We've got to keep moving."

They inched their way through tilted cattails, slogging through the marshy ground, and crawled up on the bank next to a dead oak.

"You're hurt, Tyler. Oh, my God!"

He pulled his hand away and pointed to a rock fence, which extended sixty yards up the hill, past the pond. "Let's go over there," he said. More bursts of gunfire erupted. The rounds hit the water. One bullet snapped off the surface and buzzed overhead. She took one of the pistols as they went up the hill. They walked, stooped over, staying below the fence's cap course. They rolled to the other side and collapsed onto the ground. Whitney knelt over him and helped lift him to a sitting position. She peered through a gap in the fence.

"Do you see anything?"

"No."

"They may try to outflank us. We'll follow this path to the right."

"Where are you hit?"

Ashton took off his belt, and unfastened and unzipped his trousers. He lowered them and examined his right leg. A wound at the mid-thigh was bleeding copiously from two holes. The bullet had been wide of the femur and great vessels. The muscles contracted at will. He removed his shirt and undershirt, and with a knife, cut it into large strips. He tied them around the wounds and tightened his web belt over them.

"My truck is about a hundred yards to the right of the main gate. I crashed through the fence. It's over there." She was not looking. "Look at me! The truck is that direction." He pointed.

"Okay. Let's go. We've got to get you to a hospital."

"I'll slow you down. Get to the truck, and meet me at the side of the bridge."

"I'm not leaving."

"Follow the fence until you reach the wood. Then double back to my truck. Here are the keys. Watch for anyone who might have found the truck." He took her pistol and changed its magazine. "You'd better take this." He handed it back to her. "Eight rounds."

She held up the gun.

"I said I'm not leaving."

"You have to, Whitney."

"Let's go." She struggled to get him to his feet.

"If I'm not there in fifteen minutes, leave."

"No!"

"I'll call 911. Don't tell anyone you were here, unless it's the police."

"Get up."

He pulled out the Officer's Model and examined the breach.

"I'm not going."

He heard a metallic noise, the click of a Kalashnikov safety, a sound lodged in his memory. He rose with painful slowness and looked over the fence, where a large tree encroached on the stone. He placed his pistol to the tree's left side. Someone shifted in the near darkness, making his way to the stone wall. How foolish it was for someone to approach a wounded man behind cover. Ashton fired two shots in rapid succession, and then two more. His ears rang again. He ducked behind the tree. When he closed his eyes, orange ghost images burned in his mind. From across the fence, a disembodied groan emerged from the night.

He reached into one pocket, then another. He traded guns with her, found the spare magazine, and gave it to her. After a few seconds, she seated it with a click. They exchanged pistols.

About ten yards away, a second man vaulted the fence to their right. He was stooped, but advancing. Whitney was between him and Ashton. The movement caught her eye. She swiveled toward him. Before Ashton could turn around, she began to fire the .45. Time slowed. When her arm jumped for three seconds, she hardly heard the noise. Eight fireballs erupted from the barrel. For a strange interlude, she wondered who was firing her gun. The slide locked back, but she continued to pull the trigger. Acrid residue of ball powder clung to the humid air.

The man raised both hands, tottered, and fell to his knees. He put his hands to his face, as if to hide behind them.

"Don't shoot; please don't shoot." He fell, face down, into the tall grass.

Her hands shook, but she managed to press the magazine release. The magazine dropped away. She asked for another, and Ashton gave it to her. She rammed it home, pressed the slide stop, and the slide snapped shut. Ashton picked up the empty magazine.

"Don't shoot," the man cried.

They crept close to where he lay. She stood over him. Ashton pointed his pistol at the man's head. The voice implored them again. He sat up with difficulty and raised his head. It was Geoffrey Laird.

Whitney, her eyes wide, moved the pistol to the midline. Her hand trembled. Her finger curled around the trigger.

Ashton put his thumb between the Colt's frame and hammer and pulled the gun away with Whitney still clutching it.

"I'm not going to shoot you," she said. "I'm not a monster."

Ashton released the gun, and he heard the safety snap upward.

"Some god you are," she said. "Some father." She paused. Her voice quivered. "Why are you here?"

"I came to get you," he said. His breath was short. "Moreno called me. Talking strange. He told me to get over here." His eyes moved to her. "To take you home."

Ashton interrupted. "How many people are here?"

"Four that I know of. Five, including Moreno in the house. Maybe more."

"What kind of guns?"

"I don't know. Rifles and pistols."

"Where are they?"

"I don't know. We all scattered. I tried to stop them. You've got to believe me."

"Why should I believe anything you say?" she said.

"I don't have any weapons. Please believe me."

"Where are you hit?" Ashton said.

Laird held up his left wrist. A bullet had cut through one of the bones. He had a hole through the palm of the same hand. There was a wound in the hip, extending in a diagonal to the thigh. When she fired, he must have turned away. Blood spurted between his fingers as he attempted to stop the bleeding. His mouth was agape. He struggled with his words.

"You'll live," Ashton said.

"He's too mean to die," Whitney said. Her hands were shaking. A shudder went through her body.

"You shot me," Laird said in belated, stunned amazement.

"It's not my fault." She stumbled over the words. "I didn't know—I—"

"No. It's mine." His head hung reproachfully.

She kept watch while Ashton tended Laird's wounds. He ripped off Laird's shirtsleeve and fashioned a pressure bandage about the mangled wrist. The bleeding stopped, and blood flowed to the fingers, though the hand was beginning to blanch. The flank wound was not deep.

"Stay here," he said. "Someone will pick you up."

Whitney took Ashton's arm over her shoulder, and the pair moved about forty yards to where fences intersected. When they stopped to rest, the only sound she heard was Ashton's labored breathing.

"I have to stop."

"Just a little ways more." She helped him a few steps to the end of the fencerow. He slumped against it, mouth open, panting. His nostrils flared, and his chest heaved. A growing circle of red formed ominously on his shirt. He coughed and spat a pink froth into his hand.

"It's too dangerous to go to the house," he said.

"Give me the phone. I'm calling the police."

Ashton searched her eyes. "I'll do it." He dialed 911.

"This is Dr. Tyler Ashton. Send ambulances, state police— code three, to the Moreno horse farm—Cabello Manchado, on Highway 314 east. Send a SWAT team, code three. People are trying to kill us." There was a pause. "Juan Moreno, Brendan Coulter, and some others." Another pause. "Whitney Laird is with me. Several people have gunshot wounds. Seriously wounded. We'll try to help them. We must go." And then, "No, no I can't."

He snapped the cell phone closed.

"We'll try to help them?" she said.

"You may be arrested. You don't want to be portrayed as the aggressor."

"What do we do now?"

They might be coming here. Take my truck. He gave her the keys. If you can't find it, hide in the woods below." He gestured. "Over there."

"What about you?"

"It's best if we separate. They won't find you."

"I won't leave you, Tyler, I can't."

"Just go to the road. When you hear the sirens, wave the police down."

"I love you."

"I love you." It was not difficult to say. "You cut your hair. I like it."

"Do you? I was very angry when I did that."

"Are you angry now?"

"No, Tyler."

They embraced and kissed. A smudge of crescent-shaped blood stuck to Whitney's mouth, like carmine lipstick. She licked her lips, and then wiped them with the back of her hand. She stared at the blood on the truck's key. She looked up.

"I'm not going. I won't leave you here."

"You can tell the EMTs where I am. It's my only chance." He pushed her in the direction of the road where he had crashed through the fence. She hesitated, and then, looking over her right shoulder, continued in a straight line. She bent down, keeping her head below the top of the fence. He watched as she receded into the night.

He leaned against the stone. His pant leg was heavy, and it stuck to his thigh. He gave some thought to going to the pond to drink, but rejected the idea. He checked his pistol, the safety. The grip was slippery with blood, so he pressed hard against the checkering. His breathing had not worsened. Perhaps he could walk with the leg wound.

He moved along the fence for about twenty yards, using it as guide and crutch. Through a hole in the fence, he crossed to the other side. He went tree to tree and came closer to the downed man. He lay prone, one arm extended, the other palm up, like a swimmer in a static crawl. His breathing was shallow. Ashton pulled the rifle from underneath him and checked the gun's magazine. It held about fifteen rounds.

Ashton trudged in a diagonal line up the hill. He hugged the fence. Every few yards, he stopped, trying to ration his strength. He neither heard nor saw anyone. He left the safety of the stones, crawled across a pasture, into a copse of large oaks, slugged through the undergrowth, and emerged on the far side. He propped himself up against one of the oaks and sat with his back to the tree, exhausted, panting like a dog.

After a time, a low voice came from the darkness. He pivoted slowly and looked around the tree, upward, to a gentle hillside. Mackerel clouds floated before a three-quarter moon. There was movement on the ground. Two people walked on all fours, and they were headed toward him. At intervals, they lay in clumps of fescue. Ashton waited. His breathing was better.

He put his finger inside the trigger guard and pivoted the rifle. His hands trembled like leaves in a wind. He trained the sights on the men as best he could in the low light, and pressed the trigger. He thought it would fire, semi-automatic, but instead a burst of six or seven rounds erupted, most of which shot high. Return gunfire blazed on either side of the grass. He doubted he had hit either man. They would surely try to outflank him.

He lay on his belly and dragged himself through a patch of brambles ninety degrees to the right, for about thirty yards. His throbbing leg made it impossible to go far farther. He hid behind a gum tree. The armada of cicadas droned on. A nameless bird called. He moved the selector switch one, then two notches, and then back to the first notch. He couldn't remember which setting was semi or full automatic. He press-checked the Colt and quietly moved the safety.

To his right, a twig broke. He slowly turned his head, but saw nothing. There was a slight rustling of leaves. He moved nothing but his eyes. A human silhouette appeared against the moonlight. Ashton slowly raised his rifle. He placed the sights on the center of mass and pulled the trigger. Nothing happened. Instead of changing the selector, he must have reapplied the safety. He switched the lever. The AK shot in a burst of four, then fell silent. The man disappeared.

Bullets whirred overhead. Ashton saw the muzzle flashes coming from the ridgeline. He rolled slowly away from his position after the firing had stopped, and alternately crawled and dragged his body in an arc toward them. He lay on his belly and scooted through the tall fescue. He was approaching the barn. He possessed only his pistol now.

The barn stood outlined against a security light. He limped toward the rear door, knelt next to the barn, caught his breath, and listened.

Inside the barn, a man with a CZ Skorpion opened fire. Slugs splintered a plank next to him. Fragments of wood blew out, and one stuck in Ashton's neck. He removed the splinter. Ashton dropped to the ground. More shots punched through the boards above him. He heard metallic sounds, as if the man inside were attempting to reload. Ashton crawled through the rear door, and at ground level, peered inside. Not five yards away, an eight-inch beam half-concealed the man holding the machine pistol. Ashton aimed the .45 and shot twice, and the man pivoted, and as he did so, Ashton fired another two shots. The man staggered backwards, fired a last burst into the hay, and fell dead.

Ashton stood, pressed the magazine release, and was about to insert a fresh magazine, when a second man stepped out of the shadows and into the soft light. He stood five or six yards away. They exchanged piercing looks. It was Coulter. He shot five times with a snub-nosed revolver. All missed. Ashton returned fire with his single chambered round, and the slide blew back and locked. Coulter was still there.

He rammed home a fresh load and pressed the slide stop. By the time the pistol was in battery again, Coulter was upon him. Ashton dodged and clubbed with the gun frame, missing Coulter's head, but he did strike the shoulder. At the blow, a howl issued forth. Ashton's gun was wrenched away, and it bounced on the ground behind a hay bale. Coulter was knocked to one knee, but he rose and advanced. Ashton limped to the back wall, looking for a weapon. Hung helter-skelter were a fishing net and farm tools, some of which clattered when he backed into them. A two-man saw twanged when it fell.

Ashton reached up, grabbed the net, and threw it like a fisherman. It fanned out, settling over Coulter's head. Caught and entangled, he swatted wildly, spun, hit the wall, and recoiled off the boards. As Coulter tried to extricate himself, Ashton seized a hand sickle and swung it. It swooshed and struck an overhand blow. The blade slashed through the net and glanced off the frontal bone.

Through a gash in the net, Coulter clawed at his face, horror stricken, furious. He shrieked and burst forward, ignoring the rush of blood. Ashton stepped aside, and as Coulter barreled past, he swung hard, his arm extended. The tip of the steel just reached Coulter's head. They pivoted, linked for an instant, like ice dancers. Ashton released the handle. The blade quivered and hummed. Coulter hopped briefly on one foot. He leaned, toppled, and fell into a slack, twisted heap.

Ashton moved backward one step. His teeth were exposed, lips curled. He brushed the sweat away from his eyes.

Coulter's jaw worked in spasms, but no words came. He gasped; his eyes opened wide. All breathing stopped, and then came a sardonic smile.

Ashton searched for the .45 and finally found it under a clump of hay. He sat. He brushed away a few errant straws, and blew into the breach and bore. With great effort, he arose and propped himself briefly against a post. He emerged from the barn and walked into the night, where even the cicadas were silent.

Had Moreno and others retreated to the house?

Ashton hunted for matches at the workbench, but found none. One of Coulter's pockets held a lighter. He took it and limped into the barnyard. A fuel drum stood attached to a pump. He grabbed a feed bucket, pumped in diesel fuel, and abandoning all scruple, lurched toward the house, wild-eyed, like a beast in anguish.

The bucket tore through a side window, burst through glass, and spewed its contents inside the house; some of it splattered onto his clothes. He flicked the lighter anyway, touched it to the wall, and when fire grew at the broken window, he threw the lighter inside. Flames ran on the carpet.

He reeled backward and staggered through the empty field, clutching his pistol, and then veered toward the stone fence where he had left Whitney. He stumbled, and his gun dropped, muzzle down, and stuck in the moist dirt. There it remained. He continued, bent and wheezing, until he sank to one knee. With a grimace, he managed to stand.

He turned around and looked toward the house. Orange light glimmered on the second floor. In a few seconds, he slid to the ground and sat, leaning against the wall.

Movement caught Ashton's eye as the garage door opened. Two men, one with red hair and a beard, made crimson in the firelight, ran from the house to the Mercedes. The two dogs were on leashes, and Moreno let them in the rear door. He sat in the front passenger side. A man with short hair cranked the engine. The car advanced a few feet, angled in reverse with smoking tires, and then screeched onto the driveway, heading toward the road.

The flames in the house grew monstrous. Glass melted; windows blew out. Tongues of flame licked at blistered walls. Torrents of yellow smoke snorted in a back draft. A fiery wind blew, and in the fullness of time, it lapped at the eaves; the conflagration, not without beauty, lit the landscape in a searing glow—fire begetting fire, and then the gas tanks blew up and shrapnel ripped through walls.

Ashton stared, trance-like, at the ravening inferno. The roof collapsed, and by turns, two of the four walls fell in. The implacable flame devoured the beams, heat was lost, and ash, born of flame, floated up, then down like feathers, and except for the stonework, the house vanished into the night. He was alone.

The world seemed to slow. His eyesight narrowed, but his hearing stayed keen. His head lolled against the fence. Someone was approaching. He grabbed for the Colt until he remembered it in the dirt, too far to reach. The man closed in, dragging a leg, holding an arm, and pitched forward like a zombie. Closer still—and Geoffrey Laird flopped down beside him.

"I'm sorry," said Laird. "I'm so sorry."

"Let's burn it all down and start over."

Laird was short of breath, but calm when compared to the fury of Ashton's rasps. Pink foam, streaked with blood, spumed from Ashton's nose and mouth. He was ever mopping his face with his sleeve.

"Where's Whitney?"

"She's safe."

"You need a doctor," said Laird. He reached for his cell phone and opened it.

Ashton stared into the firelight. He wiped his blanched face again. "You forget; I am a doctor." He paused. "I'm not afraid. If my body would only listen." His voice withered. "After all this time, I was just starting to understand." His features seemed to soften. His face bore no anger.

A huge bed of seething coals grew radiant. From time to time, showers of sparks flew in bright trajectories into the darkness. For a long moment, he watched them burn away. After everything, then and now, he did love still this fey life and the earth that sustained it, even with the pain, which of necessity seemed forged with its splendor.

Laird sat clutching his side.

"Whitney doesn't hate you," Ashton said. "You have to help her now. She needs you."

"I'll try to put it right."

Ashton nodded. "Tell her something for me."

Laird leaned forward. Ashton coughed weakly. He was no longer gasping. Laird saw the fire reflected in Ashton's eyes.

He gripped Laird's lapel in an effort to support himself. Laird leaned in; his ear was close. "Tell her—tell Whitney—I have no complaint. She'll know."

Laird looked distraught. Finally, he said, "I'll tell her."

Ashton released him. "And ask her to finish the orchard." He leaned away and rested his back against the wall.

"Finish the orchard," Laird repeated.

Ashton closed his eyes and in less than a minute, was still.

EPILOGUE

Just four weeks before term, Whitney's uterus descended and her breathing eased. Her time was drawing near. A week later, early one morning, the pain began, and at intervals, it increased, it slackened, and it returned. She called her mother. On their arrival at the hospital, a clear fluid ran down her legs and confirmed to all that delivery was imminent.

The floor nurse, Gwen Hathaway, wheeled her to a labor room, much like a suite in a fine hotel. Centered in the ceiling, lights in clusters hung bright and limned the room in chiaroscuro. Whitney's clothes were exchanged for a gown of white cotton. She lay in bed, studying the babe's empty warmer. Gwen started an IV. Fluid ran to her arm from a volutrol, drop by drop. Attached to a fetal electrode, a wire led to a cart, upon which sat a machine and monitor making rhythmic sounds like a living thing.

The door opened, and Dr. Conrad entered. He greeted Whitney, gestured to the nurse, and walked to the sink where he washed his hands, dried them, and slipped on a pair of gloves.

"Exam time," he said with a slight smile.

Afterward, he discarded the gloves and approached the bed.

"Four centimeters dilated, thirty percent effaced. You're doing fine," he said. "A few hours more."

"That means back to work, right?"

As though to bear out her words, her demeanor quickly changed. The hands clenched. The brow wrinkled. Her breathing came in spasms. Doctor and nurse looked at the monitor as the sinuous lines on the screen performed a minuet.

"Let's give some oxygen, three liters," he said.

"Everything normal?" Whitney said with a pained face.

"Yes, yes, fine. You really don't need more oxygen, but for the baby's sake, we'll give some to be sure. I'll check back in an hour."

The progression slowed, and Conrad ordered oxytocin to begin. The contractions increased in force and number. Again and again, she looked at the clock on the wall. The labor was eternal. She was stricken with gothic toil, but her jaw was set. Nurses came and went, checking the monitor, feeling besieged tissues, listening to fetal heart tones.

The third floor elevator doors opened. Michael Amberley emerged, turned right, and walked to the nurse's station. He asked an Asian nurse about Whitney's condition and was directed to the waiting room. Three others were seated there, two women and a year-old child. Amberley searched for something to read and settled on a newspaper. He finished a section and peered over his reading glasses as the child waddled across the room, falling occasionally, picking herself up, falling—all in high, good humor. The child came to Amberley, put two fingers in her mouth, and stared with big eyes. She walked to the older of the two women and did likewise. The woman smiled at her fondly.

"My daughter's having a baby," said Melanie Laird, noticing Amberley's look in her direction. "Three weeks premature."

"You must be Whitney's mother."

"Yes, that's right. The proud grandmother. And you are?"

"I'm Michael Amberley, your daughter's attorney."

She gestured across the room. "The little girl making eyes at you is Zoë Laird, Whitney's half-sister. And her mother, Heather." The woman smiled. "You're surrounded by Lairds."

Amberley got up and shook their hands. "A pleasure to meet you all," he said.

Zoë continued to toddle back and forth.

"Wasn't it a surprise about the will?" asked Melanie Laird. "The housekeeper and Whitney."

"Yes. I drew it up. Tyler had no family." Amberley grinned and added, "I inherited his dog, Piper."

In the labor room, Conrad changed gloves, slipped into a gown, and then infiltrated the pelvis with lidocaine. Whitney's face streamed with sweat. Her navel pouted over a striate abdomen. Gwen importuned, "Push, push!" and "Breathe deep—in—and out." Conrad stood aside, his fingers interlaced.

After twenty minutes of pushing, of waiting, the perineum swelled, and Conrad used scissors to make a small cut. The delivery stalled. He positioned and locked the forceps. He drew the babe forward, and then removed the blades of the forceps one at a time. The scalp came into view, and a few seconds later, the head and shoulders emerged. The rest of the baby slipped out and lay on his forearm.

It was a girl, small, even for thirty-seven weeks gestation. She scarcely weighed six pounds. He held her face upward with his left hand. The legs straddled his arm. He suctioned the nose and mouth, clamped, and severed the cord. The baby squalled, she clenched her fingers, and in unison, her arms shook. She opened her eyes and blinked. The nurse pressed a button on the clock.

At one minute, she called out the time. Dr. Conrad responded, "Eight." With one hand, he held the newborn at the chin, and with the other, he held the legs level with the stirrups. A slick and chubby-cheeked face with open blue eyes and matted blonde hair stuck above his hand, and she stared at her mother.

"It's a girl! A beautiful girl," Conrad said.

"Is she okay?"

"Beautiful, absolutely."

Whitney broke into a tired smile.

The door opened, and a floor nurse asked if Whitney wanted to see visitors. "Sure. Let them all in." Melanie, Heather, Zoë, and Amberley were ushered into the room.

Gwen suctioned the nose, dried the skin, wiping away vernix, and then wrapped the babe in a warm towel and handed her to Whitney. She clutched her to her chest. Whitney looked into blue eyes, and the baby looked back, blinked, and opened and closed her mouth.

"A little towhead!" said Heather.

"Be-be," said Zoë. She pointed to the ceiling with an index finger.

The flash of a camera lit the room. "Your father would like a picture," said Heather.

"I'd like a duplicate," said Amberley.

"As would I," said Melanie, standing close to the bed, staring down at her daughter and granddaughter.

"Go ahead. Shoot a roll if you want to." There was another flash.

Whitney smiled. She rubbed her finger at the corner of the babe's triangulate mouth. The full lips turned reflexively and swallowed up half her finger.

"You can feed her if you want."

"I can?"

Gwen took the baby and guided her to Whitney's breast. "Welcome home," Whitney said.

"A little peanut," said Dr. Conrad.

"I never thought this day would come."

"This might hurt a bit," the doctor said as he began to repair her incision. Whitney turned her head to look at the part of herself that now lay in a steel bowl. It seemed deserving of some sympathy, having bubbled up from nothing, nurturing without rest. Cast away. Unremembered.

Her face was serene. The pain of childbirth appeared to matter not at all, as though her thoughts were elsewhere.

"Are you sure she's normal?"

"Yes. She's fine."

"She looks like us both."

The nurse removed Whitney's oxygen line, and placed it next to the infant's nose.

The child's eyes were closed. Her damp hair, strawberry blonde, glistened under banks of light. She glowed like an ember.

"We'll find our own way." Whitney shaped the blanket like a cowl around the babe's face. "You're brave. You can do it."

She clutched something in her fingers, suspended on a gold chain. The babe's eyes remained closed. Whitney touched the nose of the baby, who opened her eyes, closed them, and then yawned.

"Have you named her yet?" her mother said.

"Yes. Ashton—Ashton Laird."

"Ashton, yes."

After the others left the room, the nurse fastened name bands to the baby's ankle and wrist. She inked the soles of both feet. She made tiny footprints. She dimmed the lights, wrapped baby Ashton, and gave her to Whitney. The door closed behind her, footfalls faded, and all words ebbed to whispers, and then disappeared. Whitney looked at her child, sleeping, at her closed eyes, and both were calm, covered in the rapture of a dream.